MARTHA'S DAUGHTER

McSWEENEY'S
SAN FRANCISCO

Copyright © 2024 David Haynes

All rights reserved, including right of reproduction in whole or in part, in any form.

Some of the stories in this collection were previously published, some in a slightly different form, in the following publications: "That's Right, You're Not from Texas" in *The Story Behind the Story: 26 Stories by Contemporary Writers and How They Work*; "Blind Alley" in *Southwest Review*; "Big Things Happening Here" in *Dallas Noir*; "Taking Miss Kezee to the Polls" in *City Pages*; "The Lives of Ordinary Superheroes" in *Who Can Save Us Now?: Brand-New Superheroes and Their Amazing (Short) Stories*; "Dear Daniel Davis, or How I Came to Know Jesus Christ as My Personal Lord and Savior" in *Callaloo*; "Your Child Could Be a Model" in *Gumbo*; "The Weight of Things" in *Natural Bridge*; "On the American Heritage Trail" in *Leon Literary Review*.

McSweeney's and colophon are registered trademarks of McSweeney's, an independent publisher based in San Francisco.

Cover illustration by Diana Ejaita

ISBN 978-1-95211-944-6

10 9 8 7 6 5 4 3 2 1

www.mcsweeneys.net

Printed in the United States.

MARTHA'S DAUGHTER

DAVID HAYNES

PART OF THE *OF THE DIASPORA* SERIES
edited by ERICA VITAL-LAZARE

McSWEENEY'S
SAN FRANCISCO

With love, to those who are still on the journey
and to those who have left the road

Martha's Daughter 9

That's Right, You're Not from Texas 127

Blind Alley 143

Big Things Happening Here 173

Taking Miss Kezee to the Polls 189

The Lives of Ordinary Superheroes 201

Dear Daniel Davis, or How
I Came to Know Jesus Christ
as My Personal Lord and Savior 223

Your Child Can Be a Model! 237

How to Be Seen in Public 257

The Weight of Things 275

On the American Heritage Trail 301

MARTHA'S DAUGHTER

THERE'S A WOMAN PACING outside my office—although "pacing" is both more *and* less purposeful than anything Janine Chalifour has in mind. She's dying for me to look over and to pay her some mind. It pleases me to disappoint her.

I remind myself frequently that some people—people such as Janine—crave the enforced bonhomie of the workplace. They thrive on the gossipy lunches and the water-cooler banter and the obnoxiously frequent potlucks, which feature the sorts of bad casseroles invented to feed poor people as inexpensively as possible.

Include me in the "not a fan" club.

I scan my office to avoid looking at Janine. The cord on my desk phone looks as if dogs have been chewing it. Almost daily I twist it and pull at it and wind it around my fingers in hopes that one day they'll replace it with something from a more recent decade—or just remove it altogether. It is as vestigial as the social contracts that keep us from murdering each other on a daily basis. Otherwise, I imagine you would approve of the tasteful undertones in this, my personal warren, a private office with a window, as befits my status, here on the seventeenth floor, high above Clayton, the regional headquarters of Synergy Enterprises. Walls that might adventurously be referred to as camel-colored are augmented with binder-stuffed bookcases. Those binders are also vestigial, pleather-bound relics from the days when paperwork involved actual paper, and they are chock full of pre-digital sales reports. It's been years since I've opened one, and to make them less imposing I have interspersed them with pleasingly innocuous and nondenominational knick-knacks: a glass bowl from the art fair, an antique tin that once contained cookies. Brown desk, brown chairs, brown woman: the lair of Cynthia Beatrice Garrison. Museum shops are stocked to the rafters with exhibition posters that match my décor. Here you will find two of them, appropriately conventional—a Monet and a Klimt, to be exact—and there, out the window to the north and west, you can almost see the decaying post-war suburb where I was raised. I swivel my chair in that direction as a plane makes its final approach to Lambert Airport. I twist and untwist the intricately knotted phone cord. I am on hold.

Beyond the door of this coveted "private" office, out past Janine, who continues to patiently pace, the cubicle farm buzzes with standard mid-morning melodrama. The new girl in Major Retail had a "date" of some kind, the Southern Illinois rep laments the closure of another strip mall in the Metro East. Janine Chalifour notes all—on the off chance she will overhear a tidbit that she might parlay into another premature promotion. She eyes me through the window they have installed for your viewing pleasure and mimes a telephone—less an invitation to "call her when I have a minute" than her way of updating herself (and others) on the progress of my workday. The voice on the actual telephone reminds me of the location of the funeral home.

So much for you, Janine Chalifour: my workday has been aborted. Observe me as I fold this or that piece of paper into a color-coded folder, some of which I stack in the inbox, the balance I place (in any damn order) into my briefcase. I will not be looking at any of it any time soon.

You would like this briefcase. Many of you have praised it; Mother liked it as well. As I have done not infrequently, I dance my fingers across the nearly invisible nub of the oak laminate on the desk, a sensation that has always given me pleasure. Here is one of those things that I will acknowledge that your kind and mine share: our quirky tactile comforts. The tantalizing rasp of a bath-soft nailbrush, the impossible smoothness of a pork rib when the meat has fallen from the bone.

But I linger too long on such musings, and this may or may not come to annoy you during our time together. As if on cue, Janine Chalifour pivots into my office to inquire if I am "going somewhere." She asks this in a tone somewhere between prison wardress and the suspicious but still solicitous wife of a serial philanderer.

I tell her that something's come up.

I have learned over the years to walk a fine line where she—or any of you—is concerned: work stuff on this side; personal things over here, with me and mine. Why is it any of your damn... and yet say the wrong thing and by lunch she'd have everyone in the building thinking I'd skulked away with the quarterly profits bundled neatly into that briefcase that everyone so admires.

I offer Janine a neutral smile, but she persists. So, I offer her more, informing her that "a little issue has come up." Two parts diplomacy, three parts performance art. Every word calibrated for nuance, brow raised and the mouth turned down to signal just the appropriate hint of urgency. I could be an envoy to the Middle East—put these hard-learned lessons to better use than placating the company four flusher.

"Anything I can do?" she offers. Janine Chalifour's voice drips with that brand of ersatz sincerity that you so often employ with us, the standard tone offered at the nurses' station of your higher-quality emergency rooms, sometimes augmented by a concerned hand on the wrist.

("I bet she's a handful, huh, your mom?" [*Wink.*]

"It's always a struggle when they get like this." [*Purse-lipped nod.*]

"After a while it may be best to have them in a more... supervised environment, *if you know what I mean.*" [*Head canted to the side—because we all speak the same language here,* and why wouldn't I know what she means?])

I simper in response to Janine, a technique I learned in much the same way I imagine that you learned how to condescend and to whom; the patronizing fake smile that is part of the give-and-take of our lives together. I decline her help and brush past,

I decline her help and brush past, knowing that you never can mollify the likes of her—but one can dream. For her part, in standard manic mode, she remains in hot pursuit, a few steps behind, inelegantly clomping across the industrial-grade carpeting. Like many of her peers, Janine Chalifour has embraced the ethos of a certain media phenomenon that highlighted the shallow and oversexed lives of single white women with fabulous careers and even more fabulous wardrobes—only a partial explanation for the clomping, as she struggles to balance herself on one of the several pairs of overpriced but not really designer shoes, footwear of which she is sinfully proud. Explaining that Clayton, Missouri, is not Manhattan and that girls as horsey as Janine Chalifour oughtn't wear knit fabrics would be what Mother would have described as a poor use of my time. More than once Janine Chalifour, a girl no doubt raised in hand-me-down Keds and garage sale Garanimals, has snagged her six-inch knock-off Manolos against the no-pile carpet and landed square on her fat ass, a twangy "mother fuck!" betraying her Jefferson County roots. As is the case with all comedy, how funny one finds this depends on one's own experiences.

Speaking as a fellow (if not quite parallel) striver, some days I laugh, other days I do not.

On this day, Janine remains upright and plods along gamely behind me.

"It's not your mother again, I hope?" she asks, more of that help-desk sincerity oozing from her lips, blissfully unaware of the verbal aggression manifest in her always wretched syntax.

And, yet another example of the reason to keep one's personal life personal. Because they are happy to remind us (are you not?), when it best suits their needs, that a rarely but occasionally cranky car once made you late for a much-less-than-necessary staff meeting, or that your mother was, to put it mildly, a bit on the eccentric side and required more of your attention than was deemed advisable. I tell Janine Chalifour I will check in later.

I will do nothing of the kind.

Janine has the good sense not to board the elevator. One might, if they wish, offer the poor creature constructive criticism, advising her to stick with her concerned expression a second or two longer—until the doors snap firmly closed—forestalling her twisted-lip sneer and thereby maintaining at least the illusion of authenticity.

One could do that, or one could instead tell the horsey-ass bitch to go fuck herself.

Shock you, does it, this intemperate language? Or does it, instead, confirm what you believe you already knew?

Oh, we are well aware of your prejudgments. *Those people with their filthy mouths and even filthier habits!* And probably for a significant number of you that is the real shocker: How often we are privy to your policing of our behavior—our manner of dress, where and what we choose to eat, and with whom we choose to eat it—judgments often punctuated with your shopworn lament: *Well, what did you expect?*

Wouldn't we all like to know the answer to that?

If it matters, *horsey* is one of Mother's words. Part of a specialized Martha Garrison lexicography, one that neatly categorized all the women of the world into easily digestible packets.

(Take notes—you may find these words helpful in your dealings with us!)

Horsey, haunchy, stringy, mannish: these would be your primary phenotypes. *Trampy, trashy,* or *stylish* covered most bases as far as fashion was concerned. And in Mother's world, only one other variable mattered—and I must tell you that I have never fully deciphered the distinctions between *loose, slutty, slatternly,* and *whorish*, even as I am keenly aware there were actual distinctions, at least in her mind. For example, her next-door neighbor was always referred to as slutty but never loose. The best I can figure, a slutty woman became slatternly once she "paraded her business in the streets"—another of Mother's useful ways of accounting for the complexities of the human condition.

Oh, and in fairness to Martha Garrison: the personal-demeanor category also included *good girl* and *sweetheart*, although no one above age eight need apply for either of those monikers.

For the record, Mother never set eyes on Janine Chalifour, but had she done so she'd have sized her up in a second: a horsey, trashy-looking slut.

Those crazy mothers! What are you gonna do? That's Janine Chalifour talking, mocking me in my own head. We get inside of each other in these places, don't we? It's an essential part of their "charm."

No doubt before the elevator reached the parking level, a certain horsey trashy-looking slut would have found her way to the VP of Marketing's office, where she will have made small talk, batted her fake eyelashes, and waited for the perfect opening to note that if anyone was looking for her, "our colleague Cynthia Garrison" stepped out for a minute and she (Janine) sure hoped it wasn't anything serious, because such things had been happening a lot here lately—"as you are no doubt aware"—and I guess we'll all just have to find ways to support her in her hour of need—maybe take some of that pressure off her shoulders, pick up the slack and what have you—because, well, this is *clearly* a trying time for her. And she has been out. (*A lot.*) (*As you know.*)

Anything you need me to do?

And, yes, since you asked, I did see her coming, this Janine Chalifour. Knew exactly who she was from the moment I hired her, five years back—sadly, the best of the crop churned out from the local tank that passes for a university, back when "special accounts" had been desperate for a marketing assistant. Janine Chalifour, who, out of the four dozen willing-to-work-cheap ingénues culled by HR, was the only one whose credentials contained a complete set of mostly coherent, mostly correctly spelled sentences. There she came, typically announcing that her goal would be to "someday be CEO of a company just like Synergy Enterprises—manufacturing and distributing a line of sportswear for teens and young adults. My own unique line, of course." Oh, *of course*, one is required to agree, and one wishes these strivers the best of luck with their dreams—and I'm sure I'm being punished to this day for having been caught lingering my eyes a bit too long on the run in her vulgar and slutty and cheap-looking pantyhose.

Ah, the days of being twenty-one and frantic to please! How did any of us live through all of that earnest desperation?

You might find it hard to believe that I felt sorry for her. Sorry for this fresh-from-the-trailer-park creature, ineptly cobbling together what she believed to be a professional demeanor. Hungry to escape her raising and everything associated with it: I know the feeling well. Hungry enough that I knew she'd get the work done—and so she has done. Skip forward to her famously successful stealth-marketing campaign for the 2019 line of sparkle tops for tweens that had gotten her promoted into the office next to mine. In my generous moments (yes, I have them!) I acknowledge her genius for anticipating exactly which tawdrily designed and cheaply manufactured casual wear will fly off the shelves of our low- to mid-end retailers. (Only one bad call, this girl—a long-shot bet on a collection of anime character tees; five years too late [or maybe it was three too early?].)

So, she's entitled, you see. Entitled to clomp around the office in those pathetic shoes. Entitled to speak familiarly to the men who run the place, believing, as she does, that they see her as a peer and not as a potential sexual conquest. Entitled to believe she is *my* peer, that we are friends. *Sisters in the work-a-day struggle.* Together on a shared quest to rise to those coveted senior management offices on the Twenty-Third Floor.

And so there it is, another thing we share, you and I: our disdain for ambition when it is both shamelessly naked and tragically unrealistic.

But we also know that they are garden variety, the Janine Chalifours of the world: spit across any cubicle farm and hit six of her type with the side spray, these various schemers with more ambition than common sense. Mostly they come to no good end, these working-class strivers, young women and men who simply do not understand that the rules of the game have been crafted with someone else's success in mind. Oh, yes, now and then one will break through—some bourgeois hero, profiled with one of those pixilated non-photos in the *Wall Street Journal* and paraded across sundry political daises as an exemplar of the dream that is America. As for the rest of them, well, when the time is right, we cull them from the herd, those of us in upper middle management whose job it is to guard the gates of the inner sanctum against the fools who dare fly too close to the sun. Or, likely, as will no doubt be the case with Janine, they eventually effect their own demise—bet once too often on the wrong sweater set or, more likely in her case, sleep with the wrong exec. Until that fateful and wonderous day, I have chosen, you may be relieved to know, to abide her unctuous insufferableness. *Patience*, Mother would have counseled; so, patient I will be.

Mother—the mother that raised me, as opposed to the mildly demented creature I have shepherded and nursed these last dozen years—knew a lot about the way the world worked, and it has chagrined me over the years to acknowledge how many ways she was spot on in her advice.

Black, tan, and occasionally navy for the wardrobe. Florals make you seem frivolous. Yellow looks cheap.

Pull your hair back, low to the scalp. They've got plenty other things to check you on, so remove the mess on your head from their list.

No laughing; don't guffaw. Chuckle if you must, but only because they like it when you appreciate their *jokes*. Smile, but never show your teeth. *It ain't no minstrel show out there.*

The list goes on, and such as it is, it has served me well over the years.

The keys to the Camry are, it goes without saying, resting comfortably on the file cabinet where I place them every morning upon arrival at this hellhole. Next to the spider plant. Which I remember watering recently (but that is mere conjecture on my part).

It rattles one, such news. Even a person as expert in contingency, as I have had to be, could not possibly prepare for "the call" when it finally arrives. When it comes, you swallow hard and you... punt. You improvise.

You start moving—and hasn't that been the plan at every step on this journey: move and keep moving? Don't let them catch you asleep on the job. *Never confirm what they already believe.*

In such moments one sometimes sees oneself from the outside in—sees a middle-aged woman with a few extra pounds on her, cradling a briefcase, pissed about forgetting her car keys, watching herself wonder if she's doing any of this right. So, she moves again—and she keeps on moving: She pushes the "up" button on the elevator and circles back to the start.

I scoop up the keys and am greeted, predictably, by the voice.

"Back already?" it chirps. These greetings are by no means special treats, reserved only for me: Why is it necessary for this woman to rise from her desk and comment on absolutely every arrival and departure on the seventeenth floor? It is like living with a hyperactive German shepherd. I spin the key ring, but as *your* elders like to say, a nod is as good as wink...

"Can we talk?" she says. Not a question, and she doesn't wait for a response and she closes *my* door, closing us into *my* office, and she traps me between *my* desk and *my* file cabinet, perching herself on the edge of *my* desk, and before I can open *my* mouth to explain that there could perhaps be no more inopportune time for one of *her* impromptu meetings, she leans forward and in almost a whisper says: "I really do want to help. I mean it. I mean, I owe you, you know." She smiles, seemingly sweetly, and grabs my hand up in hers, misty-eyed with earnestness.

You would almost believe her.

It was never in the curriculum—not Martha Garrison's nor that of any school I ever attended—this matter of how to read your behavior. Literature, yes; American history, certainly; but this matter of what exactly might be going on in your heads at any given time? Not so much. One does one's best, of course: one studies the cues and tests one's assumptions and does what one can to learn it on the fly. But it's rather like studying discrete mathematics or quantum theory. One of those fields abstract to the point where getting to the bottom of it makes your head hurt.

You remain as opaque to us as if you had landed from another planet.

(Even on my best days, when I am really forced to focus—when I am, for example, toe-to-toe with some pasty-faced web-sales manager about a banner ad, and I know I've got the poor guy by the short hairs and will therefore get the rate I imagine may lose him his job—it is still as if I were communicating through a scrim, as if he were standing behind me in a fogged bathroom mirror.)

So, I just say "thanks" to Janine Chalifour, and I spin my keys again, and spin them again, and calculate the required necessary wait time before walking out on the conversation. But Janine Chalifour—this damn Janine Chalifour—has powered herself back up on those heels and moves another inch closer. No cringing or flinching, I remind myself, but, again, a nod is as good as a wink, and my wide stance and rod-straight posture—that Mother had always insisted upon—do nothing to thwart the full-frontal assault. Janine Chalifour's zombie arms extend, and I find myself pinioned against her slightly too ample breasts, and I think, Bitch, you'll be drawing back stumps, so you better take your damn hands off me, but she hangs on tight. She inhales the extra parcels of her Janine-ness up into herself, pulls herself up erect and solid and level, and says, Let us help you, she says, We are all here for you, she says, I am here. Me. Let me, she says, help you.

"Let me help you."

Fine.

"Fine," I say. I shake myself free and say, "Come on then."

We head off to the elevator, my new bestie and me, and I do not look behind at her, because I will not be turned into a pillar of salt. Come on then. Get your horsey, trashy, useless white ass in line, and let's get about the business of dealing with Martha Garrison's finally dead body.

My tally mounts, does it not? Added to my list of crimes: a galling lack of sentimentality, alongside what you'll describe as a penchant for being "enigmatic."

On the latter charge, let the evidence speak for itself. That Janine Chalifour—a woman who couldn't solve the puzzles on the side of a cereal box—knew of my mother's demise, if anything, betrays my failure to keep my private life as private as it deserves to be. Amend your charge, please, to carelessly... indiscrete: none of this is any of your business.

Blame the antiquated phone system—the "live" operator that the boys upstairs insist lends us the caché of actually giving a damn about our customers. Blame the paper-thin walls that line our warrens. Blame Mother's neighbors for dialing blindly around Synergy Enterprises to find me, repeating, as their calls are passed forward, their horror stories to whoever will listen. And—believe me—*everyone* listens. To everything.

When it was me with the (only slightly) snagged nylons and the too-eager-to-please demeanor, across town at Brown Shoe—similar warrens, similar stale ideologies—such calls became a regular feature of my life. Me, intent on a career. Me, head of something called "urban marketing initiatives." (Comments withheld: yours and mine.) Mildred Davidson would have been among the first callers; this before everyone and her mother had a cell, before I had gone door-to-door in Breckenridge Hills, handing out cards to all the neighbors, cheery pastel standard-sized business cards that I printed up at Kinko's containing my private number, which, for the record, I had highlighted and supplemented with a personal note asking folks to call me immediately if anything came up. Code for: "If and when my mother is on the loose."

"I don't mean to bother you at work," Mildred had said. Mildred, a woman from around the block, and it had taken a moment to recognize her voice. "It's about your mother," she'd said. "I don't know exactly how to tell you this."

There's an electric charge, is there not, in such moments: the soap-operatic dialogue punctuated with the dramatic pause. Imagine me leaning up in my chair like a bad actress, noticeably drawing breath, girding for the worst. I thought, Mildred Davidson seems to be having a little too much fun delivering whatever news this was—but why would that have been true? A woman who had known me my entire life, a woman who, as had all the other women in the neighborhood, supervised the entire gaggle of us growing up in Breckenridge Hills back in the day. That hesitation wasn't about drama, it was about trying to find the right words to tell me that at that very moment my mother had been parading (a concept Mildred Davidson shared with my mother) around the neighborhood in her housecoat, that the housecoat was imperfectly fastened, and that her business (another of Mildred and Mother's words) was pretty much on display for one and all to see. Apparently, Mother had been peering in people's picture windows and calling out the names of whoever she believed lived in that house.

Similar tales had been circulating for some time—Martha Garrison wandering the Schnucks store, her head half a maze of pink rollers, half a crown of wild white thatch; Mother in an aluminum-framed lawn chair, watering the yard, again in her nightgown and even though it had rained not five minutes earlier; Mother knocking on the neighbors' doors at all hours of the day and night. Until Mildred's call I had mostly ignored those rumors, blaming it all on spiteful gossip, old hens who lorded over the neighborhood as if they were denizens of a royal court rather than the ancient residents of a couple of worn-out cul-de-sacs in a worn-out second-ring suburb of St. Louis.

"I just thought you should know," Mildred Davidson had said. "I just thought you might want to come see about your mother."

I remember noting something akin to a quiet pleasure in Mildred's voice, but Mildred was hardly the type to revel in the petty misfortunes of others. I understand now that what I had actually been hearing was the feigned casualness of someone trying to soften the blow. That and no doubt the relief she felt having transferred the responsibility to where it belonged: onto me, the only known family of the neighborhood's current and primary object of concern.

Or was it pity?

And thus, they began, my routine summons to a world I'd sworn to have left behind for good, the specifics of that first summons to Breckenridge Hills blurred into the dozens and dozens of other times I've been summoned in the years since. Today, no different than the others, with me not wanting to go, having no idea what I might find when I got there—let alone having any idea what I should do about it when I did.

Well, with one big difference: next to me, this one last time, here's Janine Chalifour, and she regales me with a charming anecdote about last weekend's outing where she and "the girls" "positively tore it up" at a "home lingerie party" out in St. Charles. Apparently, I would just die if I saw the bra-and-panty set she got—lacy with little heart cut outs.

Imagine along with me, if you will, a townhome full of similar strivers, sloshed on cosmos or mojitos or micheladas or this week's fashionable girl drink of choice, writing checks they can barely cover for overpriced lingerie that will barely cover them.

I nod and feign a convivial smile: Janine is trying to distract me from my "grief" and I am trying to play along.

"Those unmentionables weren't red?" I tease.

(If I keep the bitch talking, then I won't have to answer the questions I know she is eager to ask.)

Unmentionables. One of Mother's words: Baby, Mother's doing a load of unmentionables, if you'd like to throw anything in.

Unmentionables: I'd credited Mother's cleverness for that locution until I realized she'd borrowed it from a television commercial. Most of her crap was borrowed: from TV, from old wives' tales, from straight out of other people's asses.

"I used to get wasted like that all the time," Janine says, adding, "hard as that is to believe."

I raise my brows and hope that signals to Janine the desired state of awe at her confession.

(Regarding your tales of "partying": I never quite know what response you are angling for. Empathy? Should I be jealous? Would you like a referral to rehab? I *am* here for you, but as noted above, I don't always understand what it is that you mean…)

I have the misfortune of knowing enough about Janine Chalifour to be able to report that she lives the bifurcated life of the Saturday-night reveler, sobered up, if barely, in time for a respectable appearance in the pew on Sunday morning. This is both an example of too much information as well as a clear indication that many of you need to expand your conversational repertoire.

To wit: I pull onto 170, and she has already purged her inventory of small-talk topics. We've been in the car all of five minutes. Meaning it's my turn to talk about nothing at all. But I am interrupted:

"Tell me about your mom," she says, quietly.

I expel a noise, something between a grunt and a sigh, something that I hope signals a wistful search through the memory banks for the perfect, precise nugget to recapitulate an exemplary and well-lived life.

What are we expected to say at such times? Clearly, I've not paid enough attention to cable-news disaster coverage, where distressed individuals such as myself are called upon to eloquently summarize their unspeakable losses. Routine media banter intended to spare the anchor, back in the studio, from further misinforming America about the crisis du jour. They stand there, these pitiful women and men who had, moments earlier, just before the unspeakable occurred, been about the ordinary business of life. All hell breaks loose, and now there is a fool in your face with a microphone, familiarly close to you—but not so much to offer comfort, but only so as to be in the same frame with you when you say something worthy of digital posterity. You babble a few words that you almost immediately forget, but those sob-laden platitudes are preserved for eternity through the good graces of our major media conglomerates. Thirty years hence, on the anniversary special—not of the disaster but of this particular idiot's having joined the network—there you will be again, standing amidst splintered homes or spent shell casings, your deadened eyes the size of saucers as you stumble through a simple sentence or two. There were no words then, and there are none now.

I could tell Janine, I suppose, about the Martha Garrison who had no compunction about delaying the Washington University graduation ceremony to facilitate her photo op—said picture filed under double M (Mortification, Mine). And there's that charming little tale of how in her late years Martha succeeded in getting herself banned from the local fast-food franchise for "lewd conduct"—although that tale required the marshaling of a range of unfortunate facial expressions that are best left to the imagination.

Girl Scout melodrama. The childhood humiliation of amateur tailoring. The routine "Let's Make a Deal" aspect of everyday life in the Garrison household. "Cut to the survivor: this one's a raver!"

"She's hard to describe," I mumble to Janine. And I swallow as I mumble, in hopes that this might sound to her as if my voice has broken with grief.

And it's a lie, of course. Brilliant, manipulative, domineering, mean: I could describe my mother for days. I have zero desire to do so.

"I don't know what I'd say about mine either," Janine replies, saving me from further dissembling. "What is it? Past eleven on a Tuesday, and she's likely walking around that Dollar Store again or up gambling on the boat. If she's even out of bed. This one time... Oh, say look, we got that same Chinese buffet down by our place."

The Camry is oddly magnetized to where her finger points, and I take the exit.

"I didn't mean to suggest..." Janine protests, which I wave away. A little lunch may make this all the smoother. For Janine and for me.

I pay for both of us, grab a platter the size of a hubcap and build a plate in homage to Martha—all her favorites: some greasy-looking egg foo young patties; a few chunks of fried something with pieces of onion and red pepper adhering to their sticky shine; a tower of crab rangoon, which I slather in a sauce the color of a post-nuclear dawn.

Janine, by contrast, works her way around the entire buffet, the spoonful-of-everything strategy. When she is finished, there is no telling what is what or where one might even begin eating such a mess, but in she digs with the gusto of a girl who grew up on boxed macaroni and cheese and not nearly enough of it. "Yum," she comments on one bite, and "Yum," she comments on the next.

The food is… okay. One thing Martha Garrison knew was Chinese food, and this is miles below her standards. I can hear her now: "Too much cornstarch in this gravy!" Or: "Fried rice don't mean boiled-in-grease rice."

Back in her lucid days the phone would ring in the office, Friday at four, like clockwork: Stop up at that Chinaman's on Woodson Road on your way over here and get my usual. Remind him extra egg and onion in the rice.

Ah, the casual racism of our parents! Enchanting, is it not?

That I might have had plans for the evening and that they might not have included a stop at the "Chinaman's" or at her house were never part of Martha Garrison's calculation. They all knew her, too, all these… Chinamen, in every storefront duck-and-noodles shop between Pagedale and Creve Coeur, and their wives too. How's your mama?; Say hi to your mother; Tell Martha to come by and see me. She'd be constantly on the outs with one or another of them for "shorting" her order or for scrimping on her shrimp.

And then the calls stopped, and Martha Garrison took to wandering, and I had my Fridays to myself. I spear an onion and find a bit of the tough white root that hadn't been trimmed away. Mother would be up and into that kitchen, and there would be hell to pay.

Janine thrust in the general direction of my face something golden brown with a clear glaze. "What's this?" she asks. "Did you get any of this?"

I shake my head.

"Cause it sure is good. This sauce is like lemon or orange or something." She bites a hunk off the glob and examines the remainder as if it were a lab specimen. "Definitely orange," she declares. I smile at her triumph, and with her lips she snatches into her maw the rest of the meat from the fork.

She's a savorer, this Janine, something she'd share in common with my mother. Every bite is lip-smacking delicious. She has an entire repertoire of (thankfully) mostly inaudible noises to signal the intense pleasure this food provides her, her eyes rolled to the sky in ecstatic gratitude until the lids lower to dreamy half-mast.

"Tell me not to go back for seconds," she orders me, but I encourage her to knock herself out and blame my own lack of appetite on a large breakfast (that I did not in fact have).

Janine Chalifour procures a fresh plate and horns her way into the appetizer aisle, to the clear consternation of a stooped-over gentleman who had been waiting patiently for his egg rolls. At first, I think it is Mr. Barnett from over on the next court that she has cut in front of, but a second look reveals this man is darker-skinned and a bit rounder in the middle than mother's old neighbor.

I see them everywhere, I think—those folks from back in the neighborhood—and sometimes, in fact, I do run into them for real, but it is never the old timers, like the Wilsons or Barnett, the Washburns or old Joe Coussette. It's the ones I grew up with that I bump into—at the gym or the nail place or stopping into the Walgreen's for a greeting card. "Oh, hey, girl!" they say. Susan or Lillian or Valerie or Dot. They tell me how good I'm looking and how well they hear I'm doing over here in Clayton, and they catch me up on all the news from the hood. This one's been real sick and so-and-so had another baby, and how about you? You settling down soon?

Settling down, they ask. As if I were a pot left too long on the boil.

"No, girl, no settling for me," I tell them.

Mother made damn sure of that. But I never tell them that part.

I scan the buffet area on the off chance there just might be anyone else from Breckenridge Hills grazing away, anyone who might wonder what I'm doing here on a day like this, but all I see is Janine with a pile of pot stickers and another mound of fried rice.

"Do you mind," she asks, when we are finished, "If I have a quick smoke?" She is already tapping one up from a plastic case, the sort of container one expects to see dug out of a great-aunt's gargantuan purse.

I signal her to continue: I don't mind the delay.

"Nothing like a cigarette after a great meal," she says, exhaling. "I don't smoke, really. Not all that much. Just sometimes at the club or at a party. Maybe at the beach. Or at a picnic. You know."

She is leaning against the Camry, and I adjust myself so as not to look impatient, unfolding my arms and feigning interest in the scenery: An auto parts dealer. A nail salon. An abandoned big box store. All circling an expanse of asphalt in desperate need of paving and restriping, repairs that will not be happening any time soon.

"You ever smoke?" Janine asks, waving the cigarette for emphasis. I shake my head.

Mother didn't approve. Of smoking (*trashy, slatternly*), of eating on the streets (*what common people do*), of leaving the house looking anything less than one's very best, including hair done (or concealed beneath a fine hat) with makeup fully applied. Which is how I'd known she'd lost her mind: parading around in a housecoat and curlers. (Mother, what would you have said of yourself?)

Mother would not have cared for this conversation.

You were not raised to spend time with the likes of this . . . person. Exactly like that, she would have said it.

DAVID HAYNES

(Who instead, Mother? Who?)

"Everybody smokes where I'm from. *Everybody*. They are a mess down home, I'll tell you that. You know how you know if you're in a quality trailer park?"

"How?" I respond. (Cynthia Garrison: world's best straight woman! And nothing if not polite!)

"If the church and the liquor store by the front gate both have paved parking lots. But just listen to me up here, all hoity-toity, confirming every Jeffco stereotype." She exhales again and chuckles and shakes her head, two parts irony, one large part genuine chagrin. She blathers on, adding a story about her first Synergy vendor dinner with the "boys upstairs," where they teased her about which fork to use with the salad.

"Honest to God, Cynthia, I almost planted my face right in that salad and grazed on it just to see the looks on their faces." Even still her face runs red with fury, nary a semblance of a mask.

Neither would Martha have been amused. Every contingency in place to assure it would never be Cynthia Garrison not understanding the roles of even those lonely forks and spoons parked just above the dinner plate. Deportment lessons, youth symphonies, field trips to Washington, DC.

And then there was the local public school that she thought so highly of—stuffed to the gills, ironically enough, with the likes of Janine Chalifour.

"Watch what the better children do," Mother ordered. "That's the reason you're up there!"

MARTHA'S DAUGHTER

Many of you—liberal and conservative alike—agree with Martha on this point. Believe that our spending the day with you—with any of you, anywhere—will somehow endow us with the keys to the kingdom.

Magical thinking at its worst, is what that is, but all the same, there I was, packed off every morning to Marvin School.

Knowing you, I imagine you would smile at my "school days" photos: little brown girl in the sweetest little dress, peppered with violets, thick braid popped up off the top of her head and hanging to the left. Several lesser ones anchoring the sides. Six years old and a little toothless in that photo; same photo fading to sepia in millions of photo albums across the world.

Next photo—Remember this one? Same little girl, this time in the second row and just to the left of center, a sea of white faces around her. No *Where's Waldo?* puzzles here. I can't be missed. Forgiving sort that I am, I'll not blame the photographer. Contrast is a bitch, and he had two choices: get Cynthia right and wash out the whites, or the alternative, presented here for your viewing enjoyment, where I am an indistinct blob, nothing but eyes and teeth. Standing out like dots on rice, as the old ones used to say.

(Don't you dare pretend like you don't know what they meant.)

You have clutched inside a bit, like at the movies when the hapless teens begin their exploration of the supposedly deserted farmhouse, or when the ship speeds toward the iceberg. Here comes what you have purchased your tickets in order to witness: The drowned frozen aristocrats. The dismembered youth. The poor little black girl who couldn't catch a break among all the white devils.

Again, I disappoint.

Look, childhood *is* sometimes a bitch, and it really is quite that simple.

Was it a cakewalk in your own privileged academies? Every day a fairy-tale dream?

There's no need to answer. What we do know is that there are places in this world where our imaginations cannot comprehend the amount of daily suffering, and in those places, feelings are hurt in street games and the taunts from the neighborhood bully stab as deeply as the hunger pangs in bellies.

Childhood is a bitch.

Which is to say, then, that for this little black girl—as is true for most children—the horrors of the schoolroom are routine: forgotten assignments, misremembered answers, the day-to-day unpleasantness of your ordinary social miscreants. I would come home and pout when Tony Parlo made fun of my dookie braids. (Actual crying was not, in fact, permitted.) Mother would barely look up from her project of the moment.

"I am not sending you up to that school to pay no mind to no Tony Parlo or any of his other little trashy white friends."

One always replied "Yes, ma'am" to Martha Garrison. She'd continue with whatever chore had been occupying her in the moment and point me in the direction of my own housework.

That's all she would say, ever, never actually explaining how this whole "integration" thing was supposed to improve *my* life.

How exactly was it supposed to work, Mother Dear?

Anyone?

What exactly are the benefits of assigning oneself into a life where the majority of people, if you pinned them down, would simply rather that the likes of you were not around?

Janine grinds out her cigarette with her knock-off designer shoes.

"Tell you what," she says. "I'd sure take a quarter for every damn bad habit I picked up from my mama." Then she gets flustered and red in the face and apologetic. "Including, I guess, running my damn mouth about the wrong things at the wrong times. I'm sorry, honey." She reaches out—ready to have another moment—but I signal her to circle around to the passenger side.

She binds herself into the seat and says, "Listen to me, running my mouth about my mama, and here yours has gone and left us."

"Don't give it another thought," I tell her, but she is on a roll and just keeps on with it:

"The hard bit. That's what my grandmama calls this part. Says it don't matter if you are the Rockerfellers—that's how she calls em—or the lowest of the low, we all got to go through the hard bits."

"That we do," I concur.

And sometimes, I don't bother telling her, the hard bit feels as if the giant anchor around your neck has at long last broken loose and that maybe—just maybe—you could, for the first time in your life, move freely.

And, yes, I do admire the strength of character that is manifest as you restrain yourself from pursing your lips—in that way you believe to be subtly undetectable—and also to resist cutting your eyes slyly to the right on the likely chance you'll exchange a superior knowing glance with a fellow cynic. The like-minded are a genuine comfort, are they not? Persons such as ourselves who represent the more decent characteristics of the human species: none of this mother-bashing for our kind, no siree.

And how lucky you have been in your lives, how enchanting those sepia-tinted memories of your own sainted mothers, hot cups of cocoa always at the ready, her comforting wisdom an equally refreshing balm during the fireside chats the two of you continue to share nightly via FaceTime. Let's picture her, shall we, extracting a tray of Toll House cookies from the oven just as the doors of the school bus snap closed behind you on a wintery afternoon. In your memory, in anticipation of your arrival, does she clutch at the strand of pearls around her neck?

How lucky for you that it was not Martha Garrison waiting at the door.

There were no cookies, and what passed for wisdom from my mother wasn't worth the coffee-stale breath she wasted dispensing these truths.

For what it's worth, Martha, too, was always there when I got off the school bus, albeit the nature of that presence a willing hostage to whatever phase of life she cared to inhabit at the moment. Mother was an… enthusiast, you see. You might prefer the word *dilettante*, but that to my mind encompasses a bit too much cosmopolitan sophistication for a woman whose interests ran less toward the latest trends in contemporary art and more in the direction of joining a noontime bowling league and rescuing feral cats. Mother golfed for a while, joined an interfaith "discussion" group (long before such things became fashionable), actually did pursue painting for a spell, a fervent acolyte, she was, of l'atelier Bob Ross—ah, to have grown up in a home bedecked with dozens and dozens of grotesquely cheery paintings of "happy little trees."

Mother's enthusiasms were always worse when collaboration was required: at one point back in the eighties, just as her own child-bearing years were passing, she joined the March of Dimes, and during the annual fundraiser I would step into the house after school and be lucky to grab a saltine and a mouthful of water before being dragged right back out, whence we'd ring our way around the cul-de-sacs of Breckenridge Hills, shilling for spare change, my role, as you might imagine, a living illustration of the rewards that awaited those who practiced sound prenatal care.

Mother would pound her fist against those doors like the sheriff come to set their belongings on the curb and order me to "Smile, baby"—a manic toothy grin always her idea of a winning countenance; a winning countenance the first step in priming those endless pumps of spare change. "Go!" she would command, gouging me in the ribs with her elbow to prompt my well-rehearsed come-on.

"Good afternoon," I had been trained to cheer, immediately followed by the householder's name. There are actual scripts that use actual words such as *householder* and *affliction* and *remittance*. Householder was to be called by his or her real name if one knew it—"And remember," Mother would hector, "It's Mister or Miss to you, and just let me catch you being too familiar with anyone, and see what I don't fix your punishment at." I was to begin my little spiel about why we were there and the importance of prevention... and, no, I don't remember the rest of the damn speech, because by this point Mother would always press the eject button, heaving a big sigh and shuffling her feet in frustration. To this day, even the memory of that sigh can leave me shaking with rage—a rumbling and wheezy expulsion, a sound that most closely resembled one of those giant rigs shuddering into place right next to you on a grid-locked expressway.

"I warned you about wasting these people's time," she would whisper—barely a stage whisper, that would be—and she would shove me back into the chorus with the rest of the second-rate performers who didn't merit center stage. "The poor girl does the best she can," Mother would apologize, smiling and simpering and shaking her head, and she and householder would share a good chuckle over the haplessness of the "youngins" and then Mother would say exactly what I had started to say and then we would both smile and then the coins would come a-clattering into the can.

And, no, I did not roll my eyes the way you would like to imagine I might. Why? Because I did not care for a backhand across the mouth.

Cringe a little, did you? The thought of that brownskin ham of a hand cuffing me in the face. How very sweet of you to care. How naïve. Only in your *Father Knows Best* versions of America do parents withhold the sharp smack in the teeth when merited, and while it *is* my nature to mock your disingenuousness, I must remember the marked differences between my life and yours. The pearls, the cookies, the ongoing lovefest that was and remains your birthright? Treasure those memories, my friends. Martha Garrison wouldn't have thought twice about snatching a switch off that weeping willow and striping the back of your legs with it—not that persons of your fine character ever required such handling—and neither would any one of those householders have blinked an eye had she done so.

I am being overdramatic, surely. Having a bit too much fun confirming your beliefs about pathologically violent parenting in communities other than your own. For the record, and while we're comparing heavy-handed bullies, Mother was strictly bush league. Physical confrontations of the public variety were beneath Martha Garrison's station, or so she liked to believe; the sort of thing that the desperate and the common resorted to when they lost control of their offspring in the produce section. Right there in the aisle of every discount store in America you will find the subject of Mother's disdain, obese women in thrift-store rags, swatting aggressively at their disheveled rug rats. Right there in the aisle next to those women, that similarly obese but somewhat less poorly dressed woman is my mother, clicking her tongue in disapproval, a sound that you also are skilled in reproducing.

Vicariously thrilling, are they not, the lives of the less fortunate. It is impossible to look away. There are entire industries in our world whose sole purpose is keeping you thus entertained. It will interest you to know that in my younger days, I played a decidedly minor role in this industry, entertaining myself by entertaining others—people very much like you—with my own lurid "tales from the dark side."

That is my charmingly sardonic way for describing my witty commentaries on the life of my people.

It was an accident, really, my brilliant career as a storyteller: there I would be in the college dorm, regaled with all your pumpkin-pie narratives of life out at the lake house, those wistful memories of backyard keggers gone awry. My own coming-of-age had been highlighted by scintillating hours in a study carrel at the Overland public library; all I had to add to the tales of wayward youth was a comically slapstick tale of a course in "deportment for young ladies" that mother would drive me to on Saturday mornings. The car ride to that course a master class in derisive grievances, directed toward me for every dime spent on tuition—as if it had been my idea to go to in the first place. Barely an anecdote, the story of my debut on an improvised runway at the Northwest Plaza Sears store, less than dazzling in budget sportswear, soon drained of what little entertainment

MARTHA'S DAUGHTER

value it had, and desperately eager to remain "one of the gang,"
I diverted my young peers with tales of a crack-addicted uncle
who stole the family Christmas presents to feed his habit, and
the fact that I had five siblings that my father had sired through
five women other than my mother. An electric sparkle of adren-
aline would rush my veins as I spun out every sordid detail of
these lies. As are all well-meaning people of their ilk, my "peers"
were simultaneously appalled and titillated at the witness of an
actual person who had survived such a life, and I realize now
that my storytelling, in fact, performed a kind of public service.
I report to you with pride that any number of my classmates
went on to volunteer for organizations such as Big Brothers
and Sisters of America and the Literacy Council; some joined
the Peace Corps and more than a few of them actually stayed
for at least a full year.

I will ask you not to judge me: I was not and am not a terrible
person. It's simply that Mother had failed to adequately prepare
me for the ambassadorship duties that are a requisite part of
this experiment in intercultural community that you and I find
ourselves signed into, no choice of either of ours. It would have
been beyond Mother's ken to imagine that she'd even need to
prepare me. For what it's worth, my stint as young America's
representative from the ghetto was a relatively short-lived one.
At a certain point the gullibility of others becomes tedious,
and that would become my saving grace. All that willingness
to believe my lies, however artfully constructed, rather than
amusing me, left me disgusted in a way that hardly mitigated

my revulsion for the smoke-filled lounges and cheap flat beer that are standard features of our privileged college lives. Eventually, when my need to be loved by you waned, I found myself again contented to life in the study carrel, me and my books and my plans to simply survive until the next phase got started. I ceded the task of chronicling the life in America's underbelly to the much more highly skilled employees of our cable-news channels and to the studio executives in LA's entertainment industries—and far be it from me to begrudge them giving people what they want. It makes one's life better, does it not, to have confirmed what it has always comforted you to believe.

Before stepping aside, however, I did leave my loyal fans with one last tale—a true one, as it happens.

Throughout her life, Mother had a recurring obsession with the buying and selling of hers and other people's unwanted household detritus. She was of the class of rummagers less engaged with profit-and-loss and more enthralled with the art of the deal. Hadn't it been just a few weeks back that she called me at the office in one of her lucid moments to inform me that her favorite price club had on offer a pallet-sized bundle of paper towels at a member's-only price of $24.99, *get em while they last*. That neither she nor I had room to store many dozens of rolls of paper towels nor any imagined need for that much absorbency in our lives was beside the point; a deal was a deal.

In her heyday Mother would have set those towels on a folding table and sold them for a dime a roll, her own version of a loss leader. She was the queen of the impromptu sale—the spirit struck her and down to the main drag she'd go with her cardboard signs and her staple gun. Out on the front lawn she'd assemble an assortment of gewgaws and whatnots and plastic dishes and boxes of sad-looking baby clothes, an inordinate amount of those emblazoned with characters from the golden years of Sesame Street. 31 St. Benedict Court, just one of many thousands of way stations for the vortex of crap that spins through the bottom rung of our economy: beat-up cars, paste-board furniture, aluminum forks that bend at the resistance of a boiled-to-mush canned pea. Around and around it spins, all that crap, until the legs fall off the chest of drawers and the bottoms rust out of the Chevrolets. That stained onesie with the faded face of Elmo is now the garish center square on someone's Aunt Denise's surprise Christmas quilt, and that, too, before long, will be available on a front lawn near you—if you can fish enough bills out of your bra strap.

But I am disappointing you, I know. Back when you were being trained to conceal your disdain with that oh-so-cool demeanor that attracts so many admirers, I began my own (often failed) attempts to read the contempt beneath your plastic veneer—those of you, at least, who take the time to even bother to mask your scorn. As you might imagine, I actually prefer your ridicule to your patronizing simpers, and, yes, I do understand your frustration. You are unused to such banality when it comes to stories from my world, and I genuinely wish I could ease your suffering. Alas, my mother wasn't the prototypical ghetto monster of your wet dreams;

Martha Garrison was just... weird. An odd duck: I think that's the phrase I've heard you use.

What can I say? I learned back in those college lounges the perils of dramatizing the inherently undramatic. What is that other animal expression you say? The one about purses with ears? The one about the futility of a bad bluff and about playing the hand you are dealt? This isn't the story of a monster; it's the story of a fool.

I arrived home from school one day to discover that my mother had set my bedroom furniture out on the front lawn and sold it to whichever hausfrau had made her the best offer. Dresser, vanity, nightstand, mattress—every pathetic stick of it, the sour linens right along with it. Me, I scrounged a bundle of sheets and blankets from the closet in the bathroom, made myself a nest amidst the now homeless piles of socks and shorts and T-shirts, and over those next few weeks made considerable progress on my master plan to get myself the hell out of Breckenridge Hills.

We both appreciate the appeal of stories from the dark side; your morbid fascination with our drug-addicted uncles and bastard siblings and fists in the face. Who could resist? Many people live those lives—your system assures that this is and will always be the case. But those are not my stories to tell, and—let's be honest—mine, while arguably tawdry, is a far less scintillating one. Here's the simple truth: people at the bottom do stupid and pointless and absurd things to scrape their way through life. That's it. The usurious "payday" loans and the paper-thin cold-cut sandwiches and ketchup soup at the end of the month. Someone else's old jeans over your own raggedy-ass underwear. A rummage sale to pay the electric company or to pay for deportment classes at a long-torn-down Sears in order that your daughter learn to behave as a "proper lady" in this world. All part of Mother's own master plan to usher me the hell away from my home and my neighborhood.

More shameful than lurid, really—and funny, isn't it, the way we'd prefer to have you believe that they beat us in the face with their fists rather than know that on most days they couldn't make change for a five-dollar bill?

Ah, you say, but it all worked out, did it not? Look at your fabulous life. Or is that *her* saying that: Martha Garrison, body not yet cold and already kibitzing from the beyond, nodding wisely and tossing a little wink in there to acknowledge the general consensus among us? I might suggest that she shut the fuck up for once, but haven't I incurred enough of your wrath?

A month or so passed and a "new" bedroom ensemble, bargained from some other sale on some other hardscrabble cul-de-sac, greeted me in my boudoir, dressed in pink-and-lavender-striped sheets that were pleasant to the touch and, honestly, somewhat fetching. The woman had exquisite taste, if you must know, if often enough with little or no money to support that discernment. At no time in the thirty-two years between then and today did Mother and I exchange as much as one word about those beds, and now, it goes without saying, we never will.

It would kill her to know that I am telling you this.

But I do tell. I tell it to Janine—or part of it, at least. There'd been another lull in the conversation and a back-up on the entrance onto 270. I exert a faint chuckle—slightly snide, slightly ironic—and I tell her:

"One time I came home and she'd sold the beds." That is as much as I share.

"No!" Janine exclaims. (She is *shocked*! *Shocked*, I tell you!) "Well, isn't that just the way they are?" She laughs.

Knowing me as you (think you) do, you imagine me ready to pounce on that *they*—you know: the way we like to amuse ourselves when we get the chance (which is often) by exploiting your pernicious and almost-constant linguistic microaggressions, intended or not. But Janine saves herself by babbling on with enthusiasm:

"These moms! What are they thinking? You got to love em!"

Yes, I tell her, you do.

"Mine," she says, "she'd have dropped them beds off at the consignment shop and high-tailed it to the VFW in Arnold for another round of bingo. That's probably where she'd be right this minute if they hadn't opened that casino boat down our way. Don't tell anybody I told you that." She offers the same giggle of all naughty schoolgirls who air the family dirty linen, a volatile mixture of delight and shame. Embarrassment colors her cheeks, as it often does, but shame has never inhibited this one's confessions.

"My mama! Now that's an old gal who still loves her party, I'll tell you what."

Is that the air conditioning, or do I feel a Janine story coming on?

"Maybe not all that old, I guess," she says. "Mama had me young—real young. But you know how it is: If they're your parents, they always seem like they're ancient, don't they? I mean, I can't go to a bar down home without people asking me where my sister is. People actually say that to me. Can you believe it? And I don't have to tell you that Mama loves it. *Loves. It.* Leaves me thinking, I must be looking pretty damn old myself, you know what I'm saying? I don't know. Sometimes I just wish... You know?"

"Yes, I do know."

I offer her that much.

I have mentioned, I am sure, my abhorrence for true confessions. How does it improve my life to know that Janine Chalifour's mother is the Jefferson County barfly?

Ah, but Cynthia, you say: You are missing the point. Salacious details aside, you are two women bonding in a difficult time over the shared experience of being the adult daughters of difficult parents.

Well, maybe. And I'll certainly grant you that this is the thing we do, we women. The practically mandatory price of admission to the sisterhood, and as distasteful as I find it, there are catalogs of websites and entire television networks that are more or less venues for easing the "hard bits" by way of public mortification. Janine and I at least have the common decency to confine our confessions to a barely moving automobile—rather than, say, to the panel of an afternoon talk show hosted by an ersatz doctor.

To wit: Janine twists a hank of hair that has circled from behind her ear and—her mouth set flat and hard—she tells me, "This one time, Mama and I actually went out with the same guy. She actually stole a man from me, my mama did."

"No!" I respond.

The horrors!

I have no more desire to hear this story than you do, but the lunch-hour rush-hour traffic in North County crawls along sluggishly, and better her than me doing the talking. She, needless to say, requires little prompting:

"Yes, ma'am, she did. If I'm lying, I'm dying. She did it."

I shake my head sympathetically and look her way. Janine's face has shifted somehow. As if all the edges of everything—the ridges over the brow and tip of the chin and the apples of the cheeks—have hardened and now protrude at the wrong angles. It's that hardened face you studied in your art-history textbooks, the iconic photos of women in Appalachia during the Depression. How jealous you must be that I have something resembling the real thing here, just to my right.

"He wasn't... nothing, really. Just a piece of shit Jeffco trash—you know the type—but still... I don't know why I took up with him in the first place."

Janine snaps and unsnaps the flap on her purse, and I know she's craving a cigarette (which she knows better to light up in *this* car). She says she met him at a party, or so she remembers.

"I spent a lot of my weekends down there before I settled in St. Charles. Familiar routines, and all."

When I'd hired Janine, she shared an apartment out in Maryland Heights with some girls she'd gone to school with. That gray area between college and "real" life, when one exists in neither place, where the past has passed, but the new part hasn't yet fully formed. Janine would clomp into my office looking bedraggled and sleep-deprived, complaining about this roommate or that roommate keeping her up all night with various impromptu drama. Often enough on Mondays she'd rush in just this side of late, announcing she'd spent the weekend "down home" and had forgotten to add the extra minutes to her drive time. Even when she'd not say she'd been visiting her family, "down home" had a unique smell about it that would linger in her wardrobe. Cigarettes and wood smoke and moth balls, with an undertone of fried catfish.

Next to me in the car, she simmers in the quiet rage of her memory.

"Don't know whatever happened to old Duane. We lost track of him. Last I heard he'd headed back down to Poplar Bluff to work for one of his brother's landscaping crews. Can't imagine that boy keeping a job."

There's a mix of disdain and affection in her voice.

What do you bet that you and I are conjuring up the same image of Duane: lean, with the kind of stringy muscles that come from a job instead of from a gym. Nice-looking? Well, maybe with ten more pounds on him, he would be, and maybe if he'd gotten those teeth fixed and had a decent haircut. Cardinal's cap and the kind of wannabe-thug outfit that these days you can buy at the corner Walmart. (A trend Synergy caught right as the wave started its ascent: Thanks, Janine!)

Or beefy. Maybe that's what you see. Farm-boy type, with the overalls and the jaw full of chaw. NASCAR all the way, baby!

The thing is, we're all on the same ride, my folks and Duane's: the people who invent these stereotypes happily sell them across zip codes and county lines to whoever is lucky enough to tune in. Was Duane born the way we see him—the way he sees himself? A good-old-boy, Jeffco-hillbilly-thug wannabe? Or did his favorite reality TV show make him into one?

What the hell difference does it make?

Janine says:

"Mama, you know, she dumped him almost as soon as she snagged him. She liked the part where she lured him away—you best believe she *loved* that—but she sure didn't like paying the liquor bills or having his lazy ass underfoot all damn day. Biggest mistake in my life."

I say: "I don't know, he must have had something going, two women chasing him like that."

(See. Not the conversational deadbeat you thought I was— but) all Janine offers in reply is something between a sigh and a grunt; noncommittal, and, frankly, just this side of rude.

Perhaps it had been the man-stealing that had finally driven her away from the trailer park and out into the adult world. A year or so after I'd hired her, she'd stopped coming in on

Mondays smelling like ashes and beer, and it wasn't long before she scrimped together the deposit for the condo in St. Charles, and it wasn't long after that that she'd made the effort to dress a little better and hold herself a little straighter and to "get with the program," as Martha Garrison used to say. Still, what is it your sainted elders always say? You can take a girl out of the trailer, but...

My own extrication from the world of my raising had been somewhat less momentous, albeit what it lacked in tacky love triangles had been more than made up for with Martha Garrison melodrama.

Everything in Marthaland was about Martha, be it the diploma handed to me at graduation or the color of the cars I bought or which brand of detergent I wash my dirty drawers in.

Post-graduation, the mistake had been returning home in the first place, but what could I do? Unlike many of you—with your trust funds and your hedge funds and your rainy-day funds and your what have you—my college life was about existing one work-study paycheck to the next, with each of those signed over to the bursar to cover tuition and room and board and fees and books and, and, and... And even though I graduated with a job already lined up (at the long-defunct May Company) and would be starting the following Monday morning, in fact (no summer backpacking idylls for the likes of me), I had nothing in the bank, and I needed a place to land while I put by some cash. I arrived home with my few bags and boxes—mostly of books and class notes (I've always traveled light)—and Mother greeted me with enough wide-eyed glee that I ought to have known I was in trouble.

The furniture in "my" bedroom had turned over at least twice since I'd chosen dorm life over "chez Garrison," although the basics of the décor had been maintained, as they have to this day, a shrine to Cynthia at Sixteen: at the window, a cascading nylon sheer embossed with a faux-lace patterning (hiding a plain beige roller shade); the walls a Pepto-Bismol pink, bedecked with posters of the various exotic locales I had planned to escape to. She'd trade out a dresser, Mother would, and bedeck the new one with the same items that had graced the surface of the old one—a few favored paperbacks, a cloisonné tray, a seashell from a trip to Gulf Shores—arrayed as they have always been, sprinkled with the same dust as from before the last time she had moved them.

"Put your things away before they get wrinkled," she had ordered me. "If anything's in your way, set it in the other room."

I slid open dresser drawers and found them packed to the rim with "her" stuff. No room at this particular inn. I couldn't imagine what all this crap might be: far from a hoarder, my mother, as previously noted, preferred to slap a price tag on anything she could make a dime off of and set it on the front lawn for the suckers to buy cheap.

Exquisite care had been taken when loading these drawers. Each item folded as if for sale in a boutique. She had separated one piece from another with a layer of tissue paper, and additional paper had also been folded into each garment, the way one does when allowing the clothes to breathe a little. Here and there, tucked amidst the garments, I discovered delicately scented sachets, little pouches sewn from scraps of flannel, some of them prickly with lavender sprigs, others sprayed with cologne.

I had never seen her in any of these outfits. A bundle of burgundy satin unfolded into an evening gown, one with an elegant constellation of rhinestones arrayed across the bodice. The deep jewel tone was the perfect color for her.

Where would she have gone in this beautiful dress? I had no memory of her dressing for anything formal, ever—say nothing of highlighting her body in the way that this particular sheath would.

"Well," she harrumphed. "People do take liberties." She retrieved a piece of the tissue paper from the floor and stuck out her hand like someone demanding her change at the 7-Eleven.

"You said I should…"

She waved those words away with a wiping motion.

During the college years I'd restricted my time with her to holiday weekends and to meals where I'd arrange to meet her at one of the restaurants in the Loop. My junior year I'd spent abroad—Oxford, as it happens—and the senior year, which I had just completed, had been packed with a series of internships that were more or less full-time jobs. Which is to say that I'd honestly forgotten how peevish and persnickety she could be, and—I couldn't help it—I actually sniggered at her little fit.

"This yours?" I asked.

DAVID HAYNES

I handed her the pool of satin that she'd continued beckoning for. (To be honest, it was all I could do not to throw it at her.)

"Everything in this damn house is mine," she responded; not in an angry or aggressive way, but with a mixture of pride and haughtiness—as if she were one of those marginally educated hip-hop stars showing off the gold-encrusted flusher on his commode.

The previous four years I had located (not without difficulty) women and men on campus and at my internships to mentor me and support me as I pursued my academic and career goals. These people would speak to me as if I were someone of intelligence and ability, and I would respond in kind. I had quite simply lost the habit of being part of this sort of exchange—of being part of the whole Martha Garrison... "thing." I opened my mouth to respond to her superciliousness, but she reared her body up and tossed her head to the left, pursing her lips and daring me to say... anything. It takes but a second, does it not, for all of it to come flooding back in; all the aggression and bullying and general unpleasantness.

But I'd come too far to be beaten back so easily.

"I've just never seen you in this," I said. It came out more sheepishly than I would have preferred—perhaps because I genuinely wanted the story behind this fabulous piece of wardrobe.

She was already laying the gown out on the bed to be refolded, and I reached in to assist, but she put up a hand to stop me.

She pointed to a squat cabinet under the window, more the size of a nightstand than a dresser, really.

"Your things go there," she announced matter-of-factly. And then, circling her hands around the dresser from whence the dress had appeared, she added, "*This* would be none of your concern."

I helped her unload a few storage bags from my assigned cabinet. (Well, actually, she ordered me to "come here," and loaded up my arms and directed me to put them by her bed. "Not *on* my bed; *by* my bed. See if you can handle that.")

Earlier that same day I had heard the words "magna cum laude" said in conjunction with my name. How quickly the worm turns.

Ground rules established and satisfied that my rampage of her storage facility had been fully arrested, Mother made herself scarce, and I found a place to hang the few new outfits I'd purchased as office wear. I tamped down my irritation by reminding myself that this was temporary—a few months at most—and that Martha Garrison only had the power over me that I chose to allow her to have.

Is this familiar to you, this tale of domestic displacement? When you returned from the Ivy League, what had your old room become? The sewing room? A guest suite? Had it been turned into your privately dissolute father's unpleasantly tacky "man cave"?

Perhaps your once-beloved bedroom is now the disheveled den of some acne-strewn, down-in-the-mouth teenage male, a boy you remembered to be sweetly bratty but is now the sort of person you change course to avoid passing on the streets. He glares at you when you take too long to brush your teeth and adenoidally hisses at you under his breath, calling you names that both of you know he'd never have the guts to speak aloud to an actual woman.

Maybe our lives are less different than I'd like to believe. It's hard living with these people, but we do our best.

The following Monday morning I rose early and made myself some coffee and made ready to drive into the city. I'd been interning at this office since January—the aforementioned May Company—and by now my morning routine was... routine.

"Oh, good: you're up." Mother said that as if it were noon instead of barely dawn, as if I'd already slacked away the shank of the day. "Listen, I've got a couple of things lined up for us. You remember I told you I'd been working with Washington-Reed to raise some money to update the playground. Lots of grandbabies around here now—I told you about the Hawkins girl, I know. A fast little tramp, that one. Have you ever been to that carnival supply down on Broadway?"

"I'm on my way to work, Mother. I have a job."

A ripple of indignation flashed her face, but Martha Garrison never allowed anyone the advantage of seeing her lose her composure, most certainly not the likes of me.

"Oh, I see," she said. She couldn't help herself—she said this as if she were a television talk show host and I was a precocious five-year-old who had been plopped on a stool mid-stage and ordered to be cute. "And what exactly is it you do at this job?"

I'm the President of the World! (*Audience roars with laughter*.)

"I'm a retail analyst, Mother. The job I went to school for. You know this." Perhaps even as recently as the previous evening I'd reiterated as much, but conversation was a one-way street with Martha Garrison. She twisted her mouth skeptically and shrugged.

"And this is what you're wearing today?" she added.

(*These mothers!* What are you going to do? Right, Janine Chalifour?)

Who, in the seat beside me, gnaws on a fingernail, longing for that cigarette, trying to direct her mind away from the duplicitous cow that birthed her.

In line with my mentors' training, I swallowed the sharp retort my mother deserved, filled a travel mug I had purchased at one of my company's discount stores (also now defunct), and told my mother I would see her sometime after six. Whatever it was that she said to my back has long since dissolved into a vast constellation of similarly ill-tempered Martha Garrison last words. Something dismissive, no doubt. I'd been immune to her bitter closing remarks since middle school. And, frankly, I had almost come to enjoy these pithy little commentaries on my shortcomings: preferable, in any case, they were, to the dead cold silence she'd leave you with when you really crossed her. I'm sure you know what I'm saying: When you can hear them back there. Behind you. Breathing. And judging. And fixing you with the kind of stare that might freeze molten lava.

Those few months I lived back home, Mother resigned herself, begrudgingly, to the time I would offer her on the weekends, most often a field trip on Saturday mornings and a shared late-afternoon supper on Sunday. This, after I'd held my ground about saving my weekday evenings for leftover office work, even and despite her constant ranting about what she was "owed" and the consequences of not honoring that debt.

Every one of those Saturday errands had the quality of having been invented on the spot. Let's be clear: this is a woman with nothing but time on her hands, one who, when the spirit struck her, would get in her car and drive into the city and over to the south side for a bag of chicken wings. There was nothing needed doing that she'd not have already done, had she so desired.

In my less cynical moments (yes, I do have them!) I recognize how lonely she must have been. My father had passed away when I was in high school. His benefits and a paid-off mortgage left her no need to find work, and despite her regular participation in a variety of clubs, both civic and social, she'd cultivated few if any friends. It's hard to know how much effort she'd even put into making friends; harder still to imagine her finding folks she deemed worthy of her attention. (*All those... common types around here!*) Sometimes, indulging my sentimental side, I imagine that she actually enjoyed our Saturday mornings together, browsing at the mall or examining the produce at Soulard. Imagine: a brightly lit montage in which two elegantly dressed black women, separated by a generation or two, ambling amiably past shops and cafés whose pastel awnings are inscribed in whimsical fonts with the sweetly ironic puns with which they have been named. They link arms and lean into each other as they laugh heartily at one another's clever bon mots.

We all entertain such fantasies: Come on, admit it! We live our lives pivoted on a hinge between sweet nostalgia and

MARTHA'S DAUGHTER

bitter disdain. Here, in the seat next to me, Janine Chalifour simmers at the memory of her mother's betrayal, but give her twenty minutes (and a cocktail or two) and observe as the corners of her mouth turn up slightly while recalling when that same mother bought yet another round of drinks for an assortment of aunts and nieces and cousins, a third pitcher of margaritas at the mediocre Mexican joint off I-55 (you know the one—just up from the title loan operation). Each of those aunts and nieces and cousins has been done wrong by a whole series of loser men, too often the same one. Janine's mother tops up their goblets and offers a salacious toast at the expense of doggish men everywhere, and Janine cannot resist smiling at this memory, at the nail-tough resilience of the woman who raised her. Mother Chalifour can and has directed her own despicable worst behavior toward each of the women at this table, but let one asshole in the bar come incorrect to any one of her girls, and she'd beat him to death with her platform boots.

This, needless to say, is nostalgia of a trashy and desperate variety.

Mother Chalifour is, in fact, a conniving barfly. This is true: her daughter says as much. And, as for Saturday mornings with Mother Garrison, the Spanish Inquisition might have proved a more enchanting way to pass the time.

On a Saturday in early September, after delaying my appearance for as long as is decently possible, I came into the kitchen and reached for my favorite mug, and she said to me:

"I guess the only way this tablecloth gets changed, which has needed to happen for years—not that anyone but me attends to such things—is if I sew one myself. What is the likelihood of your being able to find that fabric store on West Florissant Road? I don't want to put you out or anything."

And no, friends, we will not be deconstructing that sentence. To begin with, it was still early in my day and the first few ounces of coffee had yet to splash into the mug, and I am, therefore, unable to vouch for the accuracy of this particular transcription—which without a doubt *under*-reports its level of verbal aggression. Also: this was routine. This is the way she spoke to me every morning for as long as I could remember. And on this particular morning it would still be hours before things turned genuinely and more memorably ugly.

"Look at this," Mother said, plucking at the tablecloth. "And this. And this and this. And this." She fingered frayed edges, further busting open already broken seams. She particularly obsessed over an ancient beef-gravy stain resembling a deformed maple leaf. One Easter, a decade earlier, the serving spoon had tumbled from the bowl as Daddy had passed it in my direction. He'd laughed, but she had growled at us and snatched up the offending utensil and was already wiping at that stain before either of us had a chance to fully perceive what had occurred. Whatever amalgamation of plastic and natural fiber this monstrosity had been woven from absorbed the liquid immediately and permanently, imprinting a new pattern atop the embossed faux herringbone, Mother's ministrations notwithstanding. Years later, here she was, reading the tablecloth's various assaults like hieroglyphics, examining with seeming tenderness the documentation of a thousand family meals, and I imagine in that moment that she allowed to surface a glistening bubble of rage toward her dead husband's many foibles, am also sure that this rage pleased her, albeit in a shabby way. Hers was a quiet, if powerful fury, irritation that in an ordinary person would have long since calcified into some less toxic emotion, something almost certainly gentler and perhaps a bit playful. As she had done with many of the fixtures around the house, she could have replaced this tablecloth *many* times over the past twenty years. It had been on this table for longer than I had been alive, but at least part of her, I knew, enjoyed the way that it put her in mind of the good old days—and especially of the bad ones. And, yes, I'm sure she had been thinking of Daddy at least a little bit as with two snips of the scissors she extracted a fairly pristine triangle of fabric.

"We'll match this," she announced, sliding the sample into a pocket on the side of her purse.

Daddy worked the rails—the Union Pacific and Amtrak—porter work and cargo work, had done the post office mail run between St. Louis and Chicago, and would be gone often enough for a week or more at a stretch. He, too, it seemed, preferred to live his life "elsewhere."

I offered: "We can stop up at Famous and you can pick out a new one. With my discount and the current sale…"

"There was a bakery up there—those German people, who make the best stollens—and I'm going to have you stop me past there, as well. As if a person couldn't run a simple hem on a square of fabric. Some people have money to burn."

Her purse dangled from her crossed arms: a regular part of the Saturday-morning show. She'd tap her foot impatiently and look from me to the doorknob and back. Like a bossy and overindulged German shepherd ready for its morning walk.

I guzzled my coffee like a drunk while contorting myself into a sweater and fishing for my keys. "We'll stop on the Rock Road for a breakfast sandwich," I offered, and all she had to say about that was "I ate." Declaimed that, she did, like she was Mark Antony on the steps of the Forum. And then she mumbled (in that non-stage whisper of hers), "Plenty of food here. I don't know why I bother." Which would be her final benediction for that portion of the morning's services.

Garden-variety mothering, you're no doubt saying to yourself; *you should hear about mine when she comes over and looks around my medicine cabinet.*

Fair enough. But indulge me please. I've asked you before to set aside your received notions of tender mothering and filial harmony and love-conquering-all goodness: such fantasies will serve you no better than they have served me. I was young when I disabused myself of those fantasies: Isn't it time you did the same?

Because no one actually enjoys breakfast sandwiches and because I didn't care to hear a running commentary on my dietary choices or on the decline in civilization that was signaled by the advent of drive-thru windows, I headed over to

70, which I'd take to Lucas and Hunt. Work had me spending an inordinate amount of time in this part of North County: the company had been in the final stages of pulling the plug on their anchor store at the dying Northland Mall; my internship involved studies of traffic at the mall entrances and in a range of the departments, including housewares and better dresses. Soon I would price the final markdowns and begin shipping the still-viable merchandise to our other stores.

To my right, the turn onto West Florissant coincided with a crescendo of sighs and clicked tongues.

"Mph, mph, mph," she grunted, shaking her head. "Mph, mph, mph."

Ignoring her and having no recollection of a fabric store along here, I settled into the center lane—all the better to maneuver should it turn up on either side.

"Mph, mph, mph."

I did not feed in.

"Emerson Electric," I pointed out, instead. "Remember when Miss Thurester took a bunch of us kids from the neighborhood to the company picnic over there?"

Mother harrumphed and mumbled something about trifling heifers. She exhaled loudly and moved her head slowly from left to right, scanning the surroundings with disappointment.

"Used to be so nice up through here. SO nice. Mmmph!"

"I think it was me and Donna—both Donnas, maybe—and Tommy and Henry that Thurester took. Little Henry, not that other one."

Words kept spilling from my lips. I'd had this belief, disproven since childhood, that if you just kept talking, she'd abandon whichever unfortunate thread of conversation she proffered. I said: "They had rides set up for us and games and all the hot dogs you could eat. Thurester got us all fed and let us take a turn or two on the games. I don't think we stayed too long. I think it must have been a union picnic, now that I think about it, and she was probably just making her mandatory appearance."

"This is the long way out of the way to go to Florissant. I guess I should have known better."

"Mother, this *is* West Florissant. See, look at the sign. Right there. You know that my company has a store right back there, and I'm in that store all the time, and up ahead at 270 there's..."

And then there was the finger in my face. (No, not that finger: By now you know her well enough to know that *that* finger would never be part of her repertoire.) Mother's preferred gesture involved placing her pointer finger diagonal to your face—as if one were to follow where it indicated, toward some critically important item above and to the side of your head—but what it really indicated was that you were about to be corrected and that attention need be paid.

"Lived in this city long before you were born. That's number one. The fabric store has been where the fabric store has been—on Lindbergh—in Florissant, in the mall by the bakery, the one with the German people. This is by all evidence too much for you, what with all your fancy degrees and all."

One. As of that moment I had *one* degree. Not that it

mattered. I signaled the left onto Chambers, which would carry me over to the other Florissant Road, the regular one, which, this being St. Louis County, is to the west of *West* Florissant. Mother continued with a range of comments about people not listening and why, therefore, one oughtn't bother in the first place.

She had been right in her own wrong way. Despite having gone exactly where she'd asked me to, I had ended up in the wrong part of town. This was a regular feature of our Saturday outings.

Mother "mmphed" and clicked her tongue and shook her head. "It used to be so nice out through here. It's such a shame." On the left we passed a rundown strip mall, anchored by a chain record store (this was back in the day when there used to be record stores). In the car, to my right, more sounds of disapproval, now bordering on the anguished.

I would not be baited; I ignored the nail salons and the payday loan operations, and I pointed out a well-maintained Catholic school on the left.

"A girl in my dorm went there, as I recall. She used to…"

"It's no secret that when those people move in, this is what happens. It's a disgrace."

I tried to hold it in, but sometimes—often, actually—she crossed the line.

"Which people, Mother?"

I already knew the answer to that, and you do as well. Textbook example, is it not, of the charmingly coded language we employ to talk about each other here in America. Does it surprise you that we have our own codes for ourselves and that more than a few of them overlap with yours? You should know that on your *best* day Martha Garrison would whoop your ass in a "those people" contest. With one hand tied behind her back, she would.

"If you ask me..." (She hadn't really, but I wasn't letting her get away with it...) "I don't see anything around here that looks any different than over where we live."

Mother waved a hand to let me know I was dismissed.

Even knowing that you are well experienced in the world of bigotry and every other manner of ugliness, I can offer no useful analyses that might aid your understanding of the nature of my mother's personal brand of nasty.

Maybe this will help: the way that you snigger (along with me) at poor Janine—the limp hair, the sometimes too coarse laugh, the upper-left canine that ought to have been corrected by braces. The there-but-for-the-grace-of-God way that we are *so* glad that, whatever the hell we are, at least we are not *that*: it's the same thing, really. We titter nervously in ways that we believe mask our rudeness at those we secretly fear becoming, or at those we are afraid we already are. How many times a day do we do this?

Mother warned me regularly: Just let me catch you being common. That was her favorite word: *common*.

Common: the deadliest of the many deadly sins in Martha's book of evils.

Worse, you ask, than *slutty*?

Well, if you're slutty, then you *are* common, and Martha and I wonder, both of us, why you don't know that.

To save you from yourselves, here's a list of things that "common" people do that we would encourage you to discontinue:

Having furniture of any kind in your front yard

Sitting on furniture in your front yard

Walking up and down the street with *your business* hanging out

Walking up and down the street

Hiccupping, farting, or belching

Acknowledging someone else's hiccup, fart, or belch

Acknowledging the existence of bodily emissions of any kind

Marrying or dating a "common" person

Marrying or dating anyone whom Martha Garrison has not herself chosen for you

Biting all the nail polish off your fingers (*Janine! Stop!*)

"I don't think I've ever been up this way," Janine says, as she spits out another hot pink chip. "We've got all these same stores down home, you know."

Yes, Janine, I do know that. I don't know if you are aware of this, Janine, but I work in the retail industry. We are coworkers, as it happens. We work for the same company in a nondescript office tower in Clayton. I hired *you*, we work on the same floor—where you are ever and forever up in everyone's grill. That's the reason—the only reason—you and I are in this car together.

There is just a little bit of awe in Janine's voice, as if the intersection of 270 and Halls Ferry didn't resemble every major arterial crossroad in every suburb in the United States.

"We are almost there," I tell her, just the way I might reassure an anxious child. I do not tell her that "there" is a funeral home.

I had said the same thing to my mother in the car that awful morning. She had been glaring at me since I'd dared compare her forlorn part of St. Louis County to another forlorn part of St. Louis County. To Martha Garrison there are distinctions in such matters. Even the poor have their standards: those in the cardboard shanty towns under the railway trestle disdain those who sleep on the subway grates downtown. That's the way of the world.

"This is nowhere near where we're going," she goaded me.

Righteous indignation being her go-to attitude, nothing gave Mother more pleasure than finding others wanting. When she came at you, her scornful tone would be underscored with a wispy trill of glee.

Thought you were smart, did you?

I've got you now!

You know you should listen to me, but you don't ever learn.

Before I could suggest she remove her ornery old ass from my car and walk to the damn fabric store, she said, "Turn right. Right up here. We should have done it my way from the start."

As if we hadn't been. But turn right we did, as it happened, onto the actual Florissant Road, called in this part of the world New Florissant Road, I imagine to distinguish it from West Florissant Road, which as I've already mentioned, is to the east of where we were now driving. In my business this kind of street is known as Residential Arterial. (Definition: good luck finding a quart of milk.) Since the age of nineteen it has been my business to know things like this. Where the markets are and how people get to them and the likelihood people in the area would be shopping for moderate- to budget-priced casual wear. It's what we do, Janine and I. If there's a developer in the Midwest with his eye on a vacant lot and the possibility he'll be leasing to a clothier, we've got his number on speed dial.

Next to me, Janine's in analysis mode, I can tell. She's scanning the developed properties along Halls Ferry Road, where the two of us are stuck in traffic at least two stoplights deep.

"This was Mike Wilcher's territory before he left."

Bless her country heart, Janine Chalifour kept a directory in her head of every manager's domain.

She asks me, "Did you ever work the field?" and at first I think it's time to remind her about getting too personal, but this is shop talk (which is in-bounds, at least to an extent).

"When I was at May, I did a tour in merchandising. Working with managers, department by department, balancing visual appeal against optimum square footage. That sort of thing. I was in the stores regularly for a year or two."

"Stores sure are trashy these days, don't you think?"

"I do. Aisles crammed with markdowns. Nothing ever gets refreshed."

"If I were a manager, I'd hire two or three high school girls just to walk around and refold and straighten the shelves."

I tell her I agree.

"Geez," she says, "Will you just look at all these FOR RENT signs. I'll tell you what: brick and mortar's dead. That's why Wilcher left. Cynthia, us two: we need to focus down on Synergy's e-commerce repositioning."

Us two, Janine? As in you and me? *These people and their familiarity.*

"You read my proposal?" she continues. "I've been trying to snag you. For weeks. I haven't wanted to press it. You know. With your mother and all."

The truth always outs, and here it is—why Janine chose to join me on the mortuary run. She's got business.

I am entitled to throw a fit, am I not? My ululations of grief, my gnashing of my teeth having been so ignominiously subverted by this shameless office troll and her base ambitions.

As if reading my mind, she apologizes. "That was tacky. Thoughtless. You don't want to be thinking about work right now."

"I don't mind, really," I tell her.

This is true. Happy to take my mind off the traffic and off the task that is just up ahead and on the left.

As for Martha Garrison, well, she'd have me reach across this car and backhand Janine for daring to pull focus.

They'll always steer you wrong, those people. You can't let them. You make sure you're about your *business, not theirs.*

That she had no interest in anyone else's business but her own was a major part of my mother's confounding hypocrisy.

No. *Hypocrite* is the wrong word for what she was. *Hypocrite* necessitates the selective application of principle, but Mother was nothing if not consistent with her critique.

"At least it hasn't gotten too bad up through here. Yet," Martha had pronounced that morning.

What Martha Garrison *was* was a narrow-minded bigot.

"Up through here," as New Florissant passes under 270, were more superfluous strip malls, albeit with more small professional offices and fewer payday lenders. Mother's demeanor shifted from high alert to noticeably less rigid. Dare I say it: she relaxed. Beside me in the seat, she seemed to deflate a bit. Her shoulders dropped and something in her face softened. She loosened the grip on the purse in her lap.

"Washington Street: go there!" she ordered. My signal had already been clicking for the turn. Mother sat forward in her seat ever so slightly, like a child eager to catch the first glimpse of the roller coaster at the amusement park. "Your father and I considered living out here," she said. "But they weren't selling to us back then. And he liked it over where we are, so..."

These were, many of them, the exact same bungalows as *over where we are*, some of them shingled, some of them brick. Blindfold me and turn me loose in any one of these boxes and

I could find my way to the bathroom and to the thermostat next to the utility room.

"Here we go, up here on the right. Finally. After you got us all turned around. They'd better not be out of my stollen. You know how much I like a cherry stollen. Or, you know, they also make a half and half in here; half cherry and half berry or half pineapple. They're not stingy with the glaze either. You know I like a lot of glaze."

For those keeping score, the Meadows strip mall occupied the corner of Washington and Lindbergh; none of the Florissants, neither hers nor mine, intersected here. The mall was sixties vintage, built as they began filling in with subdivisions the land between Lindbergh and bluffs above the Missouri River. In college, one of my first papers was about retail strips such as this one. Back in the day, they'd build them simultaneously with the new houses. A regional grocer on one end, the Rexall Drugs on the other, with everything else you might need sprinkled in between. The children of the people who shopped here have moved to St. Charles. Anything they can't get at the Walmart, they buy online.

"Go slow," Mother ordered. "The bakery's just along here."

There was a Dollar Tree, a Walgreens, a Chinese joint that badly needed new signage. Nothing resembling a bakery.

"Looks like it's closed," I said.

"You drove too fast. Pull down here by the fabric store and let me get my bearings."

"Mother, that's a Goodwill Outlet."

Evidently, the fabric store had moved on, as well.

(NB: Advice from your favorite retail analyst: fabric stores are a good bet if you're considering a stand-alone retail venture. Lots of folks still sewing up curtains and school uniforms, even more so in a working-class area like this. More than likely Mother's fabric store had moved to larger digs nearby.)

(Bakeries: Yeah, unless you're in an area populated by hipsters with a lot of disposable income and a taste for the latest dessert trend, I'd pass.)

"Circle back," she ordered, so I did. Twice more I repeated that cycle.

"Well, I'll be damned," Mother rasped, more angry than disappointed. "If those people haven't ruined this too. This is why we can't have nice things."

At which point I'd had enough of her bullshit. I pulled into a parking space; there were plenty to choose from.

"Who exactly are we talking about, Mother? Who are all these people you keep going on about? Those people over there?" I pointed in the direction of the Goodwill. The doors slid aside to let an Asian family enter, just as an older black woman with a young girl came out followed closely by a couple in their thirties. The wife in that couple wore a purple hijab. At Synergy we'd had our eyes on the smart moves Goodwill had been making with their freestanding retail. A lot of our merchandise cycled through their operation, some of it secondhand, a good deal of it overstock.

Mother side-eyed me coldly and said: "You know exactly what I mean."

I did. And I wasn't having it. Not anymore.

Across that summer and fall, practically since the day I graduated, on every one of her damn "outings," I'd put up with her running commentary about "those people" and all the ways they were ruining her world.

I was done.

"You mean people like you and me? People who, as you just said, thirty years ago, when all this was being built, couldn't even *look* at a home in Florissant or Hazelwood, let alone purchase one? I assume that's the *those people* you're going on about?"

She exhaled sharply and refused to meet my eye.

"*Those people*, like our neighbors in Breckenridge Hills, who worked right down the road at the auto factory and at McDonnel Douglas and at the airport. Those people, right?"

"You better act like I raised you, with some sense, young lady."

"The sense to look down on my own people? Bad news: you failed." The tires squealed as I pulled out of the parking space and out of the mall and out into the Saturday-morning traffic on Lindbergh. I was taking her ass home and finding myself someplace else to be. For the rest of the day and, while I was at it, for the rest of my life.

"That's right," she said. "Take me away from this dump. You should have never brought me up here in the first place."

I practiced the relaxation technique I'd learned in a college mediation class. Inhale four counts, exhale eight. Repeat my affirmation, remember my strength. Next to me, my mother's coping mechanism consisted of sharp intakes of breath followed by snorts of disgust.

"I didn't raise you," she said, "to speak back to me."

"No, ma'am," I mumbled, and she retorted: "What!"

I did not respond.

"Wasn't me who made this world, but I definitely know some things about it. You can listen or you can learn the hard way. That's entirely up to you."

By that point in my life, I'd had twenty-two years of listening under my belt. Since graduation, my existence had been work and then more work and then coming home from work and listening to... *this.*

How could this be my life?

I spotted a JoAnn Fabric in another strip mall and navigated my way over to it. I pulled up right in front of the store, put the car in park, and reached across her to open her door. She opened her mouth to object, but before she could, I said, "I'll be in that parking space, right over there."

She took her time unbuckling and unfolding from the car. I refused to look over—and what was there to see anyway? That same look of enraged reproach I'd known my entire life.

Those mothers! You and Janine will agree. *What are you going to do?*

And, okay, fair enough: my stories of overbearing parenthood are routine at best. Your sainted mother hovered, too, and it drove you crazy, and yes, I imagine it does go with the territory.

Routine also: the story of the child who tries to break free but cannot stay gone.

"Seriously," Janine says. "Cynthia, you know the trends as well as anyone in this business. Synergy needs to make a move. Now. Or Else."

"You think?" I pretend to ask. We both know she is right. We both know it may already be too late.

"It's not that complicated. We partner with a successful e-tailor while we develop a niche concept for our own store. I've got five or six viable concepts for that." Her face morphs through a maze of contradictions, part enthusiastic schoolgirl, part the confident professional that I sensed was there in her (somewhere) when I plucked her out of the lineup all those years back. A film of desperation colors her impromptu presentation, the defendant's plea before a not particularly sympathetic judge. I hold her life in my hands.

She offers her final appeal: "The supply chain's already in place. I've got the drive and the motivation. You know that's true! You know how to make the numbers work. You know how to get it greenlighted."

"We'll talk," I promise her, and she reminds me that she's secreted the proposal into a manila envelope marked "recipes." It's in the trunk, somewhere in that briefcase we all admire.

Several stoplights down Halls Ferry, on the left, I spot the Cartwright name on the sign outside the mortuary, spelled out in the assertive yet tasteful cursive lettering that is the hallmark of such places. The original Mr. Cartwright had lived in the neighboring cul-de-sac from my parents. He buried my father, our next-door neighbor Wilson; almost all the dead people I'd ever known. Likely I'll end up here myself when my turn comes, a son or grandson of the current Cartwright patiently awaiting the arrival of whoever will come to make my arrangements.

"Yes," Janine nods. "When you're ready we'll talk."

My car is in the right lane; Cartwright is ahead on the left. I should be working my way over, but I hold my position. I assume Janine won't notice—what could she possibly know about black funeral homes in North County?—but I am wrong.

"You passed it," she says.

"Oh, dear," I respond. I don't imagine I sound particularly convincing. "I guess I'm distracted."

She reaches over to pat my arm, saying, "Of course, you are. Of course, you are. We're doing the hard part right now. Right here. This is the hardest."

Ordinarily I'd twist that invasive hand off its arm and she'd be drawing back a stump, but I seem to be tolerating it. For the moment.

"Pull up in here," she says, and I follow where she points and roll to a stop under the shade of a gaudy awning of an out-of-business fast-food place. "We'll sit a minute. We'll head back up that way when you're ready. No rush."

"When I spoke with Mr. Cartwright, I told him we'd arrive before two. I don't care to be late."

Tardiness was number one on Mother's list of evils.

"Just sit. It will be fine."

Janine says *fine* as if it were a three-syllable word.

I nod. I roll down the windows, and we sit.

Number two on her list: rudeness. On that horrible Saturday morning she had emerged from the fabric store with two bags that I assumed contained material for her tablecloth. I didn't ask. She got in and I pulled out of the parking lot and said not one solitary word to her the entire ride home.

Nor she to me, but in Mother's world it was my job to engage her and not the other way around. And particularly since she'd been making it clear, with her crossed arms and her pursed lips and a concerto's worth of grunts and snorts and sighs, that she was completely undone—which was *my* fault—and that the first thing out of my mouth had better be the word *sorry*.

At home I shut myself in my room and sat at an improvised desk, a barely adequate thing I had repurposed from an ancient vanity that I had no memory of being in this house during my childhood, another garage sale find, no doubt. Soon it could return to whatever function she'd imagined for it when she'd first bargained for it.

In a notebook I revisited the budget I created to facilitate my exit. I could delay the down payment on a condo for a year or two and divert some of what I usually placed into that reserve for a cheap rental. It would not be near the office—that was for sure, not on my budget—but I was determined and knew how to keep my eyes on the prize, and I could tough it out, even in a small studio, if need be. (Which would be bigger than this room, at least.) Out in Creve Coeur, perhaps—I'd start the search in the morning. I would bargain with our outlet store manager over a few decent sticks of furniture. I could do this.

Later that evening, when I'd emerged for a cold drink, she had draped the table with the three candidates she had selected at the fabric store. As per usual, she wouldn't deign to ask my preference; I was, instead, to offer it, and then I was to be lectured as to my lack of taste and refinement.

I said nothing. Why? Because I'm *rude*: you play her game or you're rude. Those were the choices in Martha's world. I chose rude.

Furthermore, as soon as I signed a lease, what covered that table wouldn't affect my life one way or the other, not ever again. I can't imagine how I could have cared less. I glanced at the fabric and glanced at her and then, to signal the extent of my interest, I opened the refrigerator door.

"You're not kidding anyone," she said. "You and your whole 'woman of the people' act. I know you, Cynthia Garrison. You wouldn't last ten minutes living with the people you accuse me of looking down on."

I poured myself a glass of juice and grabbed an apple and a wedge of cheddar. I rummaged the drawer where she stored the lunchmeat.

"You believe thinking good thoughts about them will make those people behave, make them keep up their lawns, teach them how to raise their children. The world don't work that way."

"Tell us, Mother. Tell us how it does work? How is it that life in this crystal palace is so much more special than the poor folks over in Ferguson and Dellwood?"

"I suggest you watch your mouth. Your father and I worked hard for everything we have."

"*Those people*—as you call them—I bet they work hard for what they have too."

"You can work a thousand hours a week and live in a mansion in Ladue. If you're trash, you're trash."

"Really, Mother? Even for you, that's..."

"I know trash when I see it. And so do you. That's how you were brought up. I don't see you parading up and down the streets, dressed like a hussy and calling attention to yourself. I don't see you standing under that streetlight on the corner, eating your food out of a paper sack. You've got standards. You know what's right. You hate the same things that I hate. There's no shame in knowing what's right."

She speaks those words with the smug joy of a scorned wife listing all the things worth hating about the tramp who stole her husband. Cataloging the people and things she despised always brought Martha Garrison intense pleasure.

"Bad manners can be corrected, Mother, and bad manners don't make someone a bad person."

"It also doesn't make them someone you care to be around." She had a way of lifting her left brow and twisting her pursed lips in the same direction when she believed she had bested you with her superior wisdom. I'll confess that while enraging, this face also amused me. There was no denying the dogged self-confidence of this woman.

"Well, maybe," I responded, not conceding her point as much as signaling the end of a conversation I hadn't wanted to be a part of in the first place and, with any luck, I would be done with forever. I gathered my snack and started back to my lair.

I couldn't resist a parting shot: "It also doesn't make me better than they are."

To my back she said: "If it makes you feel better to think that, I can't stop you. You go ahead and pretend you're someone you're not. You and I both know who I raised you to be."

Which, among many other things, did not include being the sort of person who spent her afternoons being comforted by Janine Chalifour. Who says:

"When we buried my grandpa, I was fourteen, maybe. I did not want to go to that visitation, Lordy, I'll tell you what. I begged my mama to let me stay home, but she said, 'No, girl, there's just some things you gotta do, and this here is one of them.' Which didn't make it any easier."

My father's death had been sudden and unexpected, and the memories of that period blur into a collage of the faces of family members I had been meeting for the first time, interleaved with the surprisingly moving regimentation of the military service at Jefferson Barracks. All of that underscored by Mother's inconsolable grief. She could not be comforted. He was the only man she had ever known. She kept saying that, over and over. The only man she had ever known.

"I think this used to be a Sonic," Janine says. She points to the yellow awning above the car. "I mean, I never actually saw a Sonic in real life—they never had one down by us—but I think this is what this must have been. I think you'd order your food through a speaker that was stuck on these poles. They bring it out on roller skates."

Well, bless her random little heart. I fire up the Camry and determine that I will get myself into that funeral home if it's the last thing I do.

A grandmotherly type in a pale pink pantsuit greets us inside the foyer and directs Janine and me to a pair of oxford-colored wingback chairs in what must be the "parlor" part of the funeral home. Gold sconces, ginger-jar lamps, heavy velvet curtains: everything speaks to that old-school WASP taste that you've likely inherited from your predecessors, who had themselves aped it from the Victorian drawing rooms they'd seen pictured in paintings and early magazines. You would find Cartwright and Son's parlor comfortingly familiar and in no way dissimilar to the places out of which your own dead are dispatched.

Parked here, in the "home" part—a place where after you croaked in the olden days you would briefly be on display before a quick trip to the family plot—in this place of brocade and mahogany, I try to imagine this space alternatively fitted out Martha Garrison–style, a mish mash of Scandinavian modern, Early American, and late-capitalist thrift-store chic.

The pink grandma offers us something to drink; Janine looks my way to follow my cue; we both decline.

"Mr. Cartwright Jr. will be with you shortly," we are told.

We sit quietly. Janine is either nervous or has returned to revisiting her memories of the folks down home. She's back at it again, picking at her nail with her teeth. They do tend to circle back, those memories of the good old days. I guide her hand from her mouth to her lap and gently pat it into place. She giggles like a schoolgirl caught with a naughty book.

We had had a sprinkling of snow that January morning when I loaded what few things I had out of the house in Breckenridge Hills and into a small apartment I'd found through a referral from a colleague at the May Company. Mother focused on the *snow* rather than the *move*, partly because it had always been her way to carry on about any and all things weather-related, but mostly because speaking directly to the other would acknowledge that moving out was a thing that a person could do and that I was a person who was doing that thing ("to her" is implied, needless to say).

She announced to me: "This is a glare ice situation if I've ever seen one."

What snow there'd been had dusted the lawn like powdered sugar on pound cake, and the sun had already melted it away. I said something about having snow tires as I passed her carrying an armload of work clothes to be suspended on a line I'd rigged up across the back seat for the purpose of this move.

"Are those *my* hangers?" she asked.

"They're hangers," I answered.

This represents, more or less, the nature of our discourse over our final weeks as roomies. The holidays had been tough, despite Mother not being big on them in the first place. She'd lost interest in Christmas when Daddy died, after which the season mostly provided an opportunity to complain about the crowded stores and the rude customers. Not so much with the good will toward men, Martha Garrison.

I had spent more time than I'd cared to over the past six weeks saying yes to every work-related potluck and Secret Santa social I could find, the sorts of things I'd ordinarily go out of my way to avoid. Any excuse to be anywhere else.

I had signed a lease on a tiny one bedroom in Richmond Heights that had been appended onto a bungalow to accommodate someone's aging parent. It came furnished and had a separate entrance behind the main house, where there was also a parking space for my car. It wasn't fancy, but it was quiet and clean and close to Highway 40.

And it was cheap. I could pay my rent and still put a chunk away each month to buy a place of my own.

I passed back through Martha Garrison's living room to gather one final load, which included my purse and my briefcase and a stultified African violet I'd purchased to bring some cheer to that tiny bedroom. It would do much better in the sunny window over the kitchen sink at my new place.

"When can I expect you for supper?" she asked.

"I'll be eating at home tonight."

"It's Sunday. We have dinner on Sundays. As a family. Like always."

Who knows? Maybe if there had been a smile on her face, or maybe just a hint in her voice that indicated that dinner with her daughter might, in fact, be a pleasant way to pass an evening. Perhaps a softening in the brow, the corner of a lip turned up even in the slightest of smiles. Perhaps. Maybe if she'd begged or if there had been a catch in the back of her throat, the slightest crack, which others might miss but which I would recognize had contained a modicum of emotion. What if, instead of a pronouncement, it had been an invitation? An actual invitation. *Daughter, why don't you and I sit down for a meal?* What if I'd been asked instead of told? If she'd said "please." Or something—anything—remotely resembling "please." Who can know how things might have been different?

As it was, I said, "No." Just no.

I had spent my last night under her roof and inside her worldview.

Charles Cartwright Jr. slips into the parlor so quietly that he is standing in front of us before I notice him. It's part of the training, I imagine. Undertaking 101. Walk softly. No sudden moves. Placid face at all times.

"Cynthia? I am so sorry about your mother. Everyone back in the neighborhood loved her so." I stand to greet him, and he draws me into a benign hug—which seems overly familiar, frankly. I knew him only vaguely—quite vaguely, in fact; he was a generation older and had been off to mortuary school before I started kindergarten. But the neighborhood was small, and I'd surely seen him playing hoops in the playground while I was still on the baby swings. Maybe he'd teased me and all the other little ones at the community picnic back in the day.

Preempting any possible questions from him, I introduce Janine as a "colleague who was nice enough to come with me."

He shakes her hand, and she is completely smitten. She's blushing—and did she just curtsy?

Before she says anything wrong, I say, "This is my first time. As an adult, I mean. I suppose you'll walk us through what we need to decide. The arrangements and all that."

"Oh, my." He seems genuinely taken aback. "Well... I assumed you knew. Everything's done. It's all been taken care of."

And now I'm the one who's taken aback. "I don't understand."

"Please. Come this way." He leads us from the parlor and down a corridor lined with chapels. Signs outside three of the rooms feature the name of the visitee in the same tasteful cursive as the signage out front. The pink grandma directs a florist with a large spray of roses into the room for "Mrs. Mattie Clark."

Charles Cartwright Jr.'s office is as quietly innocuous as mine at Synergy Enterprises. In lieu of art prints there is a portrait of his father and a slightly larger one of Jesus. It's a standard-issue Jesus, a bearded, long-haired white guy who looks like he plays bass in a country rock band.

"Your mother wisely made all the arrangements for her bereavement care. It's all in this plan." He hands me a folder. "This is all the paperwork and receipts."

"This doesn't make any sense. My mother has not been of the soundest mind for... many years."

(Ladies and gentlemen: Cynthia Garrison, Mistress of Understatement.)

"Mrs. Garrison wisely took advantage of our pre-need services back when your father passed. I'm surprised that she didn't mention it to you."

That she hadn't mentioned it is *not* the surprise in this or any other situation. Inside the folder, the first page is a glossy flyer for a silver urn with a lid embossed with lilies. There is a photo of an elegant marble mausoleum. Stapled to the back of the folder is a swatch of a burgundy fabric that is oddly familiar to me.

"This looks terribly pricy, I must say. Can we discuss alterna…"

"It's taken care of, Cynthia. All of it."

The pink grandma steps in quietly—they're all ninjas, these people—and whispers, "The Tollivers have arrived." Charles stands and further straightens his already straight tie.

"Apologies," he says. "We have three visitations today, so it's a bit hectic. Please review the folder. It contains all her requests and instructions. I'll get the Tollivers settled, and when I come back, I'll answer any questions you have, and we can review the calendar and determine what works best for everyone."

"But… but. How did she get here? I mean literally. Today. How did she get *here*?"

"Everything was arranged. Your mother was *very* thorough. As you know."

He pivots quietly from the room.

"He's kinda cute, huh?" Janine offers.

"Wha… He's the undertaker, Janine."

"He's a cute undertaker, though."

Hoping an exasperated sigh will put an end to this thread, I inhale and heave forth a full-bodied one. Janine responds with an enigmatic "hmph" and sets to exploring the engaging (to her) charms of Charles Cartwright's office.

The phone calls from earlier in the day seem forever ago and only compound the mystery of mother's arrival at the mortuary. It is really almost as if she delivered herself.

Breckenridge Hills police officer (female): Thank you for confirming your identity. Miss Garrison, your mother was found this morning on her neighbor's porch. I'm sorry to say she had passed away. Mrs. Wilson, your neighbor, wishes to speak with you.

Lou Wilson: Oh, Cynthia, I'm so sorry. She looked so peaceful sitting on our glider. I thought she was asleep. I'd looked in on her yesterday afternoon. She seemed fine.

Breckenridge Hills police officer: Ma'am, the staff from Cartwright's have been notified as per your mother's instruction. They'll arrive shortly for the deceased. Please call them. They handle things from this point forward. Do you have the number?

As per your mother's instruction. Funny, isn't it, how words can slide right past you. I remember that the officer was a black woman—I guessed as much from the few sentences she spoke, and I wondered if she was someone from the neighborhood—and also the way that, behind the calm in her voice, Lou Wilson had sounded heartbroken. Poor Lou: living next door, for so many years she'd borne the brunt of my mother's erratic behavior. Mother would let herself in, uninvited, or stare in her windows when the draperies were open. Lou would call me—sometimes weekly it seemed—and ask me to come see about my mother. By the time I'd arrive, Mother had almost always wandered off somewhere else.

Suddenly bored with Cartwright's office and observing that I am making no headway on my assigned task, Janine Chalifour reaches for the folder with my mother's instructions.

"Let's see what we've got here," she says.

She lifts pages from the assembly and grunts approvingly at several. "Your mother had good taste. It's all so well organized."

"The deluxe plan, I'm sure. They thrive on the upsell; you know how these places are." And I knew how my mother was too.

Janine responds, "I would probably date an undertaker."

"Seriously, Janine?" But apparently the sarcasm function of my voice needed calibration, because rather than "how inappropriate!" she hears "say more!"

"Trust me, girlfriend: I've dated worse. A *lot* worse. Let's be honest: Undertaker is WAY up the list from unemployed—or in at least one case I'm thinking about, maybe never employed." Janine reorders the papers in the folder and pops her finger up and down on the top two, signaling that attention should be paid.

"I dated a guy in prison once," she says. "I don't know if you call it dating. But he was this friend of my second cousin and she said he was lonely and asked if he could call me and talk sometimes, so I said sure, and he started calling, and before I knew it, he was calling every day, and I was like, 'What's up with that?' and he said, 'We're exclusive now,' and I changed my number and told my cousin I'd kill her if she told him where to find me. An undertaker is a couple of steps up from that."

The first five years after I moved out, mother and I maintained entirely independent existences, separated by several suburbs, a ten-minute ride by freeway. I had little desire to speak with her and had also, almost immediately, begun relishing my life as a young single workingwoman. I pushed hard at my job, where I took on increasingly complex assignments. I volunteered at the Red Cross on Lindell, and I got accepted to my alma mater's prestigious MBA. I became friendly with and hung out now and then with some other sisters who worked at the company; we'd do happy hours and movie nights and such, but they were big sorors—a mix of Deltas and AKAs—and busied themselves with a lot of Greek drama. I hadn't pledged and had no intention of joining at that point.

And yes, Janine, since you're dying to ask, I did date. I like men. Some of them like me.

"Then there was this one guy," Janine offers. "It started out good—they always do, right? That's how they suck you in—and he'd take me to nice meals, to the Olive Garden and such, and we'd talk and laugh, and I thought we were getting along fine. And then it was like the fourth date, and, you know, I thought, well, it's about time to step it up, if you know what I'm saying, so I invite him back to my place, and everything's moving along, and then all the sudden he's whispering in my ear about all this stuff he's gonna do. Freaky stuff. And I was like, 'Hell, no, I'm not doing that!' and I showed his skinny ass to the door. I think he figured because I come from down in Jefferson County, I must be one of *those* kinds of girls, but I tell you what: he sure was wrong about that. That's what I get for dating people at work."

"Janine: NEVER. DATE. PEOPLE. IN. THAT. OFFICE. Do you understand me?"

"Oh, yes, ma'am, I learned my lesson, I did. Sounds like you learned that the hard way, too, huh? It's the same thing, I bet. Those frat boys who run that place, don't you know, to them a black woman and a Jeffco woman are the same thing. You can just tell."

Like many of you, Janine is one of those white women who, when speaking the word *black* in front of a black person, do so in a semi-whisper, as if it's the dirtiest word in their vocabulary. One wants to assure such people that we are, in fact, quite familiar with the word and the various and ever-expanding concepts that undergird it.

And she's right about the frat boys around Synergy, but I'd learned this particular lesson long before my professional career. I was invisible to most of the white men in high school and college, and for those who did see me, it didn't take long in the conversation for the commentary on how "interesting" I was to begin—and it was clear they weren't talking about my mind. Perhaps I can convince Janine to get some T-shirts printed up for you. We'll use this slogan: *I've Always Wondered What It Was Like with a Black Gal.* Let us know what size you want; here at Synergy Enterprises we're all about satisfying your every fashion desire.

But I don't tell that to Janine or confirm she's correct about the frat boys. But do I find myself curious about what she's saying, and since she's willing to talk, I ask:

"What about now? You got a man on the line these days?" I make one of those faces one reserves for when the hot tea is about to be spilled at the water cooler, including squiggling my eyebrows up and down. She tells me to hush.

"It's tough, you know," she continues. "I don't need to tell *you* that." She laughs.

She's not the prettiest girl, this Janine Chalifour, but she has learned to make the most of what she's been given. A while back, she'd settled into a semi-structured pixie cut, and whoever did her hair did a nice job on the highlights, a too often enough wasted effort for someone like Janine, who tended to wait too long between touch-ups—whereby the horizontal stripe lining the part in her hair sat perpendicular to the streaks down the side. And while, yes, she did fit the Martha Garrison category of "horsey," that was more because she was a bit top-heavy and was extra broad in her hips. In the fifties she'd have been called voluptuous, and a good tailor would do right by her, but that's clearly not in the Chalifour budget (and just try finding a good tailor these days anyway).

I sympathized. At her age, I was in my condo and paying for grad school at the same time I was paying off my college loans. Things had thawed between my mother and me, and one Mother's Day, on a whim, I'd stopped over on Clayton Road and picked up one of those seven-layer cakes she loved. Typically, she had tried to start a whole big thing about it not being as good as the Miss Hulling's you got at Famous-Barr, despite my insistence it was *the exact same cake*. Bill Clinton had ended his second term, and something about him didn't sit right with Martha Garrison. I am eternally grateful to the president for soaking up a good portion of the criticism that might otherwise have been directed at me.

Soon, we had settled back into our routine Sunday dinners, now featuring her obsession with the problems in our nation's capital, informing me, not infrequently, that she had visited Arkansas and that she knew white trash when she saw it. I chose to nod along noncommittally and change the subject as often as possible to alternative abominations, such as the restaurant's décor and the tenderness of the steak.

What a good daughter you are, you are no doubt saying to yourselves. Regular companionable meals in moderately affordable restaurants with a beloved parent. I am coming to appreciate your sentimental views of the world. Revise *good* to *dutiful*, and we'll be singing in the same choir. Almost.

I was a dutiful daughter. Back then I was.

My parents were already older when I came along, and by this point Mother had entered her sixties. She was healthy, as far as I knew, but she was alone in that house and had never socialized much with the neighbors. I was her only family.

Obligation is such a... functional word. But there it is. I had an obligation. And so I fulfilled it.

Lest this strike you as cold-blooded, consider the source. This was how my mother saw the world. Everything was a transaction. She spoke incessantly about what she was owed: by me, by her neighbors, by the president, by the kid at the vegetable stand down on Rock Road. No one kept a stricter ledger than Martha Garrison.

Janine completes a litany of the losers she had dated, all in the interest of telling me that she was, in fact, currently manless. She gets all philosophical on me, saying:

"Sometimes I have my Cinderella fantasies, and some days it just seems a lot more trouble than it's worth. You know what I mean? I tell you what: I bet if I hadn't gone to college and moved up here to have a career, I'd be married, with a brood of kids. Done things the way you're *supposed to*."

"You sound regretful, Janine."

She gives her head an ambiguous shake, dons a wistful smile. "I made my choices. I like my life. I can't say I wouldn't mind sharing it, though."

I cosign this idea with a nod of my own.

"What about you?" she asks. I regret having started down this road, but don't mind as much as I thought I might.

I shake my head. Shrug.

She nods, asks, "Don't you think for women like us things are just that much more complicated?"

"Us?"

"You know. Women who struggle their way up and work hard to make something of themselves. Like you've done. Like I'm trying to do. Don't you think that you have to keep aiming high? That maybe you're less willing to... settle." She waves her hand as if to wave away those words. "That sounded wrong. I can't put my finger on quite how to say this."

She has said it just fine, actually, and she's mostly right. But I might have settled. That one time I might have.

Let's call him GJ. Here is the story I do not tell Janine:

I met GJ volunteering on the Obama campaign, where I worked a phone bank at the makeshift storefront that was HQ for eastern Missouri. You've seen these places. Rows of generic folding tables with tucked-under metal folding chairs. Wires snaking the floor connecting actual telephones that are perched next to manila folders full of information on the voters we have agreed to call and encourage to get to the polls. There are no decorations because on the day after the election a rental company will come pick up everything here and the space will revert to its status as class-C retail (read: future failed nail salon or, more likely, vacant until demolition).

In case you've not been attending to the tone, fellow romantics, we will be skipping the "meet cute" and the friendly flirtation part of this trip. You'll find that the queue for that ride is in a different area of the theme park.

In its place, for your reading pleasure, I offer a standard montage. (Cue the James Horner score, the lovers tumbling into fountains, the quick stolen bite of food from the enamorada's plate.) Eventually we found ourselves regularly sharing meals and, sometimes, a bed. Along the way we told each other the various truths and lies about ourselves that shaped our personal mythologies.

GJ presented as your garden-variety survivor of the city, come of age in the West End when it was still possible for a smart kid with decent parents and a smidge of luck and common sense to work his way up and out. Back when such a person was much less likely to be shot on sight, simply for walking from the bus stop to his front door.

The real story was somewhat more complicated than that.

"Getting this barbershop up and going, it wasn't always easy," he told me. Early in our time together, he'd proudly offered me the deluxe tour of his enterprise, a four-chair shop in an oddly out-of-place new strip mall in The Ville. "But, you know, I'm proud of the joint. Regular clientele, pleasant place for my customers to hang. I keep the dealers out. Not having that here."

Along with a southern affect that would come and go, seemingly at random, GJ's shifting of "barber" to "barba" and other similar locutions came off as painfully forced sometimes, but in a way that I also found charming. His version of "his rise from the depths" both under- and overstated the nature of his struggle. On the one hand, St. Louis, even in its industrial heyday, had never been an easy place for black folks, what with the twin demons of class stratification and racial segregation. *Bad breaks; setbacks*: GJ revered Marvin Gaye. "Inner City Blues," the soundtrack for young men coming up hard.

On the other hand, GJ was far from your garden-variety ghetto kid. Scion of one of those elite families, the sorts of folks who were proud of the fine homes they'd made for themselves near Fairgrounds Park or in the West End of the city. They clung fiercely to identity and neighborhood, and how hard they'd worked to get into those homes and the social clubs that only admitted people who owned in such showplaces. A wrong turn or two and a disinterest in the strictures of formal schooling had engendered a rift between GJ and his family: they'd wanted a doctor; they'd gotten a barber. (Notwithstanding that GJ was the go-to guy of professional athletes and a cadre of the city's political elite.)

Gloomy, with the letdown of a successful campaign passed, GJ had decided seeing *The Dark Knight* would cheer us up. (Don't get me started.) On the way home, I'd diverted his enthusiasm for a brooding Batman to a recent obnoxious conversation with my mother, who had announced that until they started making films like *Imitation of Life* again, she'd be boycotting the theaters. I told GJ that I don't remember my mother even once setting foot in a movie theater.

"Not once?"

"Martha Garrison is not big on sitting still."

"You don't talk about her very much. In fact, this may be the first time you've brought her up like this." For some reason, that triggered a fleeting ripple of shame, and I tried to remember if it was true. (Which, of course, it was. I never discuss my mother with anyone.)

"We're not that close" was my excuse. I said that with the pleasantly flat tone I used to fire underlings or when seated next to chatterboxes on airplanes.

"Same," he responded, and he went on to tell me more about growing up in the city and how his family had been one of the last to move off Kensington Avenue before it had "all gone to hell."

I heard echoes of Martha Garrison in his tale, minus any of her ubiquitous "those peoples" or "elements" or "ilks."

"They went out to West County with everybody else. Wouldn't set foot in the city at all if they didn't love the Cardinals so much."

I had driven past those homes on his old street, a few of them still notably grand, despite years of neglect. Several of Martha Garrison's bungalows would nest easily inside them, with room leftover for the sleeping porches and the porte cochere.

I am amazed, now as I was then, at the ironies around the ways that our lives and upbringings both overlapped as well as diverged. Both of us raised, as we were, by parents with the archetypical standards and expectations of aspirational black folks around the world, the requisite wall of diplomas with your name on them being the minimum price of a full welcome to the Thanksgiving table. That ne'er-do-well cousin or niece: Bless her heart, she may hold down several jobs and pay her bills on time and own her own home, but unless she's got that paper: "Deanna is still finding herself. We're praying for her."

At the same time, my own bargain-basement classes in deportment were no match for GJ's afternoon "socials" with his Jack and Jill peers, and now and again he'd slip into the conversation a mention of his prep school and summers at the lake or the name of some prominent attorney that he'd "known since we were kids."

Me: I'd volunteered for the campaign out of civic duty.

GJ: His brother had gone to college with Michelle.

One still sees GJ's parents' photo on what passes as "the social page" of various newspapers and magazines. There they are, ancient, posed next to the mayor or the television anchor at the fundraising luncheon for "important" causes such as the United Negro College Fund and the Urban League. When I was growing up and Daddy would bring home the *St. Louis American*, my mother would grunt derisively at such pictures. She would flip the pages and turn up her nose at the fair-skinned women and their too obvious extensions. "Think she cute," she'd sniff.

Mother was the sort of person GJ's parents had fled the West End to get away from.

Janine wanders back in from a self-guided, self-initiated tour of the facility.

"You should see how nice they've got the lady in number two laid out. Lace blouse with a lavender jacket. They matched her lipstick to the jacket. Real pretty."

I hold my tongue and hold my face still. (What would even be the point?)

"The older gal, the one who greeted us? She asked me to tell you that the hot funeral director would be a few more minutes longer."

"Thank you, Janine." I'm sure that's exactly what she told you to tell me.

"She didn't say why, but there is some kind of a commotion up in number one. The doors were closed, so I couldn't see in, and I didn't want to pry, but it sounded like someone was just, you know, overcome. So sad. I guess I could go back and make sure everything is okay. It just makes you want to... do something, you know?"

So helpful, this Janine Chalifour. Never in my life have I been more tempted to send someone into the lion's den. Sure, sister: go right on in and ask the nice black people how you can help them grieve. But what had those poor bereaved people ever done to me? Instead, I say:

"I'm sure Mr. Cartwright is handling it just fine. That's part of his training."

"It's kind of a weird job, isn't it? Seeing after all this?" I release a noncommittal sound, something between a sigh and a snort. As weird, one imagines, as figuring out how to sell pastel knit tops out of increasingly rare free-standing clothing stores, or sculpting heads with clippers and a sharp pair of scissors. Once, I asked GJ about touching all those strange heads.

"Kind of gross, isn't it? I mean, hygiene and all?"

He scoffed at the question.

"Like you go to the salon with your hair dirty and stuff. Please." He lingered on the *e* sound in *please* as long as his breath would hold. And then he went on about how rare it was for men to ever be touched in any nonsexual way; about how his mentor had taught him to give a little massage to the back of the neck when fastening the tissue, and about the dozens of old men in the neighborhood around his shop who came in for weekly "shape-ups" that they absolutely did not need and how he knew what they really wanted was the conversation and the companionship and for someone to just see how they were doing. GJ knew all of their names and the names of all their kids and grandkids too.

"I take everyone's blood pressure," he told me on our tour. "And if you under ten or over sixty, you get a lollypop."

Meticulously and without fail, GJ shaved his own head every morning. After turning on *Morning Edition*, he'd lubricate his pate with his preferred gel and methodically run the safety razor in a pattern that reflected years of practice. Once, I'd made the mistake of interjecting myself into his ritual, a Martha-esque inquiry of the "Really? Every day with this?" school of butting in. He'd eyed me up and down and twisted his lips to the side—that way men do to let you know their business is not any of yours. I don't believe I ever saw his natural hairline or knew whether his baldness was vanity or necessity. It suited him though; what a beautiful man.

Even Martha agreed.

Wait, you say: That's a thing you actually and voluntarily did? You took this man to meet *her*?

As Janine would say: Shit happens.

We had been lazing around my condo on a Sunday afternoon, a thing that we'd come to love, GJ and I. He had arrived late the night before, exhausted: on Saturday afternoon, the shop would stack up with customers come in for their shape-ups before church in the morning. On a good weekend he'd finish his last head before eleven. After we were regular, he'd roll in shortly after with a bag of greasy chicken wings from the place down the block from him; fall asleep on the couch before *SNL* finished their last sketch.

Sunday brunches I would make him french toast, and in the afternoons, often, we would go for a drive. GJ and I shared an obsession with exploring out-of-the-way corners of the region. Between us, there were so many places we'd never visited: Carondelet Park, Portage Des Sioux, the deserted and border-line-creepy roads that wound through the river bottoms. We loved happening upon long-abandoned train depots and the crumbling remains of storefronts that once had been thriving retail strips. GJ had an eye for architecture, and I have always been the sort to drive by a quirky old house and imagine the lives inside.

One Sunday he made a right off of Natural Bridge and we found ourselves driving through an enclave of stunning homes adjacent to the university campus. I had no idea this street existed, and I told him so.

He asked, "You grew up nearby, didn't you? Why don't we go drive through there?"

I was taken aback. I told him I'd grown up out near the airport—which this street also was—but a place such as this, with its broad lawns and designer homes, each one unique: I'd never associated someplace like this with Breckenridge Hills. And also: if we were talking about Breckenridge Hills that meant we were talking about *her*. It was still *my* part of the weekend, *my* part of Sunday. In a couple of hours GJ would drop me off at my car, and I would go pick her up and take her to Red Lobster or the like, and we'd eat our Sunday supper while I listened to her weekly harangue on... whatever. I didn't need her in this part of my day too.

So, I told him, "Not too far," and I suggested we check out what remained of Robertson. Robertson was another of the black enclaves scattered around St. Louis County. My father had had good friends out there. It had mostly been cleared for expansion of the airport runways, as had been Kinloch, another black enclave on the opposite end of those same runways.

Somehow that answer put him in his feelings. GJ, a routinely pleasant and affable man, twitched his upper lip and shook his head once. Never a demanding person—generally a go-with-the-flow type—one who, on rare occasions, when he had a strong preference, would signal it with a question:

"Say, I was wondering what you thought about pizza tonight?"

"Maybe some sushi?" I would counter, and off we'd head to the place I liked in the Central West End—because GJ was nothing if not accommodating. But there it would be all evening, the ever-so-slight chilliness and the occasional petulant response to a benign request. (Okay, fine, I'll keep the soy sauce over here by me. Whatever.)

"Make the left up here at Woodson Road," I'd instructed, not caring to ruin an otherwise lovely day. Sometimes a right turn is also the wrong turn. ("Too clever!" Janine likes to tell me at my wry twists of phrase.)

As for Janine, she is antsy: tapping her feet and adjusting her body in the chair.

"Sure is taking a long time," she offers. I refrain from responding that death is the master of time (*there she goes again*!). I tell her to go outside and call the office and tell them we went to lunch and then to a meeting offsite.

Janine will find her way to the portico out front and to the place off to the side where the smokers gather and grieve. She will join them and, if she is lucky, there will be someone eager to tell them all about their lost friend or family member. Her eyes will water, and she will tell them how sorry she is. She'll say:

"I'm here with my friend Cynthia, who just lost her mom. Martha Garrison. Did you know her?"

They'll tell her "no" and that they are sorry for her loss as well.

We are the kindest people. I wonder if you know that?

I told GJ to turn onto Rex Avenue, the street to the east of the cul-de-sacs.

"This is nice up through here," he said, admiringly of the crackerbox bungalows, some bricked, some shingled, some clad with various shades of aluminum siding. That one could be Martha's. Or that one. Or that one.

"Real quiet," he said. "And I'm feeling these mature trees."

Many of these trees are older than me, planted when the first families moved out here from the city in the late forties. Colonel Breckenridge had given this land to his former slave, Washington Reed, after the Civil War. His ancient daughters had subdivided their parcels to build houses for black GIs returning from Europe and Asia after World War II. Martha told me that when I was a little girl, Miss Reed was still alive and living in the farmhouse across the street and would make snow ice cream for the kids during the winter.

"Which is yours?" he asked. I tell him to stop by the playground up on the left and point to the other side and tell him that I grew up over there, and he said, "Let's go," but I vigorously begged off.

"Not looking like this," I coyly demurred. "I mean, look at me. Can't have those old timers talking about Raggedy Cynthia. My mother would die of mortification."

"You look fine. As always."

He was correct. I did. And do. Always. (You know what Martha says about running up and down the street looking like trash.)

"Well, we'll come back then. Do the grand tour."

And for some reason I said, "I promise." And my fate was sealed. Just like that.

It was inevitable, I guess. This... "family thing" is the thing we share, all of us (you more than me, of course). I once heard a researcher talking about a study done with children in foster care, many of them survivors of the most horrendous parenting imaginable, and they'd asked the kids what was the one thing that they wanted more than anything: To go home, was by far the most common wish shared by these children. The parents might be monsters, the researcher said, but they were *their* monsters.

Oh, there she goes again, you're no doubt saying. Melodramatic and morose Cynthia, still on about what an ogre her mother was.

And you're still not getting this.

As the least insightful of your pundits insist: there's fault on both sides. You, for being a sap, and me for wasting my time.

I forget that you are sentimental. And lucky. Your kind holds filial adoration as the highest virtue. Unconditional. This is both simple-minded and naïve.

You wipe away the tears as a maudlin and tinkly piano underscores the final frames during which the repentant daughter spoons the last velvet scoops of ice cream into the dying mother's mouth. Earlier in your "real" life, you'd teased with your siblings about which of you was the favored child, reveling in the naughty thrill that the question might actually have an answer, never imagining that you would be selected to stay outside when there was no more room in the storm shelter. You'd always imagined that *she'd* squeeze the others in tighter to make room for you. You believed she'd stay outside herself so that you could live.

What if that wasn't true?

Sometimes they don't. That's all I'm saying. Sometimes they don't.

Later that day, at Mother's favorite Chinese place in Brentwood, I'd told her that a friend would be joining us for supper next Sunday.

"This is the first I'm hearing of friends" had been her response.

(Oh, Mother. Where to even begin parsing the genius layers of your digs? I'll give you this: you were 100 percent accurate. I never discussed my friends with you. Not ever.)

"My friend 'G' has asked to meet you." I steadied an egg roll in my chopsticks and brought it to my mouth for a bite, hoping the concentration would keep my face neutral. Across the table I could see her reading me, a series of squints and head tilts and pursed lips.

"He'll come to the house, then. And share our family meal, your young man."

I stumbled through a series of aborted sentence starters about what I wanted and what he wasn't and what we had intended to... Mother raised her hand, flat palm facing toward me. This woman could stop traffic on Interstate 70 with that hand.

"Dinner at five thirty. Bring him at four thirty. We'll visit."

I opened my mouth to object: this time she extended an admonishing finger, which she then lowered to a bowl on my side of the table. "Pass me that rice."

I felt my shoulders drop. No good would come of this. (I don't need to tell you that, right? You know her.) But what could I do? An audible sigh blew from my lungs. I didn't even try to stop it. Mother twisted up a smile, told me to "see about getting me an order of that chicken in a go bag," and also suggested that I fix my face.

I agonized about whether I would arrive at her house with GJ or have him meet me there. On the one hand, it would be good to have a preview of what he would be walking into—head off whatever disasters I was able to; on the other hand, even an hour attempting to choreograph the insanity that awaited us would leave me a nervous wreck and make the rest of the evening even more unbearable. Besides, who was I kidding that I could control any of it? I told GJ I'd pick him up at four and then pretended that repeating the mantra "It will be fine" would make it so.

I cursed every traffic light on the Rock Road—the long route from the city—for being, for some diabolical reason on this day, unlike any other, always in our favor. Approaching the turn into our neighborhood, I said, "Look, I guess I should tell you something. My mother can be a bit... much."

"That so?"

"She's... eccentric."

I wasn't sure if his "hmm" reflected intrigue or derision. He said, "They get strange when they get older, don't they? My daddy is obsessed with that show *The Big Bang Theory*. You know, the one with the horny physicists. You go over his house and it's Sheldon this and Leonard that." (It was just then, in that moment, that it occurred to me that the subject of meeting his people hadn't come up. Neither of us had raised it and, frankly, that was fine with me. One disapproving parent was more than enough for this lifetime, thank you very much.)

I held my tongue on all that I'd planned to warn him about— about rudeness and lack of boundaries and the very real possibility that one or both of us would be asked questions we'd prefer not to answer. Better, I thought, to let him see for himself.

We arrived and, as instructed continually since I had my first learner's permit, I parked precisely three feet behind her car. There *must be* room for a person to pass behind her car (ignoring, as one must, the yards of space in *front* of her car), and also she wasn't "going to be having cars hanging across the sidewalk" (there were no sidewalks in her cul-de-sac), and only common people parked in the street.

Martha opened the door and asked, "Are those for me?"

In my anxious state I had failed to notice the lush bouquet that GJ cradled like an infant. A stunning arrangement of gerbera daisies studded with a few pink roses. (And, no, since you asked, he'd never treated *me* with the likes of anything similar. Me, I got the past-their-peak bundles from the rack by the checkout at the grocery. What the hell!)

"I am pleased to meet you, Mrs. Garrison."

Mother gushed over the arrangement and preempted my addled and mumbled attempt at introducing her guest with her own cheery self-presentation. While offering GJ a seat and inviting him to "make yourself comfortable," she thrust the flowers in my direction and ordered me to make myself useful. GJ caught me rolling my eyes and gave me a sly wink.

(All you men reading this: Fuck You. Each and every one of you.)

"Such a nice home you have here," he told my mother, and while I couldn't see her face—rummaging, as I was, for some reasonable semblance of a vase—I knew that his praise was met with a demure simper.

"Been here since the fifties," I heard her tell him, and she went on about how my father had bought it new and how it wasn't much as such things go, but she was comfortable and there just wasn't any other place she wanted to be. "My late husband was a postal worker. Sometimes he did the mail run. Do you know about that? Back in the day, they'd load the mail going north and east into a rail car and the men would sort it right there on the train. Coming back, repeat the process for the mail going the other way."

"Is that so? That's something." GJ was smiling and nodding at her narration as I returned with his bouquet, now rearranged in a glass pitcher—that I had never seen in my life and that was also somehow perfect for the flowers.

"Cynthia! How lovely! Thank you for doing that for Mother, Sweetie. Did you offer our guest a cool beverage? Tell the girl what you'd like."

"Well, I guess…"

"Bring the man a glass of Mother's lemonade," she ordered me and told him, "I stirred it up just for you!"

Literally, I had presumed, and I suppressed a cringe at the thought of the powder from the mix still swirling around in the pitcher—until I noted the flattened lemons poking out of the filled-to-the-brim trash in the kitchen. Before pouring the drinks, I pulled the liner from the can and placed it in the larger bin, outside the back door. X a sloppy pail of garbage off the list of things GJ didn't need to see on the inevitable grand tour—and which would have inevitably and certainly been, somehow, my fault.

"Well, you certainly took your time," she chided when I returned with the glasses.

Rather than take the bait, I flourished the tray in her direction and told her that I'd done the ice just the way she liked: no more and no less than halfway—*if you want your tip tonight.*

"Serve our guest first! My apologies. I raised her better than this."

I pivoted to GJ—who offered me another wink.

(Seriously, just fuck you all.)

We sipped our (delicious! really) lemonade and Mother regaled GJ with a story about how she had almost "accidently" joined a circus, and I thought, *What the hell is this story?* (And, just, what the hell in general.)

"You know it happens, things like this," Mother said. "My daddy taught me his craft. He had been show-people back in the day. Minstrels and such. Black folks painted even more black. He'd taken me to a circus, over on the east side. I was enchanted."

I set my lemonade on the coffee table; it had turned from sour to bitter on my tongue. I made sure to use a coaster—because I was raised better than you. Rather than the anticipated juggling lesson, Mother asked for GJ's story, and she did so, as one would expect, in the most Martha of ways:

"Tell me all about you. Our Cynthia hasn't told me one single thing. Typically. Fill in all the blanks, young sir."

"To start with, I'm a barber..."

"A barber!"

"Yes, ma'am. I have a little shop down in The Ville."

"Well, Lord knows the ladies in this house could use some hair advice." She patted the turban that she sported in a way that indicated both how stylish she felt she was and that beneath it there lay a problem that only a skilled artisan such as he could remediate. For what it's worth, on this day she was, in fact, amazingly stylish, if also, somehow... wrong. Where I'd expected one of the carefully tailored and conservative suits that she wore to our Sunday dining excursions, she'd instead donned a caftan made from an African print—that she would insist, I tell you, was *not* Kente cloth. Boldly Afrocentric had never been part of her regular fashion palette, but there we were.

Mother pursed her lips and stroked her turban obscenely, and GJ laughed robustly.

(...)

"Three chairs, and we cater to a male clientele, but there's always a seat at my establishment for lovely ladies such as yourselves."

MARTHA'S DAUGHTER

(...)

"Good grooming is so important. I see these raggedy hussies out here parading their business up and down the street looking like trash. No home training, that's the problem. Tell me about *your* family. Who are your people?"

GJ drops the names of his prominent parents, and Mother's face lights up.

"Your mama, didn't she run the local branch of the College Fund? A while back, I think that was."

"Yes, ma'am. You know her?"

"Well, I know *of* her, and don't we all? Used to see her in the news all the time. Always *so* refined and well put together. Lovely hair!"

(*Think she cute.*)

"Fortunately, our family didn't need to rely on any of that Fund money. Worked myself ragged getting this one through school."

Yes, and let's skip right over your late husband's service in the war and the loans that his service gave me access to and his postal pension and the scholarships I worked my ass off to be awarded. Additionally, we'll skip the fact that I had not, in fact, attended an HBCU, as well as the various commentary from this woman over the years about the sorts of people who did.

Mother's interview proceeded through a dozen or so additional queries about siblings and what they did and where they had grown up and who was doing what now and where did you meet my daughter... And before she went any further down that road, GJ crinkled his nose and said, "Something sure smells terrific."

"Oh, now, you hush!" Mother shimmied her shoulders in fake modesty. She winked at him. "My special stuffed chops. That's the rosemary and garlic you're smelling. Let me go check." In my direction, she stage-whispered. "Don't be a cold fish: talk to the young man."

GJ's tongue pulled in his lower lip, which did a mediocre job covering the fact that he was covering his attempt not to laugh. I turned up my hands as if to say, "See what I mean?"

He smiled and mouthed the words, "She's delightful." I rolled my eyes.

I skipped the small talk; being rebuked for not "entertaining our guest" was better than her play-by-play when she revisited *everything* she might overhear me saying to him. GJ looked me over thoughtfully and nodded his head slowly, as if to indicate he was onto my strategy. Who knew if that was true? I'd like to hope so. What a kind and thoughtful person he was. Genuinely so.

Mother came and stood in front of me. "You'll be showing our guest to the dinner table."

What difference did it make whether that was a question or an order? I said, "Sure." And just then it occurred to me that GJ might be the first guest we'd ever had to dinner. Maybe the first guest of any kind, as far as that goes.

She'd adorned the table with a freshly pressed tablecloth; I remembered the pattern from the fraught excursion to the fabric store years earlier. She was using "the good china," the

MARTHA'S DAUGHTER

silver-rimmed white plates, subtly glazed with pussy willow fronds, the ones that I'd be happy to see on holidays—because that meant that after dinner I would be dismissed from dish duty, because heaven forbid things so precious be trusted in the care of the likes of me.

She announced, "Next to the green beans, that is kohlrabi."

Because of course it was.

"Roasted and mashed with a bit of cauliflower and my secret seasoning. As I'm sure my daughter told you, we Garrisons are fond of our root vegetables."

Why, yes, that is exactly the sort of thing that I regularly work into my conversational repertoire. I took a bite from what I had believed to be a respectable small serving. It was... amazing.

I tend to forget what a wonderful cook she was. This had always been the case. Memories of her unpleasant company usurped the memories of her delicious food. She had an intuitive sense of the balance between sweet and savory, knew which herbs and spices to pair with which meat. And she wasn't afraid to try new things; she'd see a recipe in a women's magazine for, say, kohlrabi—or quince, or quail—and it would find its way into her recipe box, a battered green tin thing stacked full with three-by-five cards and clippings from the food section of the *Post-Dispatch*.

"Everything here is wonderful," GJ gushed.

"Now, you hush! This is just a little something I threw together."

She was so pleased with herself. And, it *was* an amazing meal, the last I would ever eat in her house, served unbegrudgingly—perhaps another first, that. Back in the day, she'd call my father and me to dinner and select a gem from her rotating repertoire of charming incitements:

Don't hurry to the table on my account.

Some people around here think this food cooks itself.

Just let me catch you wasting my food.

If the food's so bad, why did you eat it all?

GJ told her that she could make a fortune opening a little restaurant. She beamed some more and told him:

"My mother taught me. She was in service to a family in Clayton—that was back quite a ways. Those were the jobs our people had back then."

What?

"This one here, she don't know about any of that. My mama did their laundry and all the housework and got their meals, everything. They kept a room for her out over a garage where she could stay, but unless they needed her, she preferred to take the streetcar back into the city, even in the cold and rain, she did."

Mother went on to tell him how this was a decent enough white family, but how the man apparently thought her name was Missy. (*It was Henrietta.*) Some liquor came up missing and they fired her. My grandmother hadn't bothered to tell them they'd find the empties in the back of their grown son's closet. "A full time alkie, that boy. It wouldn't have made a difference. That's how things were."

I had never heard any of this. Growing up, I would ask her about her family and her past, and she would tell me it was none of my concern and that I didn't need to know about those times or even have any of it in my head. The future—my future—was the only thing that mattered.

Did your parents have a "Missy" of their own back in the day? Do you have one now? A Maria? A Dora? Fatima? Are any of those her actual name, and how do you know if that's true? What are Maria's children's names? Does she sleep in the small bedroom next to your children's play area in the basement? Do you drive her to the "envois de dineros" and help her wire whatever you pay her to the people back home?

Mother served her banana pudding and insisted I pour the coffee and keep hers "and the young man's topped up," which I did. We sat at the table a long time, and I heard more stories I had never known—about her father's life as a young adult in East St. Louis and the money she'd raised to refurbish the playground, and about her neighbors who were siblings to Ike Turner and to Chuck Berry and to baseball's Bob Gibson.

"I could tell you some things," she teased. She tilted her head down knowingly.

Driving back into the city, GJ commented on the "remarkable" life she'd lived.

I forced myself to nod in agreement, and I did not tell him that I wasn't sure how much of it he should believe.

GJ was more like you than it would likely comfort you to believe. Your kind looks with disfavor on the sorts of people who accuse their (seemingly) charming and elderly parent of being anything less than scrupulously honest. Recently, you'll recall, a major nation was presided over by a leader who also had issues with the truth, and you'll also remember that the news media hesitated to use the word *lie*. Because, you know, *lie* implies intentionality—and who can know what other people's intentions are?

Was Martha Garrison a liar?

Likely she was just a bullshit artist, world class. One of those folks who believed that as long as they kept the nonsense flowing and the audience smiled and nodded and cheered, they were, somehow, winning.

She had impressed GJ, that was for sure, and a wiser woman might count that as a win. But not Martha Garrison. For her, it was just another volley in a game for which I never understood the rules and yet somehow always ended up losing.

The funeral director's assistant comes in and pats my arm gently. "You okay, Sweetie?" she asks, and she offers me a tissue. She tells me Mr. Cartwright is ready for her to "bring me back." "Where's that little girl who came in with you? Out front, I bet. You hold here, I'll go get her and then we'll all go back together."

The following Sunday, after brunch and after we'd had our weekly drive, GJ asked me to pass my greetings to her, and I said I would. Mother had wanted crab legs, and after I'd suggested a number of non-chain selections, she'd insisted that Red Lobster was more than fine and that one day soon these "airs" of mine would be my undoing.

The young man assigned to wait on us set the basket of Cheddar Bays on the table, and Mother loaded one with butter (that it did not need) and said, "You could have invited your young man to join us."

"Perhaps another time," had been my response, and I passed along his greetings.

She cleared her throat and sniffed. Rather than take her bait, I took a bite of the bread and told her I'd be ordering the grilled shrimp.

She side-eyed me and continued to do so and to harrumph for the rest of the meal, reserving any actual words for the server, a gangly and awkward young man with a short afro who, to this day, regrets advising the older black woman at table 16 to "wait for the hot batch that's just being pulled from the oven."

I pulled into her driveway to drop her off, and she said, out of the blue: "You won't keep him."

How different it all might have been if I had just ignored her, if I'd said "whatever" and wished her a good evening, if I'd commented on the trellis that needed trimming, if I'd just driven home and watched some bad TV. If I hadn't allowed her to... poison the well.

I asked her, "What is that supposed to mean?"

"It means what it says. You won't keep him." She took her time with those four words, goose-necking her head on each one.

I glared at her.

"You don't know anything about it," I said. "About my life, about my relationships. With that man or with anyone else.

You're a person who talks to hear herself talk. About things you know nothing about."

"Oh, my girl. You need to face the facts. He is not good enough for you." Her wicked smile looked more like a grimace.

"What a horrible thing to say. You go on in your house now. Go! What kind of person even thinks such things? Go!"

"That's not what I think."

And then she said the four words that changed us forever: "*That's what you think.*"

She opened the car door and heaved herself up and out, grunting and using the strap over the passenger seat.

Occasionally, even someone as unsentimental as me entertains a wistfully trashy moment of "what if?" When I see young fathers herding burdensomely large groups of children. When I see couples picnicking in the park on warm spring days.

GJ and I just didn't happen. Nothing between us remotely resembled a melodramatic ending. We simply faded, something like the intense scent of fireworks in the air on the night of the Fourth of July that are gone by the morning of the fifth. I ignored a text, or he neglected to respond to one of mine. A Sunday brunch skipped for some silly excuse turned into two brunches skipped. Then it's a month of skipped dates and then we were just not a thing anymore.

And, yes, I do wonder "what if?" And sometimes I spend a few minutes mourning what might have been, and sometimes there is a perverse pleasure to be had wallowing in that regret. And then I make myself busy with work and let those tacky feelings go.

Had the well been poisoned? Did I find myself annoyed by his often intentionally sloppy syntax? Was I bothered by his insistence in maintaining a business in a neighborhood where shots were fired on a daily basis and by the fact that he kept his own "piece" handy and would not hesitate to use it if he or his customers were threatened? Could I imagine my life with a man whom I would likely out-earn for the rest of our working lives?

There are poisons in the air and poisons in the water and poisons in the well and in all our hearts, yours as much as mine.

And, as Martha always says, a girl *has* to have standards.

"Okay, here we go," Janine says. She smells like all the smoke in the world. "This is hard, but we can do it."

She hands me a fresh tissue and supports one elbow while the assistant supports the other, and "back" they walk me. At the door to the room where the bodies are prepared, they pass me over to Mr. Cartwright, who places his hand on my back as he walks me to a "temporary" coffin where Mother had insisted on being "viewed" before her cremation.

She is tilted up, as if lounging by a pool. She wears a purple dress with a bejeweled bodice. I have seen this dress before. In a drawer? In her closet?

"Oh!" Janine weeps. "Oh, there she is! Oh, just look!"

Yes, Janine, there she is.

The woman who bore me, the woman who raised me. The woman who lived sixty years of her life in a Vatterott bungalow on Saint Benedict Court, and if she lived a life before that, I don't know and will never know.

DAVID HAYNES

A woman who believed that the alligators in the sewer would enter your house if you didn't put down the toilet seat, who swallowed her toothpaste because only heathens spit in the sink. A woman who accused her neighbor of bringing down the property values by planting striped petunias in the window box.

A woman who said, "If it were up to me, there'd be a hotline to call to report when a slut was on the loose," and "A wench must be blind going out into the world looking like that," and "I'm gonna stay right in this house and mind my own business, and I advise the rest of you all to do the same."

A woman who told me that a young lady never acknowledges a man speaking to her for any reason, and a person of quality always crosses her legs. She told me that only the kind of woman I didn't wish to be had a home without blinds on the windows, and that a decent person knew when to keep those blinds closed. Pants, she said, would be fine up to a certain age, but were never to be worn to work—and that the caftan period of life arrived sooner than most women knew and that she knew all the best places to get them when I was ready.

You told me to always have my own money and to never count on anyone to pay for anything. You said to never buy cheap shoes or cheap mattresses or the store-brand ice cream. You said to make those people pay you what you're worth and to only give them what they pay for. (*They won't be giving* you *nothing, not one damn thing, and don't forget I told you that!*) Stick with the plan, you said; there's ways that all this works, you just have to listen to me.

MARTHA'S DAUGHTER

Be a person of quality, you said. Watch the white kids, watch the best of them. Watch them and learn their ways. Watch how they talk and watch how they walk and watch the way that they move through the world. Be their friend, make friends with their friends. It always helps to know the right people. It doesn't matter if they like you or if they like people like you. It doesn't matter if you like them. This is not about making friends. Learn the difference between friendly and familiar. Do not get familiar with them. You do not want them in your business, and you stay out of theirs. Don't imagine they care about your life. What they think they know about you and about people like you is based on a lie. It isn't your job to fix that. Trust me when I tell you that the less you know about them, the better. Keep your eyes on the prize. Learn to put on the mask. Remember this: they will be happy to see you fall. Many of them will be happy to push. Build a solid platform and anchor yourself to it. When necessary, you push first. While you're at it, keep your eyes on the crabs in the barrel, the ones who will happily snatch you back to their level. I told you about those people. I told you who they are and what they are like and why you are to avoid them at all costs. Remember that they are everywhere. Watch them and guard your perch and remember that going back is not an option. Stay the course. Stay with the plan.

Stay with the people who don't love you and won't love you and who keep you from those who can and might.

You got it, my girl! Go on and live that dream.

Who dreamed this, Martha Garrison? Who would dream this world of halfways and in betweens, this world of neither here nor there?

Yes, Janine, there she is. And this is the world she gave me.

What is the prize, Mother, and where can I find it? How do I get there? What are the next steps?

What do I do now?

"It's so hard," Janine says, "but we figure it out and we move forward, don't we? Somehow that is what we do." She holds me tight around the waist and Mr. Cartwright backs out of the room and tells us to take our time. There is nothing but time.

THAT'S RIGHT,
YOU'RE NOT FROM TEXAS

HERE COME A COUPLE of useless sentences: We couldn't make it work. We just weren't each other's types. Think if you will about the untold millions for whom such ideas are entirely outside their ken. Their parents trade a goat and a couple of pounds of cheese for some poor creature wrapped in a sheet, and for a lot of young men a positive outcome is one in which his future life partner has all her limbs intact and whose visible anatomy doesn't feature any giant hairy moles. Makes one ashamed, doesn't it, and perhaps a little embarrassed, too, about all those who jumped off our own hooks.

Yasmine and I, both recent transplants to a godforsaken urban wasteland known as Dallas, were headed to the Melrose Hotel bar for a quiet drink after seeing a student production of *Six Degrees of Separation*. We had been going out for three months, steering through the intellectual bona fides segment of dating. I would spring for the box seats at the Myerson, and she would haul me to the sorts of movies where everything is hazy and people talk in French for a couple of hours. To my mind, tonight's play had shared the curse of most school productions—that of forcing young adults to overreach toward emotions they'd not truly own for decades. This bothered Yasmine not one iota. Yasmine is a woman who finds much of life charming—run-of-the-mill greeting cards, spitting and obnoxious toddlers, Thursdays. And don't get me wrong. I've no problem with relentlessly sunny dispositions. Prior to Yasmine I had sustained a long-term relationship with a woman whose entire apartment had been decorated with crudely drawn cartoons of balloon-headed figures, reminding me at every turn what "love is." Generally speaking, we cranky types benefit from being around people like these. It's important to be reminded that the world is basically a good place, critical aesthetics notwithstanding. In response to Yasmine's generic critique of the play, I had offered my commentary on the lead actress, saying:

"There was something very 'nineteen' about that girl," remembering how she had been unable to abandon the annoying personal habit of tossing her hair over her shoulder after every line—a tic ill serving her middle-aged character and from all evidence the only body language she could muster to support her clearly limited emotional range.

Yasmine breathed out a quiet "Rodney," shorthand established early in our time together to be used when Rodney wasn't being very "nice."

She says, "I guess it's just that I feel so much empathy with those who are willing to take creative risks and put themselves out there for the rest us." A typical Yasmine platitude. She no doubt lingered at shopping mall talent shows, dropped dollar bills into the greasy cap of the squawky saxophonist who frequented the sidewalk in front of nightspots in Deep Ellum. I was saved from having to respond to her nonsense by something that went thump thump-thumping beneath the wheels of the Camry.

A short side trip—to Europe, in fact—before I tell you my initial response to this disaster. My father—may God rest his soul—drove a gasoline tanker across German lines in Czechoslovakia. He adhered to the just-keep-the-vehicle-moving-forward school of life management, and I'd found that Dad's example served perfectly well in almost every circumstance I'd ever encountered. Furthermore, experience has taught us that there are two kinds of people in the world. Some are "Come look what I found in the dumpster, Honey" kinds of people. You've seen them out behind your own apartment buildings, prodding with some sort of arm extender, eyes squinched together, genuinely curious these people are, they never allow anything to rest in peace. Others, people like you and me, we feel that whatever the hell is in there, we'd rather not know that such things existed on earth, thank you very much, close the lid, lose the stick, and wash your hands before you handle the produce.

Yasmine, the moment the car went bumpedty-bump, craned herself up and around like a fat guy looking for the meal cart on the plane. She grabbed my arm.

"I think you just ran over something," she announced, and I said, "Oh, really," as if it were news to me, and I kept rolling down Beverly Boulevard. We were driving through the Park Cities at the time. University Park or Highland Park; I can't tell them apart. The Park Cities would be the enclave of the unnecessarily wealthy, set into the heart of Dallas like a pearl in a pile of shit. Home of the likes of Ross Perot, Dick Cheney, and the late cosmetics queen Mary Kay, I would be exaggerating if I told you that they had pictographic signs on the streets leading into town with a big red slash mark drawn through a pointedly ethnic face. This is Texas. No such signs are necessary. One look around and you just sort of knew that it was a good idea to get out of town by sunset.

It was well past sunset. I kept driving.

"Stop," she said, and this was nothing resembling a request. This was the Stop of a sun-weary border guard on the frontier between warring nations. This was the Stop of the curmudgeon physician, queried by the two-pack-a-day smoker for advice about his habit. This was the Stop of the soccer mom who, beyond hysteria, is one balled-up fist short of a date in family court. And like all hysterical mothers, Yasmine even put her hand across my chest as if to keep me from flying through the windshield when I jammed the brakes on.

Which, of course, I did.

We, both of us, peered through the back windshield to discover what I had done. Alas, like tony communities across the globe, the Park Cities are tastefully underlit by gaslights, and all that stretched behind us was impenetrable darkness, interrupted here and there with quavering puddles of golden anemic lamplight.

Yasmine, as any B-movie disaster movie heroine worth her salt would have done, had concluded and then announced, "We'll have to go back." And we've all seen enough of these films to know the drill. Lava flows would be blocking the exits to the island even as I put the car in reverse. At any moment some unfortunate extra would be sucked into Mothra's gaping maw.

I backed down the street and eyeballed this woman sitting next to me. I gave her my what-the-hell-is-your-damn-problem-anyway look. This was another move I'd learned from my father. Mom would ask him—for the twenty-seventh time—if he wouldn't mind pretty please doing something like separating frozen pork chops or handing down the double boiler from the top shelf of the pantry. Dad would slam that cleaver down into the meat, never, for not even one second, diverting his curled lip sneer from her direction, potential lost fingertips be damned. Ignoring his glare, her own face a vision of equanimity, Mom would shuck her peas, flinching now and again as the blade chopped through to the cutting board. "Supper in an hour," she'd chirp, gathering her hunks of hacked flesh into a baking dish. This was a broad who played to win and who knew how to savor a victory when she did.

I was a man who backed down dark and segregated streets at the whim of a woman I hadn't even made my mind up about yet. I rolled about as far back as I believed I'd rolled forward, announced, cleverly I thought, that there didn't seem to be anything there.

Undaunted, Yasmine bolted from the car to have a closer look at the situation.

THAT'S RIGHT, YOU'RE NOT FROM TEXAS

"Ooooh," she sighed, that sound women make when they break a nail or when their stockings run or when the man they went to the bed-and-breakfast with finds ESPN on the cable line up. "The poor, poor thing."

I warned her that I was pretty sure she wasn't supposed to be touching that. This is another thing one learns watching *MonsterVision*. Poking around strange animals always turns out badly. At any moment, whatever the hell that was would erect itself and extend its claws, and eyes would be gouged from their sockets, almost certainly my own.

But Yasmine was way ahead of me on this one. Felix had already taken the express bus to kitty heaven. I must have gotten him real good—a two-tire job, at least. Maybe I'd even dragged the bastard.

She asked me if I had something in the car to wrap him in, and I thought, okay, so we'd cover him up and leave him for the Mexicans to pick up in the morning. I agreed to sacrifice my tire-emergency towel for the good of the order.

So peaceful he looked, curled up there against the curb, and I could imagine him reclined just so in the sunny spot at the foot of his former owner's bookcase. And as Yasmine approached him with the tire towel, I entertained a trashy fantasy that the moment she cradled him in cloth and lifted him into her arms, his little kitty-cat eyes would snap open and he would spring back to life. Santa Yasmina of Highland Park, patroness of mediocre actresses, restorer of lost house pets.

But that didn't happen, and instead she said, "We have to see if anyone around here is his people." And before I could protest, before I could remind her that it was nine thirty at night and that we were in the Park Cities, a place that didn't cotton to door-to-door canvassing even in broad daylight; that we were two people of African descent in a part of town where people like us could not buy homes even if we could afford to; that what she snuggled there in her arms was most likely a stray, an animal that no one had ever wanted, a creature who perhaps, like us, had only been passing through this part of town on his way to the places where one could find actual food scraps in the street and where one could socialize with cats of a similar stripe; before I could say any of that, Yasmine was already making her way to the door of the house closest to where he had died.

It annoyed me, the fact that this woman seemed fairly non-plussed by the, frankly, icy reception she and I received from the good citizens of Highland Park. Perhaps her skin was thicker than elephant hide. Maybe the brittle disdain of the bourgeoisie meant no more to her than did the idle ravings of the homeless who lived beneath the flyovers of the Stemmons Expressway. Maybe she was just too dumb to notice. It was a blessing that many of the doors hadn't been answered at all.

"I guess a lot of folks must be out to dinner," she mused, passing me the corpse. Her tone betrayed just the slightest bit of annoyance; her ever-so-vague exasperation I heard as directed less toward the inhospitable residents of Beverly Drive than toward my having the bad judgment to run over a cat in the first place. I chose not to mention the flashes of faces I'd spied catching a quick eyeful of who'd dared ring their doorbells.

THAT'S RIGHT, YOU'RE NOT FROM TEXAS

I'd spent years selling candy bars door-to-door for the Midget Gunners football club so I'd been trained to recognize the tell-tale signs of people pretending not to be home.

Yasmine rang on bravely up and down the block. More than a few of those chimes rang to the tune of "The Yellow Rose of Texas," a song which had ruined Emily Dickinson for me forever. In my arms, the dead cat seemed to have taken on weight. I hoped it wasn't seeping, hoped that the unpleasant dampness I felt was no more than the sweaty palms I remembered from working the cul-de-sacs of Breckenridge Hills with my winning smile and my carrying case of chocolate bars with almonds.

At the next house an actual bald person (as opposed to a fashionably bald person) opened his door but didn't say anything.

"Hi!" Yasmine enthused. A person would have thought she was from the welcome wagon or from the local high school pep squad. As I've already noted, this part of her personality was a big + for me. I'd grown tired of sullen, cool women, the sort you'd have to beg for a friendly word or a smile. And then when they did smile—those ice princesses—they did so with all the ersatz sincerity of the disembodied woman on the campus voicemail. Yasmine, she had this lovely way of popping her head off to the side when she greeted people. Her whole face would open up, and she would clasp her arms behind her back. I loved this about her.

Bald guy, by contrast—he seemed unmoved.

Yasmine pressed on. She said:

"This unfortunate critter ran under our car, and we're trying to find his people." What an endearing way of putting it, I thought, although who knows what Baldy heard? From the expression on his face, we'd apparently just asked him for a donation to the Gay Communist Pro-Abortion League. He grunted—it was a Texan kind of noise—and then he shook his head. He closed the door, disappearing himself into the depths of his McMansion.

"Moving on," Yasmine suggested, though I sensed, however subtly, her veneer of optimism crumbling. Just like it did for the runners-up on the high school homecoming court, this being-a-good-sport business could really get a girl down. Even so, chin held high, she persisted, and five houses down, our heroine hit paydirt.

"Well, hi," the woman at that door said, her "hi" having somewhere in the neighborhood of seven syllables. Another mark of my character: I don't necessarily consider it a good sign to be greeted quite so eagerly at ten p.m. on a school night. Yasmine, however, had been buoyed by our reception.

"We're trying to find his owner," she told the woman, and she flourished a hand in the direction of my unfortunate cargo. Like some Renaissance Madonna, I tilted my bundle toward his viewer.

"Bless his heart, that's old Sammy-cat."

Yasmine extending a sympathetic hand, asked, "He's yours?"

"Lord, no. Old Sammy don't belong to anyone. He's a wild old tom what's lived around here for years. He's dead, is he?"

Directing this question toward his murderer, Yasmine looked over where I was standing, so I said, "He was run over by a car that had been being driven through."

THAT'S RIGHT, YOU'RE NOT FROM TEXAS

Which caused Yasmine to give me a look, which was then short circuited by our homeowner who said, "Y'all bring him right on in through here. Come on with him."

She showed us into her front parlor. She had filled the room, as had many of her neighbors, with the sorts of heavy hard furniture one imagines might have decorated medieval castles, assuming, of course, the lord of the manor had an account at the local Restoration Hardware. Leather, hard edges, wrought iron, rough-hewn cedar-beamed boxes. A dog the size of a small horse pranced through the room, ignoring us. We were not introduced.

"That Sammy-cat's been living back in here for four or five years. He wouldn't stay anywhere, and they never could catch him. Can I offer y'all something?"

Yasmine enthused over the hospitality, though she ultimately passed. What I wanted more than a drink was a place to unload my bundle of joy. Hoping that we didn't mind if she did, our hostess topped up her goblet with something brown from a lovely crystal decanter. Pioneers could have crossed the continent on her liquor cart.

"Do y'all live around here?" she asked. "I don't think I've seen you in the neighborhood."

And I thought, Here we go, but charming Yasmine bit this conversational hook like a starving piranha; unlike myself, she detected not the slightest ill intent in the query. She described my professorship and her own association with a prominent law firm in town. She confessed to her lifelong citizenship of North Texas, however recently new to the Metroplex.

"Rodney here lives right down the street, practically. Just down Douglas, over the city line."

I hefted the carcass in my arms by way of acknowledging my residence. The old tom had been a big mother. That had to be a good twenty pounds of dead cat meat I was holding, and in an uncomfortable position, too, eschewing dead-animal emissions from my immediate person.

"A professor!" the woman chirped. "I could tell you were a something." And then she took another big slug of the sauce.

Personally, I'd about had it with Park Cities cocktail hour, so I asked, "Do you have a trash bin out back?" And I once again lofted the guest of honor for emphasis.

Well, you'd have thought I'd asked these women to peel off their panties and get down on all fours.

"What?" I asked. "Isn't that what you do with these things?" I honestly didn't know. When I was growing up, house pets on their last legs had a way of disappearing quietly sometime during the school day. They didn't make dads any cheaper than my father's edition, and I can't imagine him doing anything other than making a run to the nearest dump. I bet he didn't even slow down while tossing the bag from the car. We are not a sentimental people.

Apparently, our other mourners were. The two women had reached their hands toward each other the way that women in the audience on *Oprah* do when Dr. Phil isn't making any headway with the bad husband of the day.

With her other hand Yasmine caressed the bundle in my arms. "Sammy here deserves something a little more dignified

THAT'S RIGHT, YOU'RE NOT FROM TEXAS

than that." So I said, "Fine." I might have mentioned the fact that this piece of work in my arms had no doubt crapped in every garden between here and Texas Stadium, crap no doubt composed largely of the remnants of dozens and dozens of songbirds, but I played the good boy.

Our homeowner rounded up an old fishing tackle box, property, she claimed, of her late husband (the introduction of whom provided another opportunity for the gals to bond). I was ordered to arrange my victim ("delicately, please") inside the case, which I did, and I then stepped aside so our funeral directors could fluff up the towel around him—make the old boy comfortable for the long night ahead. Then I was directed to a small washroom to remove the gore from my hands. Soaping and soaping some more and then some more, I remember having one of those moments of insight that, while on the surface are not necessarily profound, somehow resonate deeply, feel life transforming.

I thought, This is *so* not me.

And for just a moment walking out of that washroom I thought that what I would do was run out to my car and drive away from these people and never look back. I did not, and again in my head there had been the image of Dad, a man who believed, if in nothing else, in the importance of staying the course. Sure, the road up ahead may be mined, and without a doubt the woods around you are chock full of Krauts with bazookas and grenades. You are inches from enough fuel to send you to the moon and back. What do you do? You stay the course.

Later, maybe, you tell them what they can do with their f-ing silver star, but for now, you agreed to be here, so you stick it out.

I followed the women's voices to a tiny garden behind the house.

"That was one of Sammy's favorite spots," our hostess was announcing, adding the fact that her "boy," Jose, "fished turds out of there by the sackful." For just a moment I expected to be handed a shovel, but it quickly became apparent that it would be Jose's job to inter the remains beneath the azaleas. But I was not entirely off the hook.

"Perhaps the professor here will say a few words for us," and before I could suggest that perhaps he wouldn't, hands had been joined, and there we stood, gathered over a tackle box full of dead cat and two citronella candles. Yasmine squeezed my hand in a way that had already come to indicate that Rodney should "behave." And so I did.

"Friends," I began. "We gather here on this lovely Texas evening to bid a fond farewell to our beloved neighborhood hooligan, Sammy-the-cat. A fixture in the Park Cities for almost a half decade, he was known for his irascible sense of humor and for his deep interest in all things culinary. Sam never met a stranger, and, good Texan that he was, he lived free till his dying day."

I actually believe that I heard both women sniffing back the tears. Just before she closed the tackle box, I'm sure I saw Sammy's yellow fur emitting a warm glow. Yasmine intoned a quiet prayer, and we blew out the candles, backing away solemnly from the picnic table–cum–bier. Following the women inside, I actually looked behind me, though what I expected to see, I couldn't tell you.

Later, in the car, Yasmine made it clear that my graveside service had pretty much made up for running over the cat in the first place.

"That was very sweet," she offered, but I had been miffed and couldn't even thank her for the compliment.

What I said was: "The old girl can tell her bridge club about the nice coloreds that stopped by with a dead cat the other night."

"Oh, come on," she sighed, assuring me that I had the situation all wrong.

I reminded her that the woman hadn't even bothered to tell us her name.

Yasmine clicked her tongue and pronounced our homeowner harmless. She started to lecture me about old southern white ladies, then stopped and, midsentence, nodded her head and said:

"I keep forgetting, you're not from Texas." And I may have mumbled something to the effect of "Thank God almighty," but I don't really remember because, just then, she reached across the car and she caressed a hand that was still soft from when I'd washed away the dead cat stink. I loved that touch. It had been the perfect thing to do just then. It had said to me, "I get you." And "It's okay." And it felt right and good. So good in fact that we skipped the drinks that night and went directly to my place and, as they say down in these parts, we had us a whole bunch of sex, a whole bunch of times.

And I imagine you're thinking how crass I am. But people hook up over much less every minute of every day. Neither of us has anything to be ashamed of.

We hung out for almost another half year after that night, Yasmine and me. Me, through all that time, denying to myself that we would not be each other's forever "it," because I really wanted her to be, or at least for a long time there I did. But it just sort of... ended after a time.

I ran into her just once since, and we chatted for a while, and it was real friendly. I could tell that neither one of us bore the other the least amount of ill will, and that was comforting to see. It's unlikely we will cross paths again. There are four million souls in North Texas and nothing resembling a place where folks like us would cross paths. And anyway, I will leave Texas soon. If there's a God in heaven, I will.

I think about her now and again. About the night in Highland Park, of course, but other things too. Our time in Mazatlan and a Thanksgiving with my folks. I liked her and I'm sorry that we didn't fit. I'm two or three ladies down the line these days, and sadly, this current one doesn't feel like a keeper either. Call me picky, but this is supposed to be for the rest of one's life—Dad's rule, remember. A fellow just can't take any chances.

And I'd like to think that Yasmine thinks about me as well. She would still be unattached I'm pretty sure, and you just know that there's a group of girls around her age who she hangs with on the weekends and sometime after work. They go to that wine bar on McKinney or they drive up on Greenville and get the jumbo margaritas at The Blue Horse.

They are a self-sufficient lot, these friends. Each of the ladies has a good job and everyone pays her bills on time. And no, not a one of them has a live one on the wire, or at least none of them has what she'd consider a keeper. Everyone is disappointed, but they are a cheerful and optimistic lot. They buy another round and talk about the big sale at Kohl's and a potential trip to Ocho Rios. Now and again the talk circles around to the dearth of good black men and all the might-have-beens and should-have-beens.

Yasmine—she's the sweet one of the group—she wonders rhetorically whatever happened to good old Rodney. The girls have a good laugh at his silly name and try to remember which one he could have been. Was he the brother with the BMW and the bad BO? Didn't he live down there in a loft in the West End? Doesn't his mama still send you a birthday card every year?

Yasmine, she'll giggle and shake her head. There's a place in her heart for every one of those men, and we all hold on to her as well. But she'll say no, she'll say, "Rodney. You remember Rodney. He's the one who ran over the cat."

BLIND ALLEY

BECAUSE SHE DIDN'T WISH for herself that her own life resemble in any way the sordid soap-operatic lives of the rest of the women in her clan, Lynette decided in high school to marry a less-than-attractive young man named Duane Washburn. And while this decision had proved a sound one for the better part of three decades, Lynette's calculations failed to consider the possibility that bald men with goatees might rise several notches on the scale of desirability, nor had they accounted for the arrival in Breckenridge Hills of a certain Desiree Washington, about whom, in Lynette's opinion, the less one says the better.

And while women of this Washington person's ilk have been around since God invented trash, decent people prefer not to discover that her sort have been plopped down in the community like an off-brand fried chicken establishment, garish, gaudy, and smelling unpleasantly of last Sunday's supper. Just this morning, just after eight a.m., at an hour usually reserved only for calls announcing snow emergencies and the death of immediate family members, the unfortunate creature rang the damn phone, ululating over an exploded plumbing fixture.

Lynette passed the phone to Duane, who subsequently grabbed his toolbox and car keys. And now, here, some three hours later, still, her beloved Duane remains over at that... person's place of residence, doing who could even imagine what, though for the sake of everyone in Breckenridge Hills, it had better involve metal pipes and adjustable wrenches.

Johnny-on-the-spot in a crisis, Lynette's twice-married older sister Tamara has arrived with a bag of Krispy Kreme donuts and a sheaf of scratch-off lottery tickets. Ever since childhood Tamara has had a way of sniffing out trouble and arriving on the scene in time to provide her unsolicited play-by-play. Her own domestic life she operates as if it were a fly-by-night bus tour of the Ozarks. One did well to expect no apparent itinerary and lots of unscheduled stops at greasy spoon diners. It had been Tamara's almost-faded-from-memory first marriage to a star running back from Mizzou that pushed Lynette toward Duane in the first place. Fifteen minutes at the spectacle her sister had had the temerity to refer to as a wedding ceremony—a pageant that had featured, among other things, rented novelty limousines and groomsmen adorned in an array of morning coats representing a full spectrum pastel rainbow—and the then fifteen-year-old Lynette had figured she'd better start angling after something of a more stable variety. Tamara had had at least one other ghetto-fabulous wedding in the interim, and now here she comes to inform anyone within listening range that Lynette had spent the last third of a century living in a fool's paradise.

"Was that your husband's Lincoln I saw over on Rex?" her sister asks. With a long fingernail she peels free a scab of icing from a donut.

You'll see my husband's car wherever there's a neighbor in need, she wants to tell the woman, but Lynette will not be baited. She knows that while her sister might genuinely love her, she does not mean her well. Or anyone else, for that matter. Surely few people on earth derive as much pleasure in the suffering of others than Tamara, a talent each of those ex-husbands would be pleased to attest to.

Lynette pours herself another cup of coffee and evens out the pound cake that she had baked for tonight's supper. She had intended the cake for dessert until Tamara had shown up with those deadly donuts, and then Lynette thought, if only to be sociable, she'd shave off just a sliver, except the leading edge of the cake continues to look sloppy, despite her diligence with each subsequent shave. Duane hates sloppy. Unlike her mother, Lynette does not defile the tops of her creations with a lemon glaze. Her confections have always been lush and moist and crumbly, thank you very much, and need no such adornment. But they do need to be neat, and a neat cake requires a neat presentation, thus the need to continue working at it with a specialty Cutco knife purchased specifically for this chore.

Tamara continues picking into the skin of her pastries, contorting her face into the sorts of unsubtle and hackneyed expressions that bad actresses use when playing vixens.

"Do you know who has a lovely figure?" she asks, and when she does, Lynette blows up.

"Why don't you go get a job or something and leave people the hell alone?"

Fat chance that would happen. Both exes keep the alimony rolling in, and Tamara is one of those women who would walk into Harrah's, drop a few bucks in the slot machine, and walk out with a couple of grand, just like that.

"Trouble in paradise?"

Lynette brushes her shoulder against the rack of keys by the door to the carport. She'll fold sheets, she decides. She will not think about her sister or her husband or that Washington woman. She will not touch those car keys. This has been decided: she will not.

She will not do as her own mother did—like a madwoman, throw herself into the nearest vehicle, disregard even the most basic traffic regulations, linger with her motor running at the end of several of the city's scariest alleyways, engine in neutral and motor gunning just as if this were the start of the Indy 500.

Lynette had had issues with her mother's strategy that night, but held her tongue, chastened, as she'd been, by her mother's consistent refrain of "Just let me catch a nigger," each word punctuated by a punch of the accelerator. Lynette had been in high school at the time, and although by that point in her life she was certainly no stranger to every manner of domestic drama—scenes involving wide varieties of broken crockery and artfully laced-together strings of vulgar epithets that to this day have the power to induce a wince on her part—even she had admitted her mother's endgame—or that particular endgame, at least—might have gone too far.

Make no mistake. Jermaine Dupree Houston, the man who had been Lynette's first stepfather, was a good-looking man. Brownskin and bright dark eyes, and a person has to wonder if it were possible to just walk into the men's-wear department of Famous-Barr and buy shirts with buttons like that on the front. Those damn buttons. Decades later and Lynette has yet to figure out where the man procured such outfits.

"Isn't he fine?" her mother had cooed one morning at breakfast.

"Doesn't he sort of look like a malt liquor commercial?" had been her response, a serious inquiry on her part. There had been, indeed, something entirely too glossy about stepfather Houston. To Lynette he had seemed... laminated. Alas, her mother had responded only with a creamy "Oh, yes" and, all things considered, Lynette had not been entirely surprised those not-too-many months later to find herself in the passenger seat of an idling, oversized domestic automobile, in a blind alley behind a rundown four-family flat on the city's north side. Her mother was not the sort of woman to whom one said, "I told you so," and Lynette, having from somewhere or the other absorbed a modicum of discretion about such matters, held her peace. Her uncertainty about the origins of her tact stems largely from the fact that no one else in her family seems to have any boundaries at all, exemplified this very day by her sister, from whom, even back in the laundry room, Lynette can hear a steady chorus of transparent hums and sighs and sucked teeth.

Lynette bustles back through the kitchen with a load of laundry, brushing, again, this time with her left shoulder, that key rack—which she will for sure be having her husband move the position of—drops the stack of terrycloth on the dining room table and picks up a stack of mail to be sorted into the recycling bin.

"Sure is getting late," Tamara says.

"I hadn't noticed," Lynette responds, intending to place an assortment of unfolded items in front of her sister but then thinking better of it. Her plan to occupy the woman with domestic chores has been thwarted by the great crippler of fat black women all over America. Her sister has Krispy Kreme fingers. Her hands hover heavily in front of her face the way they always do after a good greasy meal. They appear to be glassy and satisfied with themselves.

"You should go have a little wash up," Lynette suggests.

Tamara looks at her fingers as if discovering them there at the ends of her arms for the first time.

"Oh," she says, and she rocks her heavy frame up from the upholstered captain's chair and sidles on off to the bathroom.

Dollars to donuts this wench goes through my medicine cabinet again, Lynette thinks, watching her sister clear the doorframe, figuring as she always does that all that extra bulk couldn't be good for a person, although being a big gal has never held Tamara back in the social department. A certain kind of man—and how to describe them? —just loves her to death, Tamara with her big old warm plushy self.

Oxen. That was it. Oxen. Uncharitable as it might seem, that is the only word she can think of to describe the men Tamara seems to attract. Ball players. Construction workers. Hod carriers. The sorts of men who drive those enormous Ford trucks and yet still seem to have to be squeezed into the passenger compartment. Those are the sort of men who just love Tamara, that sort of... hulk does. They just love her. And she treats them like dirt. She'll date several at a time, a weekend evening just might find her with two lined up for subsequent appointments. Heaven forbid they buy her the wrong present. Just here recently one of these guys, one of these Robs or JTs or Joes (they all have names such as Rob or JT or Joe) had bought the witch a purse that she had immediately determined to be imitation leather. She'd sent him out to empty the wrapping paper into the dumpster and had locked the door behind him. Good riddance, she'd said, and it rather broke Lynette's heart a little bit to imagine the big old fellow out there, tapping on the door, calling her name and calling her baby and calling her sweetie and asking her what the problem was and couldn't she please let him in. Tamara, she knows, would have placed the disgraced item right there on top of the console television—a reminder in all its pleather glory—flipped through the cable channels and sipped her cosmopolitan. She's a cold-hearted thing, this Tamara.

Oh, and a lot of these guys have gold teeth, Lynette thinks.

Lynette hears a flush, and though she's just about restrained herself, she hasn't quite done so, and—wouldn't you know it— just as she opens her mouth to tell her sister to stay the hell out of her things, here Tamara comes holding a prescription.

"What are these for?"

"Give me that. Honestly!" Lacking pockets, Lynette palms the bottle, mumbles about certain folk's lack of consideration.

"What is that, Viagra in there?"

Lynette gasps. Another thing she will not dignify with a response. She notices Tamara is not smirking or making any other kinds of smarmy faces or noises.

"Well? Is it?"

"It's none of your business what it is, is what it is."

She notices that her sister has that look on her face that she gets when she's been hooked by a topic that genuinely interests her. At such times her face tends to get all purposeful and elongated, just like that of a toddler who believes she's finally discovered the truth about that whole cabbage patch deal. She leans into Lynette, lowers her voice conspiratorially.

"Do you remember that Rob I went out with last week? The one with the F-350? Big Rob? Well, he got him some of that."

"Really?" Lynette asks, despite being absolutely sure that this is a conversation she should not pursue. For the record, and not that it's anyone's business, she and her Duane have never had problems in this particular department, and though she won't be telling her sister this, the pills are hers, a mild sedative, one that she almost never needs—though, here lately, since that Washington woman has entered their lives, a little help relaxing of an evening is nothing to turn one's nose up at.

And what could be keeping Duane anyway? What exactly has this woman done to her plumbing? Lynette knows Desiree Washington's kind, and she can just imagine the sorts of things her husband is up to his elbows in right this minute. It has become apparent to everyone in Breckenridge Hills that this Washington person doesn't have anything resembling common sense. Doretha Turner has seen her down at Bill's Farmers Market on the Rock Road wearing what she described as a pair of white satin hot pants—on a Tuesday morning, no less, and a woman her age—this is no spring chicken, this Washington person. And apparently she believes she has bought a home in Beverly Hills as opposed to Breckenridge Hills, further believing that her postage-stamp-sized front lawn is a palatial garden and suitable for sunbathing in the sort of item she might wear if dancing over at the Kapriole Room. Oughtn't one to be suspicious of a honey-brown woman who takes sunbaths? Where in the hell is Duane?

Tamara is popping Lynette on the arm with the wooden handle of the dust broom.

"Honest to God, Lynette. It was like this. I'm not lying."

As has often been the case in her life as one of the Jenkins women, Lynette can find no words.

"Honest to God," Tamara reiterates, sucking in her bottom lip and looking out over the top of her glasses to underline the veracity of her claim.

"These are non-narcotic," Lynette says, handing her own bottle of pills back to her sister. "I take them once, twice, sometimes several nights a week."

Thankfully, her sister releases the semi-lewd grip she'd taken to the broom handle and reaches to pull Lynette into her arms.

"We're gonna get through this just fine, you hear?"

Even while rolling her eyes at her sister's platitudes, Lynette does have to admit that her big sister's big body is a comfort. Warm, soft, and just pulsing with life. Not that she needs comforting. What she needed has in fact happened. The penis part of the conversation has ended, for now at least, it has—although with Tamara these things have a tendency to pop up again without warning, rear their ugly heads rather like... well, Lynette decides she'd rather not finish that particular thought. Hot dry towels await on the dining room table. Someone has made a mess of a perfectly luscious pound cake. A set of car keys hang by the back door, those same ones that she has already decided to ignore. Here in Breckenridge Hills, sometimes the day just gets away from you.

Despite her first and better instinct—to preoccupy the witch with something other than her private affairs—Lynette finds herself with Tamara in the better dresses department of what used to be the Famous-Barr store at what used to be called Northwest Plaza. Shopping therapy, Tamara calls it, and despite Lynette's protests of having neither the money nor the inclination to go to the mall, here she is anyway, watching her sister pull through racks of last season's designer dresses. She plucks a sparkly beige number from the collection and thrusts it in Lynette's direction.

"This would look fabulous on you. Really, girl." Tamara snaps the hanger up against Lynette's chin, smooths the fabric up and down her curves. The dress looks like the sort of thing women of a certain age (well, Lynette's age, actually) would wear to early evening cocktails at the country club. It is the sort of dress Della Reese used to wear when she co-hosted *The Mike Douglas Show*.

"I can say pretty much without a doubt that in my life I would never have reason to wear this dress." From the look her sister gives her when Lynette says this, you'd have thought the words had been in the language of aliens from another galaxy. The look lasts seconds, however, just long enough for Tamara to eye another prize on the rack—this one blue and flouncy with scarves. Lack of interest in the opinions (or interests or concerns or ailments or complaints) of others is one of the charms of the self-involved that has its advantages at times such as this.

The shopping gene that had so precisely passed itself from their mother to Tamara had gone recessive by the time Lynette had been born. For Lynette, shopping is what you do when you run out of milk or when you need something to wear to Duane's company picnic.

For her mother and her sister, shopping is what you do. Period.

The thing that Lynette can't figure out: if a person spends as much time eyeballing and fingering the merchandise as these women do, shouldn't they have developed better taste? Her mother had a knack of pillaging her way across every department store in town, and for her troubles ending up only with items emblazoned with ships anchors. Gold braid anchors. Silver lamé anchors. Anchors made from brass buttons and anchors made from copper ones. Who knew such clothes existed? And the woman has matching hats for these outfits. Imagine!

Tamara specializes in loud irregular prints, her palette running toward the jewel tones. When she thinks of her sister, the image Lynette pictures is of a woman in an unstructured caftan that from a distance seems purple but up close reveals itself as colored from large and randomly overlapping boxes of royal blue and raspberry and gold. Made from some kind of shiny material, of course, and her hair would have dyed into it threads of color that match their mother's ships' anchors. Mules, of course. High-heeled ones with fur trim.

Fortunately, Tamara seems to have clued herself in to Lynette's more modest tastes. The dresses she untangles from the racks to present to her are in the neutral color tones Lynette prefers, simply but elegantly cut and tailored. Even so, the one promising candidate she's selected of the bunch—a classic-looking pantsuit in an off-white linen—seems lovely on first glance, and then—and leave it to Tamara to dig up such a monstrosity—upon closer inspection proves to have cuffs encircled with rows of rhinestones (wrists and ankles both, of all the absurd things).

"Not exactly me," Lynette says, returning the item to its rightful place. (Tamara, she notes, leaves all unwanted merchandise draped across the fixture nearest her in the moment she decides not to buy it.) She ignores her sister's comments about black women needing to get into the colors that bring out the fire in their skin tones, decides that it is, in fact, pleasant to be out of the house for a few minutes—even and despite her husband's being deeply ensnared at this very moment in the lair of some vixen.

Around her, the better dresses department is filled with women much like her sister and her mother—professional shopper types who seem to know the difference between one blue dress and the next. There's a lot of grunting and grumbling and the occasional shout of ecstasy at the location of a long-sought Golden Fleece. When she was a little girl, Northwest Plaza was the ritzy white shopping mall, and in the center of the mall paths that wound through trees and fountains connected all the stores. Now the mall is called something else that she can never remember, although it surely must have *north* or *west* in the title. It's a covered mall now and also the colored mall now, the black folks' mall, and what had once been card and gift shops now sold wigs and styling products and potions, the sorts of implements that Desiree person employed when angling after other women's husbands.

Poor Duane. One of the problems with being a genuinely nice man is that there are just some things he doesn't get. He is susceptible to all sorts of nonsense: door-to-door preachers, rag-tag beggars on freeway entrance ramps with their improvised signs, infomercials. Hadn't Lynnette just the other night had to disconnect an eight hundred number the man had dialed in response to some sort of detergent offer? It's what came from growing up in a house with two living saints. Mama and Papa Washburn had been genuinely lovely people, and they'd raised their boy to be a loving and trusting human being who believes in the goodness of his fellow man (i.e., live bait for this Washington person and her ilk).

Love and trust had been rare commodities in the Jenkins household. Toward the end of her marriage to stepfather Houston, her mother had actually run a strip of black tape down the center of the refrigerator, designating a "His" and an "Ours" compartment. It would almost be fair to say that pilfered orange juice as much as philandering led to the demise of that unfortunate alliance.

"Do you think she ever loved him?" she asks Tamara.

"Him who?" Tamara replies. She's deep into a table of sweaters marked for clearance. She fishes one out and tosses it to Lynette.

"Houston. Jermaine." (Another almost, this sweater—someone needs to curb these people with their rhinestone appliqué guns.)

"I saw him the other week. Did I tell you?"

She had not.

"Out at the casino. Girl, he still looks good enough to eat. If he hadn't been married to our mama, I might've run off that hussy he was with and broke me off a piece of that pudding. Good thing I was on a hot machine. The little tramp couldn't have been more than sixteen."

There it is: another example of the sort of thing that had encouraged her to select Duane in the first place. Back in high school, Duane—the poor dear—he really had bordered on pathetic. Mama Washburn bought all his clothes up at the Robert Hall store in St. Ann, and his wardrobe had consisted back then of three colors of polyester slacks (beige, green, and blue) and an array of button-down plaid short-sleeve dress shirts. (Actually, that was pretty much still Duane's wardrobe.) Everything about the man has always pretty much screamed, "Not a player."

Storming through the house after one of her myriad battles with the pro football player, Tamara had caught one look at the teenaged Duane and had suggested that Lynette might want to "throw that one back." Which had as much as affirmed for Lynette her choice of him in the first place.

The scrawny ones, the homely ones, the tubby ones, the nerds: it had been slow going with those boys. A girl—especially a girl like Lynette—had to convince the poor things she was interested in more than their geometry homework. Because—and let's be absolutely clear about this—Lynette had been no cast off and certainly not the sort of girl who had needed to rummage through the lower rungs of the high school hierarchy seeking appropriate male companionship. Far from it. Lynette Jenkins had been an attractive—some would say comely—young thing, who was clean, had nice teeth, and maintained, and still maintains unto this very day, a presentable figure. And while she was no Tina Turner, she had certainly been a girl with options. And the thing with options, Lynette has always believed: they were worthless if you failed to exercise them.

Tamara has finally stacked up her dressing-room quota and orders Lynette to watch her purse. It is a huge black leather thing with the designer's logo embossed on the clasp. It is all Lynette can do not to rifle through this bag, turnabout being fair play and all, but she wills herself not to, wills herself to rise above her raising. Think of Mama Washburn, she reminds, as she always does when moral exemplars are in order. Mama and Papa Washburn had run a quiet and orderly home just as one would expect of the parents of Duane. Mama would prepare a delicious and well-rounded meal: a meat, a vegetable, and a starch every time. Papa would say grace, and the dishes would be passed for serving. After supper Mama would clear the dining room table so that "you children can get to work on your studies—bless your hearts." Duane worked hard for his Bs and Cs (which with Lynette's intervention began to include the odd A now and again).

"May I help you with those dishes?" Lynette would offer, already knowing the answer. Mama Washburn would put on her faux offended face and shoo her away, telling her what a sweet thing she was. Lynette would demure. Win the mother, and half the battle's won: one of the few useful lessons of a tumultuous girlhood at the Jenkins' ranch.

Tamara spins out of the dressing room in an almost tasteful number: a diaphanous black sheaf over white pants—stunning except for the fact that someone with a glitter gun and a jungle fantasy had been at work on the bodice panel. Were those tiger stripes or zebra stripes or what?

"I love this," Tamara announces. "I absolutely love this. Mack is taking me to this booya down at the Adams Mark. This is perfect."

Mack is the latest big boy in Tamara's life. Tamara spins some more and watches the sheaf flare. Her sister's eyes take on a dreamy cast. Lynette wonders whether Tamara is imagining the dress on the dance floor or imagining the other dancers watching the dress on the dance floor. Sparing them an argument (that Lynette would lose), Tamara has not bothered asking Lynette's opinion of the outfit. She spins herself back into the dressing area, scatting some jazz lyric in her off-key way.

"That sure is a nice outfit, Miss Tamara." That's what Duane would tell her, were he here instead of spun tight into that black widow's web. That's what Breckenridge Hills' smart money says: widow, multiple times, husbands dead under mysterious circumstances. Lynette's money is on serial homewrecker. Working her way, suburb to suburb, across St. Louis County, horning in on other women's men, leaving a trail of misery in her wake. When Lynette had first spotted Duane across the cafeteria at Ritenour High School, she'd thought to herself, "Now, that's one you won't have to worry where he is at all hours on a school night." And she'd gaze around at the various ones her girlfriends were angling after—dogs, frankly, and you didn't need a AKC handbook to pick them out—and she'd wanted to tell those young ladies, "Trust me, friend: that one will be sniffing around the housekeeper in the honeymoon suite."

"I've got a plan," her friend Valerie had insisted. "After I marry his fine behind, I intend on fattening him up. That'll slow him down some."

Several husbands later, dim-witted Valerie has yet to figure out that a few extra pounds on a man means nothing to a woman of the Desiree Washington stripe.

The Tamara fashion fair continues with a floor-length tunic in the brightest shade of pink Lynette can remember seeing outside the candy store. It's that chewed-bubble-gum pink that they made little girls' lunch boxes out of, and it is not even close to being a suitable color for her sister.

"Ta-ta-ta-ta-tah, ta-ta-tee-tee-tee," Tamara scats.

"Sweetheart," Lynette says, reaching out a hand to still her sister's spinning. "I have to tell you that..."

It must be Lynette's tone clues her sister in to the fact that Lynette has bad news about this particular outfit. Tamara stills, puts her hands on her hips, and narrows her eyes.

"What! Say what you got to say then. Bring it on." Tamara makes her already big body bigger the way some lizards do when defending their nests. Unnecessary, Lynette believes, for a conversation about a fashion mistake.

"All that I was going to say was that pink..."

"Just because you a woman can't hold on to her husband don't give you the right to be hateful with me."

Now this really is uncalled for, Lynette decides.

"Sister dear, you are really in no position to say anything about anybody holding on to a husband."

Tamara's hands fall from her hips. Her mouth drops into an O, and she runs boo-hooing back into the dressing room.

Dear God, Lynette thinks. The other ladies in the dress department are staring at her, pretty sure that the skinnier one (Lynette) said something mean to the fatter one (Tamara) to cause the poor thing to fall apart like that, and just look at the cold sister there, not even going in to offer comfort. Some people.

Lynette rolls her eyes. With the aid of the helpful wail, she has no trouble locating Tamara in the second booth on the left. Tamara dials herself back to the quiet rapid sob that sounds like a dog panting.

"You know how emotional I am," Tamara manages to gasp out. "This is a very hard day for me, you understand, what with all this heartache."

And although as best she can figure, Tamara's biggest challenge of perhaps the past two weeks was an inordinately long line at the Krispy Kreme drive-thru, Lynette suppresses the urge to slap her sister silly. The longer they fight, after all, the longer they stay here, and Duane should be in by now. He had better be. She once again takes strength from the dearly departed Mama Washburn. She fluffs her sister's metallic tresses.

"Bless your heart," she says. Then she goes to find a salesgirl to see if they have the tunic in a more appropriate color.

Tamara uses up Lynette's last nerve on the drive back from the mall, so Lynette is well beyond reprisal by the time they arrive back to DePorres Lane. As Tamara had coasted her way, ten miles per hour, from one full stop to the next, across St. Ann, Lynette, beside her in the seat, spent her time praying that her sister has some previously unannounced appointment for the rest of the afternoon. Alas, another prayer gone unanswered. Along with her clutch of parcels, Tamara trundles in behind Lynette. "I don't see Duane's car," her sister says, her voice a soundprint of innocence. Soon will come the obligatory post-shopping fashion show—more spinning, more scatting.

"Better check the machine," Tamara suggests just as Lynette feigns not looking at it. The message light reads zero.

So, this is the way it is, apparently. These barracudas sink their teeth into you, and they drag you to their underwater caves of lust, and you are never heard from again.

What a fool I was, Lynette thinks, imagining I could plan my way into a carefree life. How silly of me to believe that I could cheat fate.

Lynette remembers her mother's bearing on the night they stalked her stepfather. Sitting in that blind alley all those years ago, what had seemed like rage had soon dissolved into something more like a wry cynicism. Rather than mad, her mother had turned philosophical on her. Her mother had ceased gunning that engine and had, in fact, turned the ignition off.

"It's our lot in life, baby," her mother had announced. She'd taken a long drag on one of the vile menthol cigarettes she smoked. "Every sister's cross to bear, I'm afraid." And Lynette remembers the smug way that she'd assumed her mother had been wrong about that.

If you would only make better choices, she had wanted to tell her mother that night, but seeing the weariness around her mother's eyes, she said nothing. Number one had walked away from her, leaving two daughters and hardly a word in his wake. On that particular night, up in one of those flats overlooking the blind alley, number two did the thing he'd sworn he'd only do with her. She'd bury number three almost exactly fifteen years after that night in the car. He, she claimed, had been the love of her life.

"We're stronger than this shit," her mother had told her, starting the car and backing out of the alley. Back at home Lynette had helped her mother set all of Jermaine Dupree Houston's worldly belongings onto the curb in front of her Overland home while a locksmith worked his magic on all the doors. These days her mother juggles a retinue of distinguished older gentlemen, each of whose shiny brown heads is encircled like a laurel crown with a short white ring of afro fuzz. From them she expects dinner, jewelry, and a clean late-model sedan. One of these codgers had recently gotten the boot for less than pristine hygiene and for "catting around." Life goes on, doesn't it?

Tamara swirls into the room in the hideous pink tunic.

"Here's what I'm thinking," she announces, hands palm

forward for demonstration purposes. "I wear my black silk Miyake blouse. Then I wrap a couple of those coordinating scarves I got. The Hermès ones." Tamara pronounces Hermès as if he were a friend of Charlie Brown's. "Then, I top the whole thing off with that big new hat I got."

"That will just be perfect," Lynette agrees. It is the most ridiculous outfit she can imagine.

By now this Desiree Washington person will be showing Duane the space she has cleared out for his things in her chest of drawers. It won't take much, Lynette could tell her. About a half a drawer each for both the socks as well as the underwear and T-shirts. The chest of drawers will coordinate with the giant-sized round bed that she has (or that Lynette imagines that she has). Her bedding will match Tamara's tunic and will be tufted in a harlequin pattern and made of satin.

The bed will revolve.

Tamara revolves. The tunic rides open on her.

The football player left Tamara for a cocktail waitress at a bar over on Olive Street Road. Not before dislocating Tamara's jaw and knocking out two of her teeth. The second one, the rich one, bought Tamara everything her heart desired, including a fabulous dream home in Chesterfield. For himself he bought on a regular basis the companionship of the young men who frequented a certain park after dark. Tamara swallows handfuls of pills against the virus that lurks in her system, but she happily deposits his checks on the first of each month.

"Dum de de dum de de dum dum dum." Tamara spins and

taps.

Lynette will have to make sure this Washington person understands that her Duane does not tolerate any vegetables in the broccoli/cauliflower family. Keri lotion has proved to be useful on the unfortunate patch of ashy skin along the front of each of his calves. And the man has—and has had for many years now—issues with NBC anchorperson Brian Williams.

From the other room Tamara trumpets the opening of James Brown's "Super Bad." She backs into the room as if the Fabulous Flames themselves were playing her on. This outfit is either a rather sheer evening gown or lingerie; Lynette isn't sure. Tamara bumps and gyrates to her scat rendition of the funk classic. She's a great dancer; always has been.

This will be my life now, Lynette thinks. Shopping, fashion shows, girls' night out at the casino. It will be a stretch, she knows. Duane's salary at Chrysler won't make for much in terms of alimony. She'll keep the house, of course. That seems fair. She'll speak to Mrs. Alexander about picking up a few extra shifts at the library.

"I've got the move that makes me want to groove," her sister sings. Everything inside the outfit jiggles and rocks. Definitely lingerie, Lynette decides.

And she'll have to sit down with the homewrecker and make sure she is absolutely clear about Duane's medications. There is only one—which is certainly no more or no less than you'd expect of a man with moderate habits—but acid reflux is nothing to sneeze at, thank you very much, and she'll also have to warn the shrew about no green peppers in her chili or in her spaghetti sauce.

In fact, Lynette decides, no time like the present. The problem with soap operas is the way that they drag these things out for weeks, months, years. Let's get it done, and let me get on with my life in the world of discount malls and progressive slot machines. She turns from Tamara, still happily working her stuff in the lime-green peignoir. Just as she reaches for the key ring, Duane comes puffing in through the back door. He lets out a big sigh, sets his toolbox under the shoe bench.

"Man, that was a rough one there," he announces. He wipes his brow, blows out another breath. His shiny white teeth smile. (A boy with good teeth: this had been on Lynette's list back in high school.) "Hey, darling," he says, and then spying his sister-in-law, still working it over in the dining room, adds, "Lord have mercy!" Tamara squeals and runs from view.

Duane is covered head to toe with grime. Everything will need to be pre-soaked. He leans against the counter, is too considerate to sit. Lynette hands him a glass of water.

"Sloan and I ended up having to pull the whole mess out of there—sink, disposal, everything. Then the floor had rotted out underneath, so we pulled all that up. We went up to Home Depot and got it all changed out for her."

Isn't that what they have plumbers for? Lynette wonders. Contractors? Handymen? Husbands?

"You look just exhausted. Can I fix you something?"

Duane refills the water glass from the sink. Adds more ice

from the refrigerator door.

"Girl wanted to keep separate hot and cold water knobs. I forgot how tricky they could be sometimes. Underneath the sink, I mean."

Tamara returns. She's wrapped in the robe portion of the new nightie; feathers dance at her neckline, wrists, and down by her ankles.

"Hey, there Duane," she says, all flirtatiously. Lynette looks at her as if Tamara had lost her mind, flashes her eyes so her sister knows she is a dead woman.

"You girls having a slumber party, I see."

"We went shopping. You like my new pajamas?" Tamara spins and the feathers fly.

"That's very fetching on you, Miss Tamara. And did you all find something nice for my baby here?" He goes to pinch one of Lynette's cheeks with the grimy hand, but she pushes it away. "She never buys a thing for herself."

"You know, Duane, I spent all day trying to talk some sense into the girl, but she wouldn't hear it. You just going to have to surprise her."

"That I will do," Duane promises.

Later, that evening, after the clothes have soaked and after Duane has scrubbed away the caulk and grease and dirt from his fingernails and after Lynette has prepared him a delicious stuffed chop and his favorite Parmesan potatoes, after *Law and Order*, they snuggle in bed.

Duane thinks sometimes, Lynette knows, about the children

that never came, but there have been young ones in their lives. The Carter boy as much as lived with them through his high school years, and the previous weekend had been a rare one that Aunt Paula's grandbabies hadn't stayed over. It is neither one's fault, she knows, their being childless, or at least this is what the doctors always said. But Lynette never entirely believed them. She'd been the problem, she knew. Fear. Lack of imagination. Selfishness. All she knew was that any time she had tried to picture the children she might have with this man, the images in her head had disturbed her. She would get a picture of the two of them in standard family pose—Duane with his big smile, her in her sensible dress and shoes—and there were the well-groomed children—a boy and a girl—but their faces would always be blank.

Lynette feels the strong muscles in her husband's upper arms. He had been a spindly boy, she remembers, hardly anything on these bones worth taking notice of.

"That poor girl," Duane says. He clicks his tongue.

"What's poor about her?" Lynette asks. She defers the "girl" part for a future conversation.

Duane sighs. He is bone tired. "These folks get out here, all alone. Not a clue how to handle themselves or anything else. That's sad."

Lynette concurs, even though, really, she strongly disagrees about this. There are things to be added to this conversation about planning and choices and responsibility, but now is not the time.

She squeezes the muscle again. For just a second, she believes she should tell him about her temporary loss of faith this afternoon, but she thinks better of it. He is a good person, a good man—just as she has always known. It would only hurt him, she knew, her silly moment of doubt. She wonders if he could even imagine such a feeling as the one she had. Perhaps it is a woman thing.

"We do what we can," he says, drifting into sleep, a final self-satisfied sigh slipping from his lips.

"That we do," she concurs.

The next afternoon on Desiree Washington's front porch, Lynette checks her lipstick in the glass of the storm door and smooths the plastic wrap on the Chinet plate of cookies. She'd sent Duane off to the Chrysler plant that morning with a big sack all his own—his favorite: chocolate chips. Duane has done a superb job, she sees, on the new sink and cabinet (as if Lynette had any doubts!). Desiree Washington is appropriately grateful, satisfied, and appreciative, frankly, of Lynette's husband's efforts.

"I don't know what I would have did," the woman gushes, and Lynette tries not to wince at the slovenly grammar. (What could one expect, after all?) Lynette pats the woman's hand, noticing the salon nails and a couple of pieces of ice that would make Tamara's jaw drop.

Desiree Washington's medicine cabinet, Lynette discovers, contains only the requisite items any female medicine cabinet would.

The bedroom set: uninspiringly ordinary.

"A much-belated welcome to the neighborhood," Lynette says to her on her way out the front door. She then lets the Washington woman know that some of the ladies like to sit out behind Thurester's house on the warm evenings—just to visit and such, no biggie. "I'm sure the other girls would love it if you dropped by. Any time, you hear?"

Between women, and particularly between women whose lives have intersected at certain fundamental junctions, there are physical boundaries that are, in their way, every bit as real as the boundaries between adjoining nations. Think of it as a force field or as the kind of invisible electrical fence people use to keep their pets from defiling the neighbor's lawn. In these borderlands there can be warmth or there can be pain of the most unpleasant variety. Often there is both.

Lynette steps to within inches of the Washington woman's sadly over-made-up eyes.

Her nose fills with one of those noxious loud scents Tamara spritzed in the cosmetic department yesterday. You look like some kind of damn clown, she thinks to herself. What she says is:

"I wish we'd done this months ago. Don't you agree?" Her lower lip pushes her upper lip toward her nose and her eyelids contract with a flash.

She watches as some sort of ripple runs from the Washington woman's head right down to her feet.

"Enjoy those cookies, and don't be a stranger, you hear?"

"You know I will. Thank you all so much." The poor woman

seems to have developed some sort of frog in her throat. Too much sunbathing, perhaps.

"Gotta run," Lynette says. "At my place there are potatoes to be put on." She'll be making Duane's favorite pot roast tonight.

He is a smart man, her Duane. Oh, not book smart, of course, but intelligent in so many other ways. It's true what he'd said: these poor things out here on their own; sometimes all they needed was a helping hand.

BIG THINGS
HAPPENING HERE

THE FIRST WORDS SHE spoke to me were to ask what I had seen. Her voice resonated with a practiced nonchalance, not quite masking an equally practiced aggressive undertone. She spoke like a woman who knew that the hourglass was almost empty and the witch was already at the door—and yet with a solid hint, feigned or otherwise, of warmth and openness. She had greeted us on the steps of the rec center and hugged Cooper as if she were a long-lost aunt, the brightness of his eyes shining in contrast to the darkness of hers. Confident that I would verify what she already knew to be true, she reached toward me in that moment and placed her hand gently on my crossed arms. The soft warmth of that hand put the lie to what appeared to be gnarled roughness. Just that easily the words spilled from my mouth.

I told her how Cooper and I had headed out for supper at one of those ubiquitous strips of chain restaurants for which our city is universally famous. Brick cubes tricked out as haciendas, Tuscan villas, Caribbean patios; neon lights and interchangeable fiberglass roofs. We are ambivalent about cuisine, and our plan, as usual, had been the crapshoot of the shortest line. Ahead, midblock on the side street where we parked, the door to a bungalow flew open and three men in dark suits dragged a pair of scraggly young dudes from the house and out toward a white van. Another dark-suited man stepped from the vehicle and covered the captives' heads with what appeared to be pillowcases. They were tossed like last week's laundry into the back of the van, which lurched from the curb, turned onto the main drag, and headed north toward the freeway.

For the record, we do not reside in a third-world backwater, lorded over by corrupt oligarchs and soldiers on the take. This is a major American metropolis in a large southern-tier state. Freeway flyovers loop our downtown, where glass and steel boxes point toward the sky. It is the nature of this story that I cannot tell you the name of our city, but you would know it by sight and reputation. People have been killed here—famous ones—and the syncopated country/disco rhythms of its theme song may be echoing in your head at this very moment.

The woman—the kind woman with the soft, gnarled earth-colored hands—nodded when I told her what we witnessed on that day. The nod communicated that she knew just what I was talking about: she *understood.* A barely perceptible gesture, that nod, accompanied by a modest swipe of teeth at her full lower lip. It was an expression with which a funeral director might reassure the young widow that he has seen plenty of women with smeared mascara and red-rimmed eyes. Apologies were unnecessary. You are among friends, the woman seemed to be saying to me, and for whatever reason I felt like it was true.

It is my nature to be suspicious of moments like this. Sincerity is often ironic, I find, and moments of even marginal mysticism send my eyes rolling and set off in my head the cliché horror-movie soundtrack with the screeching violins. But the world has turned (or so we are told), the old rules have changed, and all bets are off. These are post-ironic times. And so I, with Cooper at my side, accepted her fellowship alongside a cup of watered-down coffee, and followed the warm and sincere and earnest woman to a cluster of open chairs set to one side of an air-conditioned community center in an obscure corner of our fair city. The meeting was about to begin.

What I had not told the woman was that I doubted my own truth; that even still I test the reality of it in my head, continuing to create alternative explanations for the abductions. Coop and I sat on that side street for what felt like twenty minutes, looking at the place where just moments before we had seen two young men snatched from their home. And wouldn't we all like to imagine ourselves doing the right things in this moment—the things that Cooper and I neglected to do: scratching down license-plate numbers and details about hair color and clothing. Dialing 911. We replayed it in our heads, again and again: the wresting from the door, the high-pitched squeal from the curb. Eventually I reached for my phone, but Cooper grabbed my hand and pressed it into my lap.

BIG THINGS HAPPENING HERE

"It's starting," he said to me, and collapsed into a hysterical fit, his open-palmed hand slapping his ghostly shaved head. His torso beat back and forth to a silent rhythm heard only by him. "Oh, man," he said, over and over. The good people of the central city continued with their usual business of deadheading petunias and walking their dogs. A golden retriever sniffed casually at a burgundy-colored stain. Beside me my best friend quivered and rocked and disintegrated and moaned.

I got him home and got him inside, but he could not stop pacing and mumbling to himself. Eventually he collapsed on his bed into some sort of trembling sleep state. I went into the living room and watched the local news on every channel, waiting for a mention of missing persons from somewhere around here—which never came.

Later that night, Coop wandered in and lowered himself stiffly onto the couch. "You're surprised by this?" he asked, but it wasn't really a question. His voice had been enervated with the same deadened but still punctuated edge as late-night callers to AM radio stations. He began chain-smoking, as he would do whenever he got into one of his states. "I keep telling you about shit, but you never believe me."

The blue glow from the television was the only light in the room, and I could hear Cooper's raspy draws on the cigarette and the exhalations of smoke. He had always been subject to fits of melancholy and had told me lots of stories over the years—about military-created mosquito-borne viruses that killed only birds and people; about a laboratory not far from where he spent his days processing insurance claims and I taught AP English, where a team of scientists sequestered and trained a group of super-intelligent young children. He'd been drawn to such nonsense since our college days. I had been ignoring such bull for the better part of a decade.

"You see for yourself now," he chided, aligning me in that moment with those like himself who have known such things long going. And then he said that he wanted me to come... *somewhere* with him, that there were some people I needed to meet. There'd be a woman there, he insisted, who would be someone I should hear.

"She knows things," he assured me. "She knows."

It calmed him that I agreed to tag along, and thus the following evening, there we were: Cooper, me, the woman with the hands. A dozen or so others, as well. A ring of beige metal folding chairs circling us together. Next to me, I felt the calm poise of the woman. Upright she sat, her straight spine standing away from the chair, but in a natural and not uncomfortable way. You wouldn't know that she breathed at all. According to her introduction, she was *not* the leader of this group, but it was obvious that she owned this room and that these were her people.

Before she said another word, I felt the need to speak with her privately. At the first break I implored her to join me for coffee—soon, if she would. She agreed.

The woman (I will not say her name) wore a hand-crocheted vest over a purple turtleneck. Apparently, people still crochet.

This sort of woman—the kind who hangs around the public library, women with recycling bins, these Whole Foods types—my interactions with them had been limited at best. She seemed like the type who would be a quirky friend of my mother's, someone with whom she might get together now and again to do the holiday baking or study Bible verses.

There, that night, in the circle of beige chairs, I felt myself oddly attracted to her, someone not remotely my type. She was older than me (though that has never been a criterion). She was heavy: not fat, but solid, and it looked good on her; still, we must have seemed a Laurel and Hardy match, the two times we would have been observed together in public, me being whichever comedy star was the lanky one.

An older guy, one of those university types, all gray beard and serious-looking spectacles, called us to order and insisted that we knew why we were there. Cooper and the woman moved their heads in grave concurrence. The woman radiated heat, pleasant in that cold community-center classroom. I remember leaning into her as the storytelling began.

When it was my turn, she caressed my fingers and nodded toward the group. "Tell them," she said, but Cooper interrupted, offering his own version, which was essentially the same as mine, if ever so slightly more turgid and ominous. If any in the group were surprised, you'd not have guessed it from their body language; the vague movements of heads and quietly clicked tongues—the low-energy response of people busy accumulating a bit more evidence for a case that to them has long been closed.

"The things people don't know," said another woman, in one of those blue power suits that your lawyer types wear, ready to take her turn. She stared at her feet the entire time she spoke. She sounded like a parent telling a child that the dog has died.

She said that because of the work she did, "certain information" crossed her desk on a regular basis.

"Large sums of money are moving," she whispered. And then she added, "They think I don't get it. They think that I'm too stupid to understand their codes. They think we're all stupid."

Next to me, the woman with the hands smirked; on the other side, Cooper shivered violently.

The woman suggested a meal instead of coffee, so we went to a vegetarian place she said she liked over in the gayborhood. It's an old bungalow painted in psychedelic graffiti, and all the food is yellow and orange with sprinkles of green. Some guy who acted like the owner nodded at the woman—she was clearly a regular—and showed us to our seats.

"There are good people out here still," she said, almost in a whisper. She told me it was important to remember that. She ordered tea for us and then soft pureed foods to be picked up with tasteless gray triangles of pita.

She told me this about herself: "My father taught high school biology. In the summer he drove the ice-cream truck and his route sometimes took him deep into the city where we lived. It broke his heart when the children didn't have a quarter for the Dreamsicles and Bomb Pops he sold, and sometimes he would just give them away."

We ate our mildly seasoned foods, spices so delicate as to be imperceptible. We talked about the weather. Later, after dinner, she insisted I drop her at a corner in a part of the city riddled with struggling clubs and galleries and the sorts of goth girls who seemed to exist only within these few blocks. I asked to see her to her door, but she dismissed me with a wave. I watched her walk briskly into an alley between two buildings.

Cooper had begun to keep a bag packed by the front door of the apartment for some reason, and one day I stumbled over it as I entered. I cursed him and his damn suitcase while a stack of spiritless sophomore essays scattered to the floor.

"What the hell's this for?" I asked him.

"It's because you never know anymore. And it's because whenever it comes—whatever it is—I'm going to be ready to go."

I scoffed, as I always would when teasing him, and I assured him that I didn't think anything would be happening on this fine spring afternoon. I suggested we screw the damn papers and whatever the hell was going on with the world and head out for a drink or two.

He made some snide comment about fiddling in Rome. It had a sardonic and ugly tone to it. But even on the last day of the planet, he'll be one you can count on to bend an elbow with you, so he rallied and we walked toward the bars in the trendiest part of town.

"Go to work today?" I asked as we headed past the ranks of new townhomes and boutiques that lined what had once been ghetto streets. I'd been asking this with increasing frequency, and Cooper would always shrug, as he did now. It was a glorious afternoon, and everyone in town had had the same idea, and the streets were full of the young and rich and thin.

We settled into a banquette at an obnoxiously trendy joint that was all velvet and chrome; our regular place—a low-key sports bar—had been shuttered, as had several other places up and down the block. Times were hard in the late aughts: my school had had layoffs too, and more than a few folks had thrown in the towel and just walked away. The rest of us did what we could do, picking up a class during our preps and subbing at after-school activities.

The server dropped off our cocktails, and I pressed again at the question of how he'd spent his day.

"What's the point? What's the point of any of it?" he mumbled.

"Oh, I don't know. Keeps us in the hooch, I guess," and I raised my collins glass in his direction, a half-assed toast. Cooper was always one for self-pity, but he was also an easy mark for cheering up, and I got something of a smile out of him.

"I got sick days," he rasped, but I couldn't tell if this was an extension of my lame joke or simply an explanation of his idleness as of late.

I fought a strong impulse to mention the fact that our lives, for the most part, continued on their normal trajectory, that we had not been witness to any other people snatched off the street or subject to mayhem of any kind. Don't get me wrong: this is a big city, and any given day finds its share of tragic accidents

BIG THINGS HAPPENING HERE

and random violence with a few odd disappearances thrown in for the good of the order. You develop a thick skin or you leave, and I'd always assumed Cooper had one. But witnessing that... abduction had broken him. I fought the impulse to bring it up; any mention of the subject—or of the group meetings or of the suitcase—tended to end poorly.

I asked instead if he wanted to head out to the IMAX after supper, and he said it sounded good to him.

Up at the bar, paying our tab, the TV blared as it always seems to in such places. On the twenty-four-hour news channel, a woman much like the blue-suited woman back at the recreation center interrupted the host's question and looked directly into the camera. "I'm going to say this while I've got the chance. There are things going on..." she began, but they cut to a commercial for expensive dog food. I tried to drag him away, but Cooper insisted on seeing the rest of the interview. Back on the screen, a famous football player had taken the lady's seat. Cooper went into the bathroom and vomited into the sink.

I did not return to the "support group," and I told Cooper that I thought it did him no good to hang out with those people. He froze me out after that; the most he offered me was a barely companionable grunt when we passed in the center of the apartment. I ran into the woman with the gnarled earth-colored hands in the produce aisle of a health-food store, and I found myself happy to see her again. She agreed to let me buy her a smoothie. We took our drinks to the patio, and I chatted with her as if she were an old friend—rather than an odd acquaintance who happened to share the same conspiracy-oriented imagination as my roommate. Still, I felt drawn to talk to her again and found something soothing about sitting there under the trellises with her. She asked me about my work, and I wondered if she was from here, or, if not, what had brought her to the city. She'd come in the wake of a corporate giant—*I used to live that life, you know*—where she'd done various kinds of public relations and advertising. She sang a jingle for a consumer staple that she claimed to have a hand in, a song I remembered from early childhood—from the *Transformers* days—and I realized she must be even older than I'd first guessed.

I still found her appealing, in a way somehow not quite sexual. I wanted to be her... friend. She made me comfortable in some way.

"These corporations," she said, "they're their own little kingdoms, with their own cultures, their own ethics, their own everything. We had a song we would sing every Friday morning, at ten o'clock sharp. At your desk, at the coffee cart, sitting on the toilet: it didn't matter. The clock struck ten and you stopped what you were doing and sang. It's all about making you feel part of it. One big happy family, and all that garbage. You reach a point and you realize that there is no *there* there. If you're smart, that is. Much like your job, I imagine." With her index finger she tapped at a bead of sweat on her plastic cup as she spoke, releasing a waterfall of condensation to the patio table.

"What are you doing these days?" I asked.

"This."

BIG THINGS HAPPENING HERE

That was her reply, said as flatly and as matter-of-fact as could be imagined, and while clearly "this" had not meant to indicate idylls on the veranda of a grocery store, there was zero irony in her voice. I waited for her to say more; but she simply drew on the straw, and I watched the tube of peach-colored liquid reach her lips.

"Your turn," she prompted with that same flat tone.

I told her about life in a twenty-first-century high school and how despite all the tests and paperwork and budgetary constraints, the kids were the thing: they were what kept you coming back every day. I told her about a few of my seniors—Tasha, Ramon, Zeke, Kiana—and how hard they were working to get ready for college in the fall. They were great kids, I told her, and I tried to make it clear that my enthusiasm was sincere—which it was.

"They've got great things in store for us, this crew," I told her. "This next generation. They're going to change the world."

I mistook her warm smile as approval of my hard work teaching the city's youth. Instead, she said: "I wasn't sure before, but I'm now pretty sure you are just some kind of a fool."

Around us on the patio shoppers munched on their kale casseroles and organic quesadillas, not noticing, I hoped, the taken-aback look on my face.

What exactly had I done to deserve her reproach? And how the hell was I supposed to respond?

I opened my mouth to speak, but she put up her hand to silence me.

"The complacent burn in the same circle as the complicit," she said. "I've got little time for either."

She glared at something over my shoulder, and before I could tell her what she and her ersatz Dante could do to each other, she rose and pulled me up by the arm and demanded I accompany her to the dry-goods bins.

"Don't turn around," she whispered. "Look like we're together."

In the store she peeled open a plastic bag and began purposefully scraping through a bin of dried cranberries.

I inclined my head toward her ear and implored an explanation.

"You *know.* Don't be stupid." She scooped up oats and hominy and a small cluster of dried apricots. Dutifully she wrote the bin numbers on the strips of paper twist ties and lined them up on the counter. Then she stealthily slipped the last of the ties into my pocket.

"I'll... I'm... Look, if that gentleman in the madras shirt follows me down the aisle, you know what to do."

She strode quickly toward the meat department, turned the corner, and was gone. That was the last time I saw her.

For a few long minutes I waited there with the food, but I knew she wasn't coming back. The man in the madras shirt bagged up coffee and a selection of nuts. He seemed more interested, frankly, in the lentils than in me or in whomever I'd been standing with moments earlier. I felt badly about the abandoned dry goods, so I loaded them into my arms and purchased them myself. I don't even like apricots.

BIG THINGS HAPPENING HERE

I texted some friends to meet me over by the college for pitchers, and we ended up closing the place down for the night.

A few weeks later, cleaning out the change tray, I came across the twist tie, which I'd forgotten she'd slipped me. On the back she'd inscribed nine numbers. One short of a phone number, but I dialed it anyway, trying a few logical digits up front to round it out. "The number you have dialed..." was the only answer I ever got.

Cooper by this point stayed mostly holed up in his room, but he would emerge now and then for a glass of water or some crackers. I stopped him that evening, and I realized I'd not seen him at all in many, many days.

"You look terrible, dude. Really terrible."

"Huh?" I'd been perhaps his only human contact for weeks. He seemed to have forgotten how the conversation thing works.

"Say, take a look at this." I handed him the strip. He looked at it, alarmed. "I thought you'd be interested. That woman gave it to me. You know, the one from the rec center." He burbled a bit, like someone with too much liquid in his mouth.

"Oh God!" he cried. "God Almighty! Oh my God!" And he collapsed against me.

There was almost nothing to him anymore. Holding him up, I could feel the ribs and elbows piercing through his skin.

The next morning, I acted—did what I ought to have done months earlier. I called his parents, who came that afternoon and fetched him home to the small city in the piney woods where he'd grown up.

For a while there, I would call to check on him. Daily for a while, then days turned into weeks, and so on. The last time I called, it was the "the number you have reached" woman again. The Coopers had lived in that town their whole lives. I can't imagine what happened to them.

As for me, I press on with life here in the city—and an odd enough place it is, this *metroplex*. The South, but not really the South; the West, but only sort of. A little bit of everything mixed in, which produces a quirky personality all its own. There are plenty worse places in the world.

Which has not come to an end, at least not yet. There are rooms full of people out there who are expecting it to, soon, at any moment, tomorrow, this afternoon—but the thing is, if you don't know those people you don't ever give it a thought. Which is a good thing, right?

I remain optimistic, then, despite the city's craziness. I teach the kids, who continue to amaze me. I hang out with friends, do the dating thing when the spirit strikes. I am determined to stay in this game, to see it out to the end, whatever and whenever that might be.

There have been no more abductions.

And yet, sometimes I, too, find myself collapsing a bit on the inside, when the noise gets a little too much—when another mother kills her own children, when another bank fails, when another tornado scrapes a town off the prairie—and I find myself, like Cooper, plastered to this couch, exhausted by the thought of it all.

BIG THINGS HAPPENING HERE

Still, I push through. I like my life here and, as I said, all and all, it isn't so bad when you run the numbers.

So, I sit tight. I am resolved, fixed, stolid, and mostly a very satisfied person. Unable to imagine where I might even go that wouldn't be here.

TAKING MISS KEZEE
TO THE POLLS

THE RUBBER BAND "PLINKED" as I popped out the next three-by-five card. It said Miss Xenobia C. Kezee, who had voted faithfully in every election since 1925—local and national—was "in her 80s," was a lifetime resident of St. Paul, and had lived at 887 Dayton for thirty-five years. She was a Democrat, although independent and opinionated. Her polling place: Hill Elementary on Selby. A college roommate, John—now Pastor John—who organized this "get out the vote" drive cautioned me that Miss Kezee would be ready to vote at one p.m. She expected promptness, courtesy, and cooperation. He would hear about it and there would be consequences if she were in any way disappointed. Anything for the cause: I rang her doorbell with minutes to spare.

"Who is that and what you want? If it's you damn kids again, I'm calling the police."

"Looking for a... Miss Kezee? I came to take her to vote."

"Stand over here so as I can see you in my peephole. Who sent you?"

"Pastor Thomas from the church. You do remember that it's election day, Miss?"

"Hell, yes. Thomas didn't say nothing bout sending no man. He usually send one of the sisters."

"Maybe you should call him."

"And maybe you should close your fresh mouth and stop giving orders." She opened the door. "You sit yourself down while I finish fixing up. I got me a gun back here. I'll blow your black ass back to Mississippi if you tries anything, you understand me, boy?"

"Yes, ma'am."

This was not what I expected.

She scurried like a nervous squirrel around the visible areas of her house looking for valuables to hide from my pilfering hands. She was as thin as a willow branch and from the side curved like a question mark, her wrinkled face and hands the color of an old penny. Tied across her head were two silvery braids. She hustled back to her dressing area.

"What's your name, boy?" she shouted from somewhere. I imagined her loading her gun.

"David Johnson, ma'am."

"You related to them Johnsons over on Inglehart?"

"No, ma'am. I don't know of them."

"Can't stand them fools, no how. Now, as I'm remembering I ain't seen you up to the church neither. Let's see, you from around here? Seem like I know you."

"No, I originally came from St. Louis."

DAVID HAYNES

"St. Louis, huh." She popped her leathery-looking head around the corner like a turtle to get a better look at me. "I married me a man from down that way must be going on thirty years back. You familiar with some Hueys?" Before I could say no: "Ornery nigger. Put his ornery butt out a here twenty-five years ago. A lazy dog. How you like my house, sugar? You don't see no dust, do you?"

"No, ma'am." But there was a dusty smell: like trunks of old books. The maple (or were they mahogany?) tables and chairs in the tiny sitting room and attached dining area were polished to a high luster. My fingers stroked velvety thistles and brambles that snaked upholstery on a comfortable couch and overstuffed chair. Heavy draperies drawn against the afternoon sun matched in a flowery blue. Doilies saddled the arms of the seating and strangled the tables like spider's webs, and the wide mantle of a little-used fireplace carried framed pictures—so many that, one face blended into another in nightmarish collage. "Everything is beautiful. You have a lovely home, ma'am."

"You don't see no dust, do you? You let me know if you do. I got me a girl coming in to help me out—this little yella gal what live next door. She as lazy as the day is long. You let me know if you see any dust and I'll take care of that heifer. And don't you be ma'ammin' me! You call me Miss Kezee like other folks do. You got that, boy?"

"Yes . . ." It was getting late, and I had two yet to get to the polls. "Are you about ready, Miss Kezee?"

She emerged from the back of the house wearing a fire-red wig, pink knee socks, and a faded dress with tiny roses on it.

TAKING MISS KEZEE TO THE POLLS

"You in a hurry, sugar? Miss Kezee don't need no rush. You like this wig? I got me two more, not counting my church wig." She was chewing; one rumpled cheek blown up like a rusty balloon.

"You look very nice."

"Let's go, then." I held the screen door while she locked a half-dozen dead bolts. "Take Miss Kezee's arm while we walking to the car, sugar."

"Afternoon, Miss Kezee," a round, dark woman fanning herself called from the porch next door. "How you feeling today?"

"Feeling just a little poorly today, May Ellen. Got a touch of this summer cold. You tell that Tonia she done a good job this week, and I'll be paying her when my check come."

"Don't you worry about that now. Looks like you got a new gentleman friend. Go on for yourself, girl."

She waved a hand at her. "I'm on my way to vote. Best be getting your own self down there stead of messing in other folks' business."

"All right, then, Miss Kezee. You all have a nice trip."

She sputtered to herself as I let her into the car. "Ignorant, big-ass, trifling gal. Bitch wouldn't vote if you paid her. All she got is baby on the brain. Done had a baby by every man in town—got five or six of em. Come in every color, they does."

"Now, you don't know that, Miss Ke..."

"She got one bout your color. Maybe that's where Miss Kezee seen you before, huh?" She laughed like a coughing fit. "What kind of car this be, sugar?"

"It's a Dodge Colt."

DAVID HAYNES

"Sure is uncomfortable. Make a left up here."

"J. J. Hill is on Selby, Miss Kezee."

Her look said, Is you crazy? I made a left.

"Left again and go on down here a ways on Marshall toward Central." She hummed quietly to herself and did double-takes at everyone on the street. "Who that?" she'd mumble.

"Stop!" she hollered at the top of her antique lungs. "Pull it over right here, darling. How you roll this window down?"

I showed her. We were stopped in front of a ramshackle vegetable stand on a vacant lot. An old couple like crows guarded a table of halfhearted melons and pathetic tomatoes.

"Mattie! You got any kale today? Or spinach?"

"We bout out of everything today, Miss Kezee. Check back on Saturday."

"Uh huh." She waved and cranked the window arthritically. "Damn! Can't get nothing fresh. But you like donuts don't you, sugar? Make a right up here at Lexington."

"We should be getting to the polls. We wouldn't want them to run out of ballots, would we?"

"Don't get an attitude, darling. Miss Kezee don't vote without donuts. Another right up at University."

She hummed some more—noisy, tuneless songs—while I tried to figure out how to pay John back for this "little favor." She spit an oily wad into a napkin or rag she'd fished from my glove compartment.

"You keep your eyes open, sugar, and let me know if you see any hos out there on University so as Miss Kezee can give a little piece of her mind. Walking the streets day and night like they owns it. And look up here. You see this dirty movie mess up here on the corner? That's the problem. They only put this here in the colored neighborhood. Can't even walk down here to the store no more."

"Don't get yourself too worked up, now..."

"Lord, look who coming out of... Miss Henry's neph... Stop!... Roll this window down!"

"Miss Kezee, I'm driving!" She got it halfway down by herself as we cleared the intersection.

"Get your black ass away from that nasty stuff before I call your mama and..."

"Miss Kezee, please!"

"What you hollering for? Donut place just up the next block." Miss Kezee's wig sat crooked on her head where she tried to force it out the car window. She bounced around like a sack of laundry as I turned into the steep and rutted parking lot.

"You come on in, in case they try to get smart with Miss Kezee. You may have to knock some heads for her."

There were only three or four trays of donuts left from the morning rush. A pimply faced high-school-aged white boy gave us a friendly can-I-help-you. She stared him down.

"What you got fresh back there?"

"All our donuts are made up fresh daily, ma'am."

She looked at me over her glasses with a see-what-I-mean look, pointing the fire-red wig in the clerk's direction.

"These here chocolate crullas fresh?"

"Yes, ma'am."

"Better be. Give me four. No! Not that one. This one here with all the chocolate. How bout these long ones? They fresh?"

"Yes, ma'am. All our..."

"Better be. Give me four. Uh huh. You getting the idea now. Why ain't a child this age in school?"

"This is a work-study pro..."

"These chocolate cakes fresh?"

"Yes, ma'am..."

"Better be. Give me four. That's an even dozen. You want anything, sugar? Pay up, then, and let's get to voting. Miss Kezee don't have all day."

I was in shock: I glared at her.

"Go ahead! Pay him!"

Good thing I'd brought some extra cash. I paid and Miss Kezee snatched up her box of donuts, clutching them to her chest like her own newborn baby.

"Have a nice day," the clerk chirped.

"If these donuts is stale you go back in there and beat his ass, hear?" she whispered, loud enough for him to hear.

"Miss Kezee, I didn't expect to..."

"Used to be when you went in them places it was 'Auntie this' and 'What y'all want in here?,' you know what I'm saying? I can't stand them."

I dropped it and drove toward the polling place.

"You want some of these donuts, sugar?" Miss Kezee stuffed herself with chocolate, which smeared her face. She wiped her hands on my vinyl seats. "Bastard didn't put no napkins in this box. Have we got time to go back so you can rough him up?" She coughed her laugh again.

"No, ma..." I caught myself just in time, and laughed with her. "I think I will have one of those." They were half gone.

"Who we voting for today, baby?"

"This is the primary election for the general elections in the fall."

"You must think I'm crazy or something. I asked: Who are we voting for today? We!"

(Oh, that we.)

"Don't know that there's a recommended candidate as such. None of them seem like their interested in our issues much."

"Haven't been a good one since Mr. Humphreys—H.H.H.! At least it seems that way to me. Voted for him for years. Is you married... how old is you, twenty-five, thirty?"

"Twenty-eight, and no."

"Why not? Can't find you one? I got a few little gals up to the church be interested in making a home with you." A damp, sincere hand gripped my arm.

"No, thank you anyway, Miss Kezee." (I'd met John's parade of future homemakers on more than one occasion.) Miss Kezee hummed to herself and looked at the neighborhood.

"Things be changing fast. New houses, new people. Seems like I don't hardly recognize it no more. Sad." She nodded off to sleep.

"Miss Kezee, time to go in and vote." I shook her arm. This time her wig had slipped forward on her head. A drizzle of drool interrupted the chocolate beard she'd smeared on her chin.

"Just a second, sugar." She wiped with a perfumy handkerchief. "Do I look okay, baby? Might be some eligible mens in here of a certain age, if you know what I mean."

"You look fine. I'm eligible, aren't I?"

"What I want with a man with a cheap-ass car like this here? Open the door for Miss Kezee and help her in."

"Good afternoon, and who have we here?"

We have an old black woman who will cuss your condescending white self out if you keep it up, I thought to myself. Miss Kezee was unusually quiet. Leaning weight like a sack of potatoes on my arm, she didn't answer.

"This is Miss Xenobia Kezee, here to vote," I said. Miss Kezee looked down from my arm to her shoes and back.

"Honey, is this your usual polling place?" The worker shouted as if to a small child. No answer from Miss Kezee. "Your granny's hard of hearing, huh? Is this where she votes normally, or is this her first time?"

"Miss Kezee has voted in every election for over fifty years."

"Oh, yes, here we have her... on Dayton? Do you know... does she know how to use the booths?"

Since before you were born, I answered in my head. "She'll be fine," I said instead. I walked Miss Kezee to the booth.

"How we doin', sugar?" she whispered.

TAKING MISS KEZEE TO THE POLLS

"You can't go in there with her," Miss Loud-Mouth masked her contempt with saccharine. I waved my hand at her in disgust. I heard cursing and harrumphing coming from within the booth: damn crooks—fools—cheats. Miss Kezee ambled out all weak and lost. I grabbed her arm and headed for the exit.

"See you in November, Granny. You tell your granny I'll see her in November, okay?"

"Fuck you too," I half-said over my shoulder.

Miss Kezee brightened up and lightened up considerably by the time I'd closed the car door.

"Sugar, Miss Kezee don't approve of no swearing. I'm a church-going woman. Besides, ain't much good in saying what can't be heard, what with that meek whispering you does." Once again, her dry hack.

"You were awfully quiet in there, Miss Kezee."

"Gotta give folks what they 'spect, baby."

"It's the nineteen eighties, Miss Kezee. Nobody expects anything. Things have changed."

"Have they, sugar?" she snapped, and silently eyed me the two blocks back to her house, where, in her parlor, she seemed remote—out of range.

"You sit a spell. I be right back." Moments later she returned wigless and wilted.

"You still here?" and then immediately, "I kindly thank you for all your trouble today, Mr. Johnson. I can't offer you no money."

"I wouldn't think of taking it. I enjoyed myself. Guess I should get my other two now."

"I won't be keeping you." She opened the door. "Thank you again." She gripped my arm.

I squeezed the wrinkled hand. "Goodbye, now, and take care."

"Sugar, I was one of the first, you know." And she closed and locked the door behind me.

I looked at my next address: two blocks away. Spying a chocolate-stained seat, I wiped it down with a forgotten, perfumy handkerchief.

THE LIVES OF
ORDINARY SUPERHEROES

THE OLD MAN AND I had done enough interventions in this part of town I didn't need to be told it was a bad idea to leave a car filled with high-end stereo components unattended for any length of time. He'd always say: "Son, folks round here steal anything not nailed down." Don't get me wrong: the man had faith. But just like the rest of us, sometimes his cynicism ruled the day. I told myself that the ragged quilt I'd strewn across the lot of my precious audio would fool all but the most dogged smash-and-grab artists—the garden-variety delusion we all share, all of us hiding comfortably behind our flimsy dead bolts and reassured by the whine of our alarms crying out in the wilderness.

I'd put off taking my leave of him until I could postpone it no longer. Glo and the kids were on the plane to Portland, the house keys had been transferred after the new owner's walk-through this morning, and as soon as I finished up here, I'd chase after the Mayflower, determined to beat that punk driver

THE LIVES OF ORDINARY SUPERHEROES

across this continent if it killed me. The Toyota was gassed and the passenger seat laden with enough junky snacks to clog the arteries of a moose.

I guess there was a possibility that I might not have found Bill Jenkins here at the Third Generation, but then, the sun might rise in the west tomorrow and they might cancel *Wheel of Fortune* too. Old Bill as much as had a barstool grafted onto his ass since his "retirement"—the polite way we like to talk about his change in career trajectory. I'd get calls pretty regularly for a while there—from Little Reggie, the owner of 3G, or from that girl over at Hadley's before Hadley's barred him—telling me he was in again and acting a fool again and wouldn't I come and see after him please? Which I did for a while, until Glo put her foot down, insisting that the old man was not my problem, and she wasn't about to have her husband running out every damn night shepherding some drunk has-been superhero out of the corner tavern. But what can I tell you? I felt guilty. Who else did he have after all?

You know the story: his people had all been blown to bits when that dastardly Roscoe the Blingmaster aimed his diabolical Disintegro ray at the project where the Jenkins family lived, immediately vaporizing everyone, except poor little William, who, shielded by the ancient lead-lined porcelain tub, where he'd been eluding his sister during a marathon session of hide-and-seek, was miraculously spared with the only apparent effect being his new ability to, when needed, make himself invisible (except to dogs and small children) and his uncanny ability to

DAVID HAYNES

shame even the most hard-core evil-doer into thinking twice about what he or she was up to. Evermore he has trod the lonely path of all such... dare we call them men? The passionate pursuit of truth and justice, his anonymous and solitary life of self-sacrifice.

What were the chances even one of his fellow midday drunks knew the storied exploits of the man who had once been known as Ghetto Man? And make no mistake, these were drunks, all of them; the hard-core kind, even the old man himself these days. Barely past noon and each of them already more than a few highballs into their daily journeys to oblivion. 3G was that kind of joint, "Home of the Long Pour" printed right there on their cocktail napkins, less a promise than a warning, I assure you. I sidled up to Bill on an angle, all the better not to take him by surprise. Your retired superheroes tend to get nervous about being sneaked up on. He spied me, flicked his mustache with his thumb and harrumphed.

"Hey, yourself," I said. I may as well be from the collection agency, so cold are the eyes he cut me with, and it's clear that will be the extent of his greeting.

But make no mistake, this isn't the casual dismissal of those who have lived too long for friendly discourse, nor is this the ironically comical snub of the secretly lovable curmudgeon. Bill Jenkins is an old-timer with a grudge. Long story short: I'm blamed for the revocation of his superhero license. It's because of me he's glommed onto that barstool, pickling his liver and longing after lost glory. He sniffed or snorted or made some

THE LIVES OF ORDINARY SUPERHEROES

other dismissive noise and took a long pull from his seven and seven—and if that was to be the worst of my punishment, surely, I'd gotten off lightly.

I persisted. I had a mission. I signaled Little Reg to snag me a bottle of water and perched on the stool next to the old man.

"So…" I began. It was that "so" you hear on bad blind dates, after the lucky couple has exhausted their conversational repertoire, nothing further to note about the weather or the high price of gasoline. The old man sighed, rolled his eyes. I'd seen this brand of exasperation more times than I could count; it was standard in his arsenal, a trusted saber most often employed against gangbangers foolish enough to try to explain why they're shaking down the owner of the corner confectionary—the same kind soul who'd extended credit to their mamas during that fourth week of the month when the money ran a little thin.

One of the drunks two drunks down the bar wanted to know "why the boy ain't drinking." Bill answered by pursing his lips in disgust.

"I'm driving," I responded. "Hitting the road. Today. I just wanted to holler before I took off." I kept my eye on the old man while I said this, and, in fact, I did see a flash of something in his eye. Something… hopeful. Well, to me at least it was. You don't spend half your life as sidekick to a superhero without learning to read even the subtlest of signals.

Fifteen, I'd been, when I met this man, strutting my hopeless teenage behind home from high school. Don't ask me why—a bad grade or a bad attitude, who knows—but I'd been ripping papers out of my satchel, wadding them up, and leaving them littered in my wake.

"Excuse me, young fellow," he'd said; and I swear I had not seen him there, seen anyone there. I gave him the evil eye.

"What's all this?" he said, indicating my trail of trash.

"…the fuck business is it of yours?" I hissed.

"Come on, now, son. There's no call for that."

Who did he think he was messing with? I was J. B. Henderson, toughest little MF on the Northside—or at least in my feeble imagination I had been. And I wasn't his damn son—for that matter I wasn't anybody's damn son, my actual father never in the picture past his hit-and-run sperm deposit in my mom.

But he had those eyes, Bill Jenkins did. There was something in those eyes. He tsked, and he shook his head.

"Poor Miss Harris in that house right there—we don't want to see a sister out here picking up after us. She's trying to keep it nice around here. Come on." Bill snagged a wad or two, and—damnit—I found myself snagging the rest.

"Bring it on down here," he ordered, and I followed him to the corner. Along the way he bent for a few more scraps of other fools' litter, and so I followed suit. We deposited the lot of it in an oil barrel outside the barbershop. "Good man," Bill praised.

"What the hell ever," I sniffed, and turned on my heel to head home to my game console.

"Just a second, there, young man."

I turned to see what he wanted.

"Well?"

THE LIVES OF ORDINARY SUPERHEROES

"Well, what?"

"Don't you got something to say?"

I shrugged.

"Come on, now. Your mama raised you better than that."

"You don't know my mama."

"Come on, now."

"All right, then. Sorry. Satisfied?"

"Sorry. And?"

This is what the old man was like back then. He would ride a brother ragged, wear him down like twenty-grit sandpaper. All of this, by the way, with puppy-dog-soft eyes that appeared ready to brim over with tears.

"I am sorry, sir, and it will never happen again." I had hit that *sir* heavily with sarcasm and had been about to ask him if I could get the hell out of there now. He grabbed my hand and congratulated me.

"And now your mama's proud," he cheered, and he dismissed me—pointing me on my way, trilling his fingers in that "run along now" way that people who are through with subordinates do.

I complied, or started to, but—I couldn't help it, I was hooked—I turned back and just had to ask him:

"So, this is what you do?"

"Say what, now?"

"This. You do this all day? Walk the hood and tell people how to behave?"

"I can see that you're a young man with a lot of issues," he responded.

I mumbled a vulgar name and headed home.

"What's that?" he questioned, but when I turned back I realized that he had not been talking to me. His hand was pressed to an earpiece, his head bent forward slightly as if to improve the reception. "Over on Vandeventer, you say? Twenty minutes. I'm on it."

That damn headset: still today pinned above his left ear, radical—even magical—back in our heyday, today however only slightly more obtrusive than every garden-variety earpiece on every garden-variety workaholic; alas, no more likely to ring these days than the alarm at an abandoned firehouse, it weighs his ear like the medals on the jacket of an ancient vet, reminding himself, surely more than anyone else, that once he'd had his day, that once he'd done his part.

On that fateful afternoon he keyed open the locks on his rusted Gran Torino and asked me if I was coming. Owning no better judgment, off I went on the first of fifteen years of making the greater Jeff-Vander-Lou community safe for its ever-struggling citizenry. Regrets: only the day I broke this man's heart. But I had done what I had to do.

Our first case had been a bar fight: a couple of down-and-outers who'd been aimless and most often intoxicated since the carburetor plant closed back in the seventies were having their weekly shoving match—foolishness that, frankly, you'd

THE LIVES OF ORDINARY SUPERHEROES

let pass, were it not for the grade school on the corner and the kids getting ready to walk by on their way home.

"Gentlemen," he'd cheered. They called him "Jenks" and asked where the hell he'd come from. He introduced me: "Y'all know my boy, Little J?"

And I got a round of handshakes and how-you-doings and plenty of insistence that I was a chip off the old block. Five minutes later we were inside, a bar not unlike the 3G, a round of Busch Bavarian for the three of them, "And a Coke for my boy here."

That's how I became Little J, sidekick to the greatest super-hero the Northside has ever known. And, for what it's worth, that's what it's like most days, the lives of your ordinary super-heroes. Surprised? Honestly, I had been too. Like you, I'd been raised on images of larger-than-life figures; their glossy and impossibly souped-up sports cars; their fortresses of solitude and high-profile, world-redeeming escapades. And, hey, I'm not hating: If it's a choice between being devoured by humanoid robots from Zortron and having all the media sucked up by some guy in a red cape and leotards, I choose the cape and leotards every time. But you know the drill: we can't all be Academy Award winners. For every Denzel with his guaranteed percentages of screen time and points on the gross profits, there's a hundred guys who are lucky if they get to shout the line "I'm tired of the man!" while being shoved headfirst into the back of the squad car. And for every Green Hornet, there's a half dozen guys like Ghetto Man, tamping down the petty crime, keeping a lid on the little stuff so that the glamour boys can focus on saving the world. Are they jealous, these journeymen of justice? Well, surely a little: but there's no shame. Bill Jenkins: he spent forty years happily routing drug dealers from the playground and giving the evil eye to parking scofflaws. He rounded up stray house pets, kept your alley free of abandoned tires and most likely is the reason there's still treads on the jungle gym in what passes for a neighborhood park. If only there were dozens of him, if only he were still at it today. If only he were twenty years younger, and if only there had not been that little incident with his false teeth sunk into some delirious stick-up artist's leg.

But all that water had rolled off to the sea. And I was rolling on my way as well. There was just this one last thing.

Bill signaled Little Reggie to turn on the TV: their story was on. Despite no one talking much that afternoon, the drunks all shushed each other.

"Still watching *Days*, I see. I bet that Sammy is still up to no good."

"That girl: I swear if she was my daughter, I don't know what I would fix her punishment at."

Leave it to the *Days of Our Lives* to finally get a response out of the man.

"She means well," I offered.

Bill nodded. Meaning well: as important to Bill Jenkins as actually doing well or doing good. Cynical, yes, often enough he could be. But as I already told you, this is a man who believed strongly in the goodness in each of us. Despite the hungry and neglected children he'd rescued from crack houses, despite their drug-addled mamas, despite the landlords who left those abandoned houses to decay and to become infested, Bill Jenkins remained an optimist at heart. He can and will forgive me.

The hourglass popped up, signaling a commercial break, and Bill looked me in the eye for the first time.

"How's all yours doing anyway?" he asked, and this is real progress—the most he's sent my way in months.

I told him that everybody's doing fine and how excited the kids were about the move—especially Jerry Jr.—and how I'd sent them ahead and was looking forward to joining them later in the week. He lifted a brow in that way that indicated he wasn't sure it was a good idea sending a woman and two youngsters off on their own, but it was a mild admonition only. He'd known Glo since I met the woman, and he also knew the smart money would be on her should any problems happen along the road.

We'd met on a case, as it happens, Glo and I did. I'd been rolling with the old man about five years at the time, finishing my senior year at UMSL (where he'd insisted I enroll) (and where he constantly monitored my grades) (and where—and although I've never been able to confirm this—the "Northside scholarship" that funded much of my tuition I'm confident was actually money provided by him) when one late afternoon we got called to the playground of the school up on Cass Avenue.

The future Mrs. Gloria Henderson we found in the last phase of shooing a crowd of rowdy sixth graders back into the building.

"Is there a problem, Miss?" Bill had asked her.

"Hell, yes, there's a problem," she responded, pointing to a sketchy group of male perps gathered by the swing set. "And where are the damn police? And who the hell are you?"

As shocked by her beauty as I'd been by her sharp tongue, I, as was my assigned role in such matters, helped usher the youngsters clear while Bill did his magic, all the while assuring their teacher that my employer was on the case and that things would be copacetic momentarily and could I have her phone number, please? She'd hardly finished giving me the evil eye before Bill ambled in and announced it was safe for the kids to finish their recess.

"Is that so?" she scoffed, but she let the restless youngsters back out anyway.

Frankly she was no more or less suspicious than anyone else we helped over the years. She had quickly coursed that always predictable path from mocking disbelief to begrudging gratitude that the problem had been solved. Who knows, perhaps had we worn the tights and codpieces and gotten us a couple of capes with a crafty logo affixed, we'd have gotten the respect we deserved. Somewhat dumpy middle-aged black men in denim and plaid work wear; well, they're as common as houseflies in these parts and about as uninspiring.

Look at him here; look at all these harmless drunks, sipping their beer and watching but not really watching Sammy and company emote and cry and otherwise explicate the obvious: Would you even imagine any of these men might be anything other than what you see here today? And, okay, so perhaps for one or more of them, what you see is what you get. But, again, perhaps they are not. I sauntered to the window, grimed over with smoky yellow film, checking on the car. I'd been itching to hit the road; I'd promised myself to hit mid-Kansas before bedtime, and even with the long summer evening, that might be a stretch.

"Ain't nobody studying your stuff," the old man admonished me, his signal to get on with the matter at hand. The others scoffed and mocked my caution. They'd sat here long enough to know it was too early for the neighborhood riff raff to ply their nickel-and-dime trade.

And you had to give this man his props: Bill Jenkins knew people. He knew how to sweet talk those girls who worked the corners to come and have a cup a coffee and rest their feet a few minutes and to get them to tell him how it came to this; knew that sometimes the few dollars he'd passed them would help more than the service organizations he'd try to connect them with. He understood that unless Bobby C. happened to be incarcerated, on any given night he would likely break out somebody's back window and rifle through the medicine cabinets and dresser drawers, and that he was likely to continue doing so until he got tired of climbing through broken glass and of running from the police and of thirty-day stretches in the workhouse. And wouldn't you know Bobby C. is now Deacon Bobby—Deacon Anderson he prefers these days, thank you very much—and he spends his afternoons dropping off supper to the same homes he'd pilfered from, the same homes where the old man and I had spent many an afternoon reinforcing the windows with iron gates and decoy security stickers.

"So…" I said again, and again he flicked his mustache. Fifteen years I'd ridden with this man. He won't make this easy—this leave taking. This much I knew. He waved a shaming finger at the screen—that dastardly Stefano DiMera, once again risen from the dead. What Ghetto Man wouldn't have given to have a chance at the likes of a villain such as he.

"So, I wanted to say…" I started, but he put up his hand and stopped me, reminding me that as far as he's concerned, I've had my say.

They're to be expected, I guess, such resentments. You see it all the time—even in freelance tech support, my main work these days. You just happen to be on-site on the day some lifer well past his sell-by date, one of those who didn't have the sense to walk away on his own volition, is finally shown the door. It's never pretty: the lady from human resources supervising the packing of the cubicle, the rent-a-cops standing by just in case it turns ugly, the dispossessed speechifying as to how he'd given his life to this damn company and how he can't believe people could be so cold.

Back then Bill's decline had seemed rapid to me, but in hindsight there had been signs for years, really. Routine calls—rumbles that had once taken moments to disburse—would drag on for way too long. A rowdy group of teenagers who in the past would have moved along quickly now lingered and made

THE LIVES OF ORDINARY SUPERHEROES

it clear that whatever happened was going to happen on their schedule, some raggedy old Negro be damned.

This one time, we'd taken a routine belligerent drunk call, and, as was the program, I'd stationed myself on the opposite end of the room, setting about diverting the audience's attention to a more entertaining spectacle—me making a fool out of myself with some badly executed magic tricks. (First cure for your acting-out types: lose the audience.) I'd been about to unfurl some scarves from a wine glass when I heard Bill's raised voice in full argument with the drunk. Threats were exchanged, the N-word got aired. This was *so* not his way—and had the police not rolled through just then I don't know where that might have ended.

The thing was: you didn't confront this man. I'd learned that years back, back with my paper wads and that chip on my shoulder. Instead, I waited a few weeks and raised the subject in a way I thought was clever.

"Still thinking of moving to Sarasota with your sister?" I had asked him.

"You trying to get rid of me, boy?"

There'd been some humor in his eyes, but frankly, I'd have preferred a bit more warmth in his tone. It was Glo, in fact, who wanted rid of him—or, rather, who'd wanted a full-time husband and who knew that the only way that would happen would be to end my affiliation with Ghetto Man. At the time she'd been five months pregnant with Jerry Jr. and had enough of me spending my off hours riding shotgun through the Northside.

DAVID HAYNES

"I'm just thinking how you might want to slow down some, is all."

"Slow down and do what?" he asked, and as if to demonstrate he coasted the Torino to a crawl and glowered at some lowlifes on the corner of St. Louis Avenue and Grand. Before I could muster the courage to mention some of the recent debacles, he began lecturing me on the evils of idleness.

"Lots of these folks out here, the problem is they ain't got enough to do. Always keep yourself busy, young man. That's the key to everything."

Believe me there was no pleasure in the irony of him among the midday drunks, busy with their bourbon and soap opera. Was it that there had been nothing to attend to on that screen or had they been too benumbed to raise their eyes to the histrionics? Bill and all the rest focused laser-like on the nicked wood of the bar as if it were a bottomless lake.

"Look..." I began, and I placed a hand on his shoulder, which he jerked from my reach.

"You didn't have to," he protested—and he'd not been protesting my touch.

But I did. Someone had to.

It had been a dangerous call as our calls went: a jittery older man threatening a duck-and-noodles shop with something inside the pocket of his trench coat. Bill had been testy with me that entire evening—I'd announced earlier in the week my decision (Glo's decision) to cut back my time on patrol with him. His usually genial small talk—orations on the glory days

THE LIVES OF ORDINARY SUPERHEROES

of Sportsman's Park and of when he and his boys had tried to integrate the pool at Fairgrounds Park—had been replaced by one-word answers and grunts and silences. Bill Jenkins was a seether, and the car was hot with the energy of his disdain.

At the chop suey joint he made it a point to offer me unneeded direction as to my role and on where to position myself. I'd been hiding in plain sight since before I shaved regularly, but I said nothing about his condescension and found my spot where the glare from the sun off the windows would render me invisible.

For the record, the "diffuse and ignore" strategy had been the right choice that early evening and, ignoring the panicked eyes and subtle hand warning offered by the clerk, Bill sauntered up to the plexiglass, announcing:

"Some shrimp fried rice might just hit the spot. Or maybe I'll have me one of them happy boxes." Bill Jenkins at his best: he relished playing the naïf, almost certainly could barely contain his glee at the disbelieving looks of both clerk and perp.

"Ain't nobody getting shit till I get me some cash," the perp announced, and I remember the poor man's almost violent shaking—so convulsed that I considered walking to the corner and buying him a bottle of wine myself.

Bill gave him a heartfelt "Oh, come on, now" and started in on his spiel about how these poor people didn't have nothing in here and was just trying to make a go of it and serve folks a decent meal. Over the years I had seen this speech work its magic literally hundreds of times. And on much tougher customers than this one—once I'd seen a clearly borderline psychotic crackhead lay down a lead pipe and walk away shame-faced from the man he'd been in the process of mugging. And when that jittery old drunk removed his hands from his pockets and raised them in the air—revealing he'd had no more weapon than his bad breath and bad attitude—I figured we'd have wrapped another one and call it a night and maybe get us one of those happy boxes after all. Until...

Until the drunk shoved Ghetto Man. He lowered those jittery arms and mustered whatever strength he had left in his wine-addled body, and he shoved Bill Jenkins, shoved him right up against the menu board, which came crashing to the ground in all its cardboard, handwritten glory.

"Oh no you didn't," came Bill's response, and perhaps if I'd not been so relieved that there wasn't a gun in the perp's pocket, I might have noticed Bill coming apart on me.

The drunk took a big inhale, ready to unload on Ghetto Man, but apparently the exertion of the shove and the excitement of the (now) foiled stickup had been too much for his delicate constitution. When the perp unloaded, what he unloaded was about a gallon of cheap wine, vomited from his gut.

"Oh, hell no," Bill protested, and then he added: "You get your black ass out of here right this minute, you hear?"

That was the first time I'd heard the man curse, and to show that he meant business, Bill actually grabbed hold of the drunk's raggedy jacket and proceeded to drag him to the door.

From my perspective, this was all happening both instantly and in slow motion, and I'd found myself obsessing over that

THE LIVES OF ORDINARY SUPERHEROES

puddle, which I was pretty sure I'd be ordered to clean up. By all evidence, however, Bill hadn't obsessed on it enough, because between his zeal to eighty-six the drunk and the drunk's outrage at being manhandled, they both slipped in the slime and found themselves entangled on the floor.

Where even more vulgarity spewed from both men's lips and a variety of weak slaps and punches were exchanged. And that's when it happened.

How Bill ended up with his mouth next to the man's ankle is both a mystery and entirely beside the point. What isn't beside the point is the fact that he decided to bite his opponent. This, the man who'd warned me a thousand times that as such things went, a human bite was about as nasty as they got. Here he was with his teeth sunk in another man's calf.

"What the hell?" the drunk screamed. "What are you doing to me? Lord, have mercy."

From the concentration on Bill's face you could tell that he had bared down hard, and it seemed that the louder that the perp screamed the harder he bit. The perp rolled and kicked to dislodge Ghetto Man and, successfully shaking him loose, he rose and fled from the door, the shiny white and pink dentures still firmly attached to his leg.

"My teef!" Bill hollered. "Stop that nigger. He got my teef!"

And so you see: What choice did I have, after all? Handing my hero his now broken dentures, retrieved from the alley behind the restaurant, and seeing him there with those broken teeth; seeing him filthy, reeking, confused: What choice did I have?

"I run him off," Bill had mumbled.

I'd been too disgusted to respond. And I was determined not see him humiliated again. The next morning I'd made the call that started the process that led him to this barstool.

"I did stop him," he reminded me again. He took another pull on his seven and seven. "I did run him off."

"That you did," I concurred.

He dismissed my acknowledgement with another harrumph, and again I wondered what's better: a well past-his-prime old man, messing in things well beyond his powers, or a well past-his-prime old man wasting his days on *Days* and cheap booze?

"You didn't have to," he mumbled, and I knew that it shamed him to say so; knew because this was the first time he'd said the words out loud to me.

But it had gotten late, and I was way behind schedule and knew there was nothing I could say that would change any of it. And even if there were...

"I just wanted to say..." I started to say, but he waved his hand to shut me off.

He'll not hear any of it, whatever it is. My "thank you" as meaningless to him as those of all the people over all the years whose lives he made better in some way. It's the humility of superheroes—thank them for what? For doing their job? For doing the right thing? Who would expect less? That's how these people think.

"What you staring at, boy?" he asked me before I realized I'd been doing so.

THE LIVES OF ORDINARY SUPERHEROES

Busted in my attempt to drink in as much of this man as I could, I suppressed saying "you." This is not a sentimental man—I've known that for half my life—and my eye twitched as I felt the trashy to-sir-with-love goodbye I'd long entertained fade away like a bad pop song on the ancient jukebox.

I chugged the water, stood, gathered the car keys in my fist, signaling my leave-taking as broadly as those actors on the TV and with just as obvious a purpose. Last chance, I thought. Last time I'll see him in this life. That ancient plaid jacket of his caught my eye. Lined with some sort of fleecy material that explodes out into a collar, it was way too much outerwear for this time of year.

"How long you had this old thing?" I asked him.

He chuckled—his warm chuckle. "Longer than you been alive, I imagine." For a moment there, his eyes were young again, and I saw in them the little boy who had to become a man way, way too early.

A person has choices then, doesn't he: he turns on the world and pays it back for all they've taken. Or: he makes a myth of it all, and the deranged dealer who broke down the wrong door becomes Roscoe the Blingmaster, and the stolen piece he used to shoot your loved ones becomes a Disintegro ray.

For a moment—for just a moment—I considered reviving our long-shared fancy: he used to relish my yelling things such as "Floor it, Ghetto Man!" or "When will these criminals ever learn? There's no hiding from justice!" But all that had passed. The neighborhood watch folks (a.k.a. Superhero Central) long ago lost his number, and here we were in the lives we had now: me, the computer geek, following his intellectual wife off to her next step up the academic ladder; him, another of millions of retirees, lonely and at loose ends.

"You could come with me," I offered. I mumbled it, really, afraid to further affront his dignity. And I couldn't place his propulsive laugh as being either mocking or ironic.

"Oregon: that'll be your territory," he told me.

And that would be that, I figured. I made for the door, for real this time. I did not look back and I did not linger any longer. I walked straight out of that joint and straight into the new adventures ahead. I was optimistic even, even as I crossed the threshold and heard behind those final words, my ultimate punishment, his final curse that: Son, you go on out there and do good, you hear?

DEAR DANIEL DAVIS, OR HOW I CAME TO KNOW JESUS CHRIST AS MY PERSONAL LORD AND SAVIOR

I HOPE THIS FINDS the light of our Lord and Savior, Jesus Christ, shining in your life and that he extends to you the grace of his love in everything you do. Let's clear up one thing right from the start, because I don't know what they may have told you. (Many lies, I imagine.) But I have not turned my back on Him, nor has He ever turned away from me. That's all I need to say about that. Neither have I forgotten my son, and they keep telling me to try to connect with you, and I keep telling them that that is not what Mrs. Janet Williams wants, and they tell me to try again. So, I try again.

Across the room from me is a "mirror," which is not a mirror, and on the other side of that mirror, Nurse Jeannie is sitting with her pad, watching me complete her "assignment." I don't know what the bitch thinks—like maybe I'm going to stab this ink pen into my wrist and bleed to death before she can get in here with the Bactine and the Band-Aids. Actually, I do know one thing Nurse Jeannie thinks—which is that when I look over in her direction that I'm looking in a mirror. That's how simple she is. Sometimes I make my crazy faces for her. I look all around and circle my eyes and around in their sockets, and sometimes I let my tongue hang out of the corner of my mouth. Nurse Jeannie writes it all down. Just look at poor Keisha. She types up her little notes on her fancy computer and makes sure the corners are straight before she staples them. Then she drops them into the folder that Dr. Marianne keeps on her desk with my name on it. Dr. Marianne is too busy to sit on the other side of the mirror watching Keisha making faces and writing a letter to her son. Writing the letter is Dr. Marianne's idea, so you'd think she'd pay attention, but no, she's got some other bitches she's got to sit and have her pleasant little chats with. And you'll notice that while Dr. Marianne is happy to provide the latest computers and printers and software for Nurse Jeannie, Keisha has to write it out longhand, just like the old days back at U-City High. Same shit, different day. What do you need a computer for if you're rotting in jail for the rest of your life, right?

Now, Keisha: try to remember that part of our plan is working on our sarcasm.

This is how these bitches talk to you in here. Like they are the mommies, and we are their precious baby girls. You are *so* pretty when you smile. And: you are doing such a super job in the dish room. As if shoving a load of trays into one end of the dishwasher and stacking them out of the other end were a major accomplishment in life. They all have these sweet little baby-doll voices and these fake-ass smiles to go with them.

Thank you, Nurse Judy. Kiss my black ass, Nurse Kay.

In our part of this place, that's what we call them: Nurse Judy and Nurse Jeannie and Dr. Marianne. Because "We want you girls to feel comfortable here."

Please, bitch. I sleep on a hard cot in a room the size of a refrigerator. I pee into a shiny metal bowl. You talk to somebody else about comfortable.

When they read this, they'll say, Oh, Keisha. You know we've talked about putting our best face out for the world. And, well, language like that...

Dr. Marianne will say that (won't you, bitch?), and when she finishes saying it, she'll tilt her head all to the side because she is so damn disappointed in Keisha.

It's all about the therapy, you know. Loading up those trays all greasy and nasty with other people's chewed-over meals, and scalding myself when I pull them out the other end, and sitting with Dr. Marianne for our little chats and then writing this letter.

"It will help 'Our Keisha' to have a responsible job to go to every day."

This is how Dr. Marianne sold it to the warden, I'm guessing. And what does Dr. Marianne care if they've got to have an extra guard on duty while I'm working? In case I try something, I guess. Or more likely in case one of those other heifers in the dish room starts in on me. But I ain't worried about it. I am blessed and watched over. And these other heifers? Well, let's just say the dish room is the place where our "special" population earns its keep. I'm about the only bitch in there who can write her own name, and one or two I'm pretty sure don't even know what theirs is. God bless em, I say. He's got His purposes, and we don't always understand.

I'm not going to lie to you, I can't help but laughing sometime. (And I suppose we'll be having one of our little talks about that, huh, Dr. Marianne?) But it's funny to me, all that drooling and grunting and carrying on. This one time a big old fat one who was a white girl fell down and started thrashing around on the floor. Help her! Help her! this guard said. I was just standing there laughing because it was funny as hell. She looked like one of those whales couldn't get back in the water. She was all wet from the dishes and her blubbery pasty white arms was jiggling around and shit. Why don't you help us? the guard asked, and I said, Help you what? I ain't no lifeguard. I guess she musta thought I was Nurse Keisha or something, instead of Keisha what stacks the red-hot trays for tomorrow's breakfast.

"That's not very nice."

That's what Dr. Marianne says to me, because of course I get written up for laughing at the fat whale white girl and at the guard trying to get her fat ass up off the floor. I couldn't help it, though. It was just funny to me, that's all. A person can't help what's funny to them.

These other girls in the dish room are getting "vocational" training, so that when they finish up the couple of years they got sentenced to because some man had their retarded asses out on the corner holding bags of rocks, they can become productive members of society. A couple of these girls got ho'd out by their mamas, and I'm thinking, Damn, you gots to be on a tight budget if you paying for one that's drooling and can't say her name.

"Now you're just being hateful."

Which is why I'm in the dish room. It's all therapy up in here.

I tell Dr. Marianne all the time that if she doesn't like my hateful attitude, then she knows what she can do. (Didn't I tell you that? You know that I did.)

But that's not how it works, she tells me, so I tell her to explain it to me, she knows so much.

You are entitled by law to be healthy, Keisha.

So, I say, get me some aspirin, bitch, cause you're giving me a headache, and that makes her laugh. I make her laugh sometimes when we talk. She's not so bad.

If I put up my hand to let her know she can stop flapping her skinny white lips at me, usually she stops. Sometimes I just want to sit here.

There's a lot of sadness in you, she tells me.

And that's your problem, bitch, that you say all sorts of obvious things to people. If I know I'm sad and you know I'm sad, looks like we're all agreed on that, so don't get all offended when I go off on your ass. Move the fuck on. When you read this letter that is addressed to my son—and don't even lie and say that you didn't, because I DON'T BELIEVE YOU—I want you to remember what I said in it too. We can save us a lot of time, you and me, if you'd pay attention, and we didn't have to repeat the same shit over and over again. Now, where were we?

Oh, yes. Write a letter to my little boy. That's what the bitch says to me. When I asked her why, you should have seen the look on her face. Like she's offended and surprised and shocked.

I think that would be obvious, she says. I'd think you'd want to.

Well, first of all, the only thing obvious in here is that you're being watched all the time. Hey, Jeannie! Don't think I don't see you through this mirror. When the light hits it just right, there you is, and, and, girl, you need to slap whoever put them highlights in your hair. Looking like frosting dribbled on a sweet roll.

It's obvious that food must be eaten between six and six fifteen and that the lights must go out at eleven. It's obvious that the soap dries your skin and that the shampoo makes your hair stiff and breakable. The black girl who drives out from the city to "hook up" the sisters' hair asked me what I wanted done and I told her to shave it off, all of it, every last nappy inch of it. Leave me bald. What does it matter? (Isn't Keisha's hair cute that way, Nurse Judy? So *cute*!) Fuck all these bitches. Really.

What isn't obvious is why any of this happens. Who makes the damn rules and what purpose do they serve? Why these jumpsuits, and why can someone force a pill down your throat?

And don't do what I did. Do not ask the wrong question around this dump. Why? I asked this one bitch. What's the problem with me getting some lotion for my ashy legs? Why is that too much to ask?

We're not running a cruise ship here, in case you hadn't noticed. You probably want a mint on your pillow too—and if we'd been someplace other than here, I'd have knocked a bitch's eye out over getting smart with me.

You can use some of mine, Nurse Jeannie says. She squirts some of hers onto my hand. It's white-girl lotion. Smells too sweet, like berries. But you take what you get in here. She *is* nice to me, Nurse Jeannie. Hey, out there, Nurse Jeannie. Your hair's not too bad. Maybe just wear a scarf over it or something while it grows out.

Maybe your family can bring you some lotion. We could let you keep it.

After we x-ray it and all.

Nice, but dense. Must be from running herself ragged keeping up with passes for my visitors.

You're being sarcastic again, Keisha.

And if you were really a doctor you'd know to have somebody take a look at that mole on your neck.

As for what I want to do—well, everyone here is an expert on what Keisha wants to do.

You'd enjoy walking outside today, wouldn't you, honey? Or: I thought you'd enjoy more time out of your room.

My cell. It's a cell, so call it a cell.

I don't know, Keisha. It's just that I think you've got a lot of unfinished business.

She makes that sound like a disease.

I don't know, Keisha, but I think you've got pneumonia. Or: I don't know, Keisha, but that's a nasty-looking pimple on your butt.

I tell her I'm done, and I'd walk out on the bitch, too, but that's not how we operate around here.

How we operate around here. Maybe the most important thing we learn in life. Don't kid yourself. They'll talk all kinds of mess to you, but all they care about are their rules—the ones they wrote—and whether or not you follow them to the letter. They'll post them in the front hall and carve them in granite and block the courthouse door. Thou shalt this and thou shalt that. In this case, *thou* is me and not them, and it's my name in that ledger book not theirs.

Dr. Marianne keeps after it like it's a chicken leg with some meat left on the bone. If you're done, then be done, she says. So I ask her what the hell that means. And she tells me that she thinks I know what she means.

And, see, there you go again, bitch, telling me what I know. That's what it's all about over here, reading a bitch's mind. That's why Nurse Jeannie sits over there, counting the number of times I blink with one eye locked on the pen should it slip and slice through my wrist.

I leave Dr. Marianne to stew for a while. I ain't got shit to say to her, and the fact that it's her job to snoop into other folk's business is not my problem. Let her sit and look at me for a while, and if she's got a question, let her ask it direct. I am not a mind reader and wouldn't read hers if I was.

It's been Dr. Marianne for four years now, the longest one of all. Before her was Dr. Kendra, but take one look at that bitch and you'd know she wasn't sticking around this joint. Hell, no. She had her eye on a nice house in Ladue, a fancy car and a fancy man to go with it. She wasn't finding none of that around here. You could tell by the way she talked to you what she was like. Uppity and proper. One of those bitches thought she was white. Keisha, you just let us know when you're feeling poorly. Poorly, and I wanted to say to the bitch, Where on all those diplomas on your wall does it say you're licensed to speak to me like I'm stupid? In fact, I did say that to her, and she got all offended looking like in all her years in school they'd never told her what to do when someone called her on her bullshit. Hell, no, she didn't last long around here.

Before her the doctor was a man, and before that I don't remember.

Dr. Marianne came and stayed.

Either a door is open or a door is closed, Keisha, she says.

Which made me shake and grunt, because you know who that reminded me of? She would go around the house sometimes and push the doors all the way around open or pull them all the way closed. What she said was ('cause I asked her) that a draft would blow shut a partially opened door, and she didn't need to be startled in her own home. It was always some shit like that with her. Why the sponge had to sit a certain way in the basket by the sink, or how it was "common" to sit on the front steps of a house and how we weren't common people. But I am common, I would say back to her, and she would give me that look.

DEAR DANIEL DAVIS

Dr. Marianne got impatient when I did not respond to her "open door" comments. When she first came, she would tap her pencil when I did not answer her questions, but she has gotten much better at her job over the years.

Take all the time you need, she used to say, but the tapping let you know she didn't mean it. Eventually she stopped, and I'm thinking it's because she caught me staring at the pencil and giving her the fisheye about it. You have to train these people. Nowadays she doesn't tap, but she breathes out long through her nose, like she's counting how long it takes to blow all the air out of her lungs.

(See. I do know you, girl. Don't even front.)

Let her blow that air until she empties out like a bathtub with a pulled plug. She might be rushed, but I've got nothing but time on my hands. I have sat in this chair for days sometimes, twirling my hair when I had some, and looking out the window, out into that empty field. We live in the middle of nowhere, in the middle of fields of corn, behind trenches and behind tall fences wrapped in barbed wire. Sometimes in this office the light flashing off the corn stalks turns the inside of Dr. Marianne's office a yellow color. Where I sleep, I don't have a view, because I don't have a window, because none of us do. So, she can breathe, and I can sit here all day and watch the corn grow.

There are alternatives every day, Keisha. To open one door or to close another. You've lost some of your choices being here, but you still have others. You always will.

Which makes me want to snap on the bitch.

Because you don't know me, bitch, and you don't know anything about me. You don't know that maybe one of the things I like best about here is not having to decide what to eat and what to wear and when to go to bed and when to get up. Not having to worry about who to be friends with and how to take care of all these people.

I used to snap on Dr. Marianne all the time. Before she'd open her mouth, I would yell, "What bitch?" to her. But sometimes they wear you down, these people. Dr. Marianne, she's the kind you could yell at all day and she would sit and take it and come back the next day for more. And, Marianne, I know you do care, because if you didn't care that would mean that you like to be treated that way, and, believe me, no one does. You don't like it, you're just patient with it. Eventually I got tired of being hateful all the time, so I just stopped it. They wear you down.

She brings me a little treat now and then. A little piece of coffee cake or some home-baked cookies, and I know that she is not supposed to be doing this. Feeling ornery once, I said, I could get you fired for this you know, and she said, Don't do me any favors. The pictures on her desk are of her two little girls. They are little stringy-headed white girls. One is cute and one is homely, and I wonder what that's like. Sometimes she tells me stories about them, and I know she's not supposed to do this either, but I don't stop her and I would never tell. And since you are reading this, I want you to know that I like hearing about your little girls, and I will never tell on you for this. Or for the cookies. You think I don't know why you tell me about your girls even though it's against the rules, but I do. As you like to say, I think we both know what's going on here. And that's all I have to say about that right now. And don't you push me on it, bitch.

But I do say to her, Okay, Dr. Marianne, you know so much. You and your damn doors. You can open a door all you want, and somebody on the other side can slam it right shut in your face.

I am so tired of having doors closed in my face.

Control your own doors. Open them or close them. But you be the one in control.

And this pisses me off, but it interests me, too, dammit. So, I start to argue with her, like I do.

Other people... I start to say. And she says, We aren't talking about other people, which makes me madder, but I don't go off on her like I might have some other time.

So, I choose closed, I say, and she passes me this pad and pen and says:

Close it, then.

And I say, Because I tried before and they never wrote and they never came. Which makes her nod like she's so smart. Nod the way she does when she says we're making "progress."

Like I said, I say, I'm done, and she says, Okay.

Okay, Keisha, she says. If you're done, I just have two questions. Have you closed *your* doors, and do you want them to be closed?

And this is my problem with these bitches, always putting it back on me.

Like always, I can't figure out what the hell they want me to do, and I tell her that.

Which is when she tells me to write a letter to you.

Why doncha? she suggests in her perky white-girl voice.

So here I am, sitting in the room with the two-way mirror. It's the one they use for family visits, in case you're interested. Through that wall, Nurse Jeannie is bored out of her mind, I know.

Hey, girl. You hang in there. I won't be but a minute longer.

Poor thing. How much fun can it be watching my pen move and the pages flip on this legal pad? I guess you can't be too careful.

Open or closed? How the hell would I know something like that? When I fold this letter, my assignment's done. Or I suppose you will be the judge of that, Miss Thing.

I pray every night to the Lord Jesus that He look after Daniel Davis, wherever he is. He is real, and His love is everything and all that we need. If through some amazing magic of the universe this letter should actually find Daniel Davis and you are reading this letter, please say hello to my mother, Mrs. Janet Williams. Tell her that I understand and that I pray for her too.

Yours in Christ,
Keisha Davis Williams
Prisoner #01121563

YOUR CHILD CAN
BE A MODEL!

FOOTBALL POOLS. RUMOR MONGERING. Daylong seminars on the changing face of the twenty-first-century consumer. This is what Americans did at work. Sheila had no idea. Eighteen months ago she'd been a housewife. Who knew the glass on top a copy machine could support a grown man's behind?

When Whispering Pines Junior High School rings her to tell her that her son Briggs has been sent home from school for misbehavior, Sheila is arrayed across the entrance to the office of her boss, Marketa Winthrop, in the sort of pose a really bad exotic dancer might mistake for sexy. She is trying to keep the production manager from stabbing Marketa Winthrop with an X-acto knife. The knife is right there in his hands, its edges serrated with bits of rubber cement and trimmed copy. Marketa Winthrop wants the blushing beauties on the bridal-announcement page arrayed in alphabetical order. Ralph Johansen has his own scheme. He waves the paste up in Sheila's face.

"Ugly, bootiful, ugly, bootiful." He fingers the alternating faces and assumes the bizarre and unrecognizable accent he adopts when he is angling after a date with her. Roma or marginally Latino, she thinks, but who could even imagine. Ralph is from Eau Claire, Wisconsin.

"It's ten o'clock in the morning," Sheila says to the assistant principal. "What do you mean 'sent home'?"

"Dismissed. Until you bring him back for a conference."

"You can't just send children home," she says. She keeps Ralph at bay with her foot.

"I weel now keel her with my ber hends," he seethes. Ralph Johansen is crazy and handsome and exotic. Olive-skinned and vaguely ethnic like the villains on daytime television, he has steely black eyes and a goatee, the same sort of face as did pictures of the devil on low-budget religious tracts.

"Important call," Sheila mouths, but Ralph ignores her.

"Che ees evil, no?" He grabs her free hand and kisses the darker side, licking it with his tongue. Why did cute men have to be so nasty? Or maybe it was the other way around.

"I've got a district policy manual right here, which says that I *can* send Briggs home. And my file says you agreed to this plan, two weeks ago. Right here at my desk."

She did? Sheila doesn't remember any such agreement, but she might have agreed to anything John Antonio said. Twenty-five years later and still intimidated by junior high assistant principals.

"Jou are bootiful when jou are engry." The slobber on her hand tickles. She stifles a giggle.

"I'm sorry you find this amusing."

"I don't." Sheila clears her throat to indicate just how serious she is and also to stifle her laugh. Just what these people didn't need. More ammunition against her. She bares her teeth at Ralph. Ralph growls in response.

"Where is my child?" she demands.

"He should be landing on your front porch any minute now."

"Briggs doesn't have a key."

"That's for the two of you to work out. Can I expect you for a conference in the morning?"

"You can expect me in twenty minutes." She tumbles into Marketa Winthrop's office, mashing Ralph's fingers in the jamb and locking the door behind her.

Sheila is Marketa Winthrop's personal assistant. Sheila gets Marketa Winthrop's dry cleaning. Sheila gets her oil changed. Sheila picked up snack cakes at the 7-Eleven. Marketa Winthrop is a victim of magazines like *New Black Woman* and *Essence* and *Self*. She reads in these magazines how successful entrepreneurs of the kind she imagines herself to be all have personal assistants. Camille Cosby, Linda Johnson, Jada Pinkett Smith. Those gals snapped their fingers and mountains of annoyance disappeared. Marketa Winthrop believes this can happen for her. She believes that by modeling herself on rich and glamorous women, she, too, will become lithe and loved the world over.

The Fresh Prince of Bel-Air will move into her bed. Who is Sheila to disabuse her of this notion?

"I need to run up to school," Sheila tells her boss.

Marketa Winthrop flips the page of another magazine. "Did Ralph redo the wedding announcements?" she asks. Her boss subscribes to dozens of magazines. Sheila delivers them each morning with a Jumbo coffee and a bear claw from the convenience store. Marketa Winthrop spends much of her day paging through the glossies, dreaming of the big move she promises Sheila they will be making soon to the national publications scene.

"ABC brides," Sheila lies. As if the order of suburban princesses mattered.

"Good girl. Because one thing Marketa Winthrop won't be having is a bunch of pissy mothers-of-the-bride. I'm not having it." Marketa Winthrop always uses both names, always introduces herself as if the person she were speaking with had been hearing about her for years. "Hello, Marketa Winthrop," she'd say, extending her hand, this despite the fact that as the owner of a chain of suburban weeklies, the only place they might have encountered her name was on the masthead of one of her throw-away shoppers, just above the announcement for the garden club meeting and a full-page ad for Cooper's Super Value.

"Pick up some Twinkies on the way back." Marketa Winthrop shoos her on her way with a trill of fingers.

* * *

Sheila makes a left by the trusty 7-Eleven, onto the road to Maple Villas, where she and Briggs reside. Saint Charles County scares her. What were farm roads three crops ago are now lined with strip malls and condos and industrial parks, each cluster of buildings shamelessly jury-rigged. Cheap Tudor veneer on Ye Olde Shoppes. Wet, rusting boulders leaking an anemic drizzle of water in front of an office building named Fountainbrook II. Months old and the whole shebang already looked worn out. There are no landmarks out here. Down in the city, where they had lived with the ex, you navigate using the brewery, the steeple of St. Francis de Sales, the smokestacks at the abandoned auto plant. In Saint Charles County, not even the old-timers know their way around. "I think you turn down by the old Jamison place. Go another mile or so to where they tore down the silo." Pale old faces eye her with mild contempt, as if a black woman doesn't deserve a home on the grange. Or perhaps they blame her personally that the distant city has landed on their former cornfields in all its four-laned glory. Sheila turns past the crumbling sandstone cairns that marked the entrance to her apartment complex. There are no maples, and the villas are peach-bricked generic boxes, with opera balconies and too many yucca plants.

One thing for Briggs: he has the good sense to know when not to push his luck. He is waiting on the porch, just as he knew she'd expect him to be, one less thing to go off about. Fourteen years: she'd depleted her repertoire of responses to the boy. Hysterical mom. Frustrated mom. Blasé. Rageful. Shaming. She could mount a full season of one-woman shows—hey, there was an idea: the Psychotic Divorced Mother's Repertory Company. Rent out a church basement. Sell gin and tonics and Prozac at the concession stand. Begin each season with *Medea*.

"Start talking," she orders. She'd save the small talk for the suits at school.

"Well, you see, the only thing is, it was just that me and Cedric... Oh, by the way: you're looking fine today, Ma. That's a really nice dress."

"Don't even, Briggs." Sheila rolls her eyes. Instead of a theater company, how about an anti-charm school? She could make piles of money training philandering politicians and your garden-variety teenage males alternatives to being unctuous when caught with their pants down.

"Out with it," she orders.

"Like I said. Me and Cedric..."

"Cedric and I." What did they teach in these damn schools anyway?

"Yeah, that. We were sitting in class, and we were just sitting there, and this one kid said that Cedric had ashy legs and then Miss Stephes said turn around and then Cedric said your mama's breath smells like socks and cheese and then I laughed and then Miss Stephes said go to the office."

Sheila monitors Briggs's face while she negotiates a turn. Sincerity to contrition, dissolving too quickly to oily self-pity.

"You don't even believe that story yourself," she chides.

"Yeah, I do. That's just how it happened. Except..."

And there it is: there's always an "except." Sometimes Sheila thinks she should carry in her lap posterboards with large numbers written on them that she could raise and vote on the most promising rendition. Version two of the story is parallel to version one "except" for the fact that Briggs had been the one making the comment about socks and cheese, and said comment had occurred after numerous attempts on the part of Miss Stephes to quell the squawk fest. Briggs looks gravely off into the distance as he delivers this tale, the same way the elderly grandfathers did on Masterpiece Theater. A gullible person would be moved to tears. Version three of the story, also fairly parallel, goes into great detail about the baneful Miss Stephes, who evidently had installed a torture chamber directly beneath her classroom specifically for the purpose of making Briggs's life a living hell.

"She's evil, Ma. You don't know." Briggs quakes a little, remembering, no doubt, the grip of thumbscrews, the pull of the rack.

Sheila sighs. Another Briggs three-pack. Somewhere in the middle of all those words is the truth. Or *a* truth. The frustrating thing is that Sheila knows that her son isn't really a liar. His father: now that was a liar. There was a man who could drag himself in at three in the morning, reeking of knock-off Chanel and with a pair of panties slung around his neck, look you right in the eye, and tell you he'd spent the evening at the bowling alley. Briggs on the other hand is basically an honest boy. It's the "basically" part that troubles her. Briggs views his role in these affairs as something like a hard-working reference librarian. His job: to provide an array of plausible facts and information—make of them what you will, dear patron. Like filling out your income taxes, with Briggs it's a game of approximations. Round up a little here, round down a little there. This is America: you develop a poker face, tell your best story, and stick with whichever version doesn't get you audited, and what Briggs and his father have in common is that they both believe every word that comes out of their mouths. Sheila, she spends sleepless nights worrying about quarters she'd neglected to return to petty cash. Briggs sleeps the sleep of angels, as serene and innocent as his first nights on earth.

Sheila makes a left onto a short and nameless freeway that had been constructed for the sole purpose of carrying people like her from one side of the county to the other. What is she doing in a place like this? People like the kind of person Sheila had intended to become live in the city, in red-brick and ivy-festooned neighborhoods, with coffee bars and cute restaurants that serve foods such as couscous and tiramisu. These days it's the ex and his various sluts who get to sit under the ailanthus trees, read the *New York Times*, and sip espresso. Sheila gets to go to the 7-Eleven and to junior highs and drive on nameless roads past buildings too slick for growing things.

"Honestly, Briggs," she says. "What am I supposed to say to these people?" That smug and priggish AP, who fires statements at you about your child and then dares you to come up with an appropriate response. He'll say something such as "We discovered your son and his buddies beneath the bleachers during a pep rally with a pair of binoculars and a flashlight," and then wait with his fingers folded on his desk.

"Boy, I'm sure you hate to see something like that," Sheila would like to answer, though this is not the sort of response that wins you the prize money. "He'll be dead by sunset." That's the sort of thing they have in mind.

Briggs's bleacher excuse had been too lame to discuss with John Antonio, and as to what Sheila is supposed to say about today's mischief, once again and conveniently as always, Briggs has been struck deaf. These cute boys: sudden onset deafness apparently is provided as standard equipment along with the sultry eyes and bee-stung lips. Ask for the report card or next week's production schedule or for the source of that suspicious pair of red lace panties, and your basic pretty boy's face falls into a pale imitation of deep thinking. Furrowed brows. Wistful pondering. Bad actors, each and every one.

"We were collecting the money that dropped from kids' pockets." That had been Briggs's excuse for the bleachers, though he really needed to work on his delivery. A truly unfit mother would have given some pointers. Smile and nod, son. Show some confidence. Try not to make each statement sound like a question.

Briggs, Briggs, Briggs. Just look at the darling boy. Wasn't it only yesterday he was burbling in his crib, taking his first baby steps? Now he argues with lunch ladies, cruising the hallways like a shark, firing off Vegas-style one-liners. Sunrise, sunset. A veritable storehouse of smarmy remarks, her son: "Hey girl, bring them twins over here." "Stop by my locker so you can meet my friend." "Baby, you know I could rock your world." Briggs could give Ralph pointers on gross. She considered sewing his lips together, but that still left the hands.

"Your son had better learn where those mitts of his belong," Antonio had warned.

Sheila remembers the sweet and endearing olden days at her own junior high, when squeaky-voiced boys would put an arm around you and maybe try to grab a feel. Silly things: They'd pretend to walk into walls. They'd bang their heads into lockers, because you were such a knockout. When you wake up one day and it's your son with the smart mouth and the fast hands and the too smooth demeanor, the word *endearing* goes the way of Quiana blouses and the Jackson 5.

"Understand our position, Miss Braxton. We're responsible for these young women." That was what the assistant principal, John Antonio, had said, a leaky hiss on the *S* in *miss*. But Sheila had thought, Fine: slap a dickey over the cleavage on that one over there with the C cups and tell the rest of these hussies to stop calling my house at all hours of the day and night.

Don't any of these people have children of their own? Wasn't there one person at Whispering Pines who had ever been fourteen? Maybe everyone here had been like those AV club boys who at sixteen already wore white shirts and looked like they were about to knock on your door and sell you a subscription to the Watchtower. Maybe they are all like Miss Stephes, right out of teacher college and fresh off the farm. An ordinary brownskin boy like Briggs sets her atremble. Imagine! Briggs! Harmless as a calf! What on earth would she do if she ever comes across a truly tough customer?

No wonder they won't help you.

Sheila had pleaded with Antonio for advice.

"I'll do anything," she'd begged.

He'd inhaled sharply through the nose in that way that all former coaches had of letting you know that they were about to tell you something that anyone other than an idiot such as yourself would already know.

"Have you tried disciplining the boy at home?"

Briggs is a child. Of course he needs discipline, and she gives it. How did his squirreliness in the hallways get mixed up with what went on in her house? Around the junior high, apparently help only comes in the "self" variety.

"Bottom line, Miss. Boys need a strong hand. You either find a way of getting him in line, or he'll have to find another place to go to school." Antonio had lectured her in his flat-handed fundamentalist way.

What is it they were always saying about how it takes a village to raise a child? Sure, sounds good, but try being a mother with a son. Then it becomes "You squeezed the bastard out, now you do something about him, or else."

YOUR CHILD CAN BE A MODEL!

*   *   *

Traffic on the nameless expressway is backed up at the last of its two exits. Traffic is always backed up here, as unfortunately there are no other non-dirt roads connecting the two ends of the county. People in Saint Charles seem to all have jobs that required them to drive around all day and talk on their cell phones. Sheila does a fair amount of this herself. The strip malls where she does her errands are tricked out like the fancy shopping districts in Manhattan and Beverly Hills. They promise Sheila and the other strivers that if they keep pushing hard, the real Rodeo Drive looms in their future.

In the seat beside her, Briggs's long legs have begun bouncing in that way they always do when he worries.

"It's a beautiful day today," he cheers, brimming with false enthusiasm.

"I'm not doing nice," Sheila responds. "Does the word *mortification* mean anything to you?"

"Ain't she the mom on *The Addams Family?*"

"Don't try and make me laugh." She gives him the evil eye and then laughs with him anyway. Damn cute boys. What could you do but shake your head, throw up your hands and join the fun? She'd even gone to her boss for help.

"I'm having some problems with Briggs," she had proffered.

Marketa Winthrop riffled a page in her *Black Enterprise.* "This Briggs is your boyfriend, right?"

"My son." Which Sheila had told the woman a thousand times.

DAVID HAYNES

"And he would be how old?"

"Fourteen. The school called again and..."

Marketa Winthrop had cut her off by waving her hand. "Look, honey," she'd said. "Fourteen. Hair on the balls. I can sum this up in two words: military school."

Ralph, who that day had been compositing personal ads on the computer, shared Sheila's outrage at this comment.

"It would be my hunnor to keel for a bootiful wummun lak jou," he'd said, and proceeded to squint and flash and flex his eyes at her. She had recently had the misfortune to observe her own son practicing these same faces in the bathroom mirror.

"Oh, but you mustn't," she'd demurred. She wondered if the mothers of fourteen-year-old-boys were allowed to be ingenues.

That Ralph: just too dang cute. The sticky, inked fingers. The demonic eyes. It's hard being a single woman in the workplace. Temptation is everywhere, even embodied in a ridiculous guy like Ralph. Ralph had asked her a while back if she was single, and she'd told him she wasn't sure. He'd given her the once over, lingering on her hips and breasts, and she remembers thinking, This is what Eve must have felt like when her big snake came along: scared and excited at the same time.

"Lat me tek jou avay to peredize," he had cooed.

Sheila declined. As a consolation prize, Ralph had offered her a list of reputable male-only boarding schools, the efficacy of which he could personally vouch for.

"Jes look vat thev dun for me."

YOUR CHILD CAN BE A MODEL!

Indeed, she thought. She received similar advice from her parents and even from Briggs's father. Everyone so anxious to dump adolescent males. What is up with that? Maybe there is something she wasn't being told.

"But he's such a sweet boy," she'd told Marketa Winthrop.

Marketa Winthrop had snapped her gum and taken a drag on her Kool and said, "Hun, that's about ninety-eight percent of your problem right there." She'd then sent Sheila off to the 7-Eleven for more donuts.

Ahead, just off the unnamed freeway, Whispering Pines Junior High looks to Sheila like the sort of building where secret plans are hatched to assassinate third-world leaders. Beige trapezoids of white-stuccoed concrete, no windows. The school sits in the middle of parking lots, which sit in the middle of bulldozed fields, which back up against farms, which still have cattle grazing in the field. No pines can be seen, and nothing and no one here whispers about anything. When they'd come over here to register, Sheila and Briggs had been escorted on a tour by a helmet-haired woman who was advancing her career in public education by spouting phrases such as "child-centered" and "high tech, high touch, and high teach." The woman was well put together for a school person, but around her eyes she had applied her makeup in a way that indicated to Sheila that at some point she had lived an at least marginally wild life. Did she ever imagine, back on those nights, haunting the bar at the

DAVID HAYNES

TGI Fridays, that she'd be spending the rest of her life escorting herds of mothers and their sullen-visaged offspring on a tour of the public school? She had chosen as her junior tour guide one of those student council treasurer types, a girl with a little too much bubble-gum-commercial enthusiasm for Sheila's taste.

"This is where we eat lunch. It's really neat. That's the library. It's really neat." Everything had been neat, not just all the classes and teachers but also the girl's fingernails and hair and brand-name sweatshirt. She was the sort of girl that Sheila and her friends would have backed into a stall in the girl's bathroom and glowered at until she broke down in tears.

The former wild liver had described Whispering Pines as the Triple-A+ Magnet School of the Future.

"Your children can take aikido, mountaineering, reader's theater, cooking with math. It's a rich and dynamic environment."

Did they have any regular classes here, anything resembling literature or history? These were the sorts of questions that Sheila had wanted to ask, but the whole business of finding a place to live after the divorce and a school for her son had numbed her into silence. She had discovered that in the years she had been out of circulation, the leasing offices and schools had replaced all the people who used to answer questions— simple questions such as "Where's the laundry room?" and "Does this school have bus service?"—with well-groomed robots who only knew the words memorized from scripts. If you interrupted them, they had to go back to the beginning of the tape.

"Your child will absolutely love it here," helmet hair had said, and for the most part Briggs did love it, but then Briggs could make friends anywhere. He'd probably win the congeniality award on death row, which is the place these people would like her to believe he was headed.

She should have known this was the wrong school. Too much perkiness in the hallways. Too many straight white teeth in too many expensive outfits. Too many Jennifers and Heathers and Jacobs and Sams. She'd had to resign from the Whispering Pines PTA after one too many conversations with parents who'd already put down deposits on their children's Ivy League educations. "What do you have planned for Briggs?" they'd asked. I was kind of hoping he'd impregnate your daughter Brittany and move into your house. Of course, Sheila hadn't said this, but it was the sort of environment that drove a person to extremes. Parking lots full of suburban assault vehicles proclaiming their owners as parents of an honor-roll student at Whispering Pines Junior High. Sheila wants the bumper sticker on her Neon that reads "My C Student Kicked Your Honor-Roll Student's Wimpy Ass."

Whispering Pines Junior High School is no place for someone like Briggs Braxton, but what can she do? A single woman has to live in a place that is safe for herself and her child. Sad, but young men like Briggs don't figure into the fantasies of suburban planners, and what will she do when he figures that out?

Thank God he is resilient. These Whispering Pines people could stamp their damn cookie cutters on him all they wanted, and Briggs would still be Briggs, at least that's what she hopes. But doesn't resilience wear down? Isn't it like the rustproofing on your car? A year of rain, fine, but five years and all warranties are off. Her real fear: they'll keep on stamping and stomping and fussing and cajoling until they squeeze all the life from her child, until he becomes one of those empty-eyed monsters, rotting on some street corner down in the city.

She eyes him there in the seat beside her. Head nodding gently to some tune in his head, oblivious, whistling—against fear perhaps, but it's hard to say with Briggs. He's never been the whistle-in-the-dark type. All Briggs knows of the hard streets that he's been spared from he learned from the make-believe videos on MTV. Damn cute, silly, silly boy. He really believes he is the life of the party, everybody's best friend. He doesn't even have a clue as to how much trouble he is in.

The point of all of this, of course, is to raise them up and send them off into the world, into their own happy families and into fabulous careers of their choosing, but thinking of this only causes Sheila to shudder. Frankly, she is barely employable herself. Twelve years! Diapers. Volunteering at school. Cooking nutritious meals. Then, just like that, she's out on the street. And while child support looks good on paper, she isn't about to rely on regular checks from a man who can't figure out to at least take a cat bath before leaving some whore's motel room.

Publisher's personal assistant: that seemed like a glamorous enough position. On the days Sheila feels great, she even believes that she is the glue that holds her office together. She believes that were she not setting schedules and routing invoices and generally keeping Marketa Winthrop's eye on the ball, things would grind to a halt. Most days, however, she knows this is hubris—a good former-English-major word. For the most part Sheila gets paid for returning clogged nail polish and to shop around for humane poodle groomers.

Even so, despite spending her days with a woman who believes it's a good idea to wear cruise wear to the office every day, Sheila knows that there are many worse jobs. Winthrop and Rolle left plenty of time to make another plan, and for her, as of late, weekly visits to Whispering Pines Junior High. The only really bad part is the hourly trips to the 7-Eleven. It had occurred to her only last week that the Pakistani man behind the counter believed that she herself consumed the mountains of junk food she hauled out of there each day.

"Not for me," she'd shouted, waving her hand over an assortment of Ding Dongs and packaged nuts.

"Very good, very good," he said, which at the time she thought was polite, but she now believes is the Pakistani version of "whatever."

That could be Briggs, she thinks. My son, spending his life trapped behind the counter of the convenience store, bagging up junk food for lying binge eaters.

"He's coming to no good end." That's what that assistant principal coach person had said. And what if that were true?

What if they made it come true? Schools had a way of doing that. Sheila had seen it happen. Children she'd grown up with, condemned in kindergarten to a lifetime in special-education class. Whether or not they were slow going in, they sure were coming out the other end.

She pulls into the visitor's parking space by the front entrance.

"Sorry I'm so bad," Briggs says.

Something in Sheila's chest does a somersault. She feels herself filling up with that sensation she remembers so well from when Briggs was an infant. She would get this way when someone, usually an older woman, would lean over the carriage and cluck over her adorable child.

"Yes, he is precious," she'd concur, despite his being covered at the time with chunky yellow bits of gummed zwieback. She has always thought of this emotion as tacky and unnamable. What would you call it? It isn't pride, and it's something other than love. It's a kind of ecstasy, and mixed in with that the absolute conviction that if anyone so much as plucked a hair from the angel's head, she'd hunt the barbarian to the ends of the earth and peel him alive with a dull vegetable knife.

The parking lot bustles with her fellow happy strivers, picking up their children for the orthodontist or delivering them from the pediatrician. Shiny, bright faces of the kind that Ralph pasted into ads suggesting "Your Child Can Be a Model!" Antiseptic and crisply pink, the children in those ads, you'd order them out of the catalog, you really would. Call in your

Visa number and receive in the mail one perfect blank slate, ready to mold to order. Operators are standing by.

No, honey, she thinks, you're not bad. Bad kids torture the family dog and put the hamster in the microwave. Bad kids push toddlers out of seventh-floor windows. They bring automatic weapons to school and blow the faces off girls with mousy brown hair and chewing-gum-stained Bibles.

Tomorrow Sheila will take some personal time and drive all over this godforsaken wilderness and find some sort of school that makes sense for her child. She will take the whole day, the rest of her life if she has to. Later today she will make sure the little stud in the seat beside her understands that he has gotten on her last good nerve, that he's not anywhere nearly as funny and cute as they both know that he is, and—on the off chance he thinks she's playing—that she has a list of junior service academies that will permanently erase that smirk right off his handsome brown face.

For now, she leans over to her son and hooks a fingernail beneath his chin. "Listen up, Al Capone," she says. "We're going in there and we're going with version two. Tell it so even I believe it's true."

HOW TO BE SEEN IN PUBLIC

SHE KNEW HER KID: a statement both true and offensively cliché. Jason was behind her, trying to get her to pay him some mind. She'd know this even if the rank odor of his T-shirt, fished no doubt from beneath his bed, hadn't preceded him into the kitchen.

There were hundreds of novels about this—about mothers "knowing" their offspring. Thousands maybe, and Amy Anderson had read lots of them, many of them absolute dreck. She'd focused her original scholarship on representations of motherhood in nineteenth-century fiction, having become fascinated in college with the fact that children, if present at all, were a punishment or curse—or both! Have the misfortune of getting pregnant in a Victorian novel, you'd be dead before the second half—and one needn't dig far into the character's history to discover that the sin for which she paid the ultimate sacrifice was also the act that got her knocked up in the first place. A few years back, prodded by one of her postdocs, she'd explored more recent fiction to see what having a baby got you these days. Supplanting suffering, a pervasive belief in motherly superpowers had inhabited the minds of contemporary scribes, literary and otherwise. These mamas could read minds, predict the future, and, through the powers of their big brains and bigger hearts, will their children back to health from all manner of affliction, often enough under the guidance of the neighborhood "wise woman," who would brew up some herbs, incant, and remind the mother, as Glinda had done Dorothy, that the power to heal had been there all along: just click your heels.

Amy had yet to meet the Breckenridge Hills conjure woman. When she does, she will ask the witch for strength in moments like this, strength to continue to ignore the noxious and obnoxious teenager behind her. She will implore her to bring back the other Jason. The tiny, sweet-smelling one who would sit in her lap and cuddle.

This one smelled like dirty socks.

This one had resumed a favorite pastime of the tinier one; he took great pleasure in sidling up to his parents as close as possible before being noticed. Ninja-mode no longer required the head-to-toe black camouflage or the employment of a yardstick to stand in for a sword. These days it was something closer to creepy perving. She had never once startled nor responded in any way at all—then or now; she'd always known he was there; had done so even before the doctor had confirmed she was pregnant with him. (Another trait shared with the fictional heroines she studied.)

Today's game: Say something about my wardrobe. I dare you.

Disgusting, inappropriate, no doubt ill fitting. No doubt filthy: he knew and she knew that no sixteen-year-old male would stroll into school looking and smelling like this—even if it was just summer school—and she knew that he knew that she knew that his actual wardrobe was stuffed into the backpack (along with cologne he'd purloined from his father's dresser), and they both knew this was about starting shit for the sake of starting shit—because that was a thing that teenage boys did. Everyone knew this!

She would not feed in. She would scan pages of the *Post-Dispatch* and scan them again if she had to. And because of all this she would be late (and so what?) for her brunch meeting with Amanda Detweiler: still, she would not turn around and say one damn word to this child.

"Ready for school, slick?"

She heard it but couldn't believe that his father, Kwame, was actually patting him on the back—that he'd actually touched that filthy tee. She turned and waved her arms up and down at the outfit and said to her husband (and not to her son—a critical distinction, thank you very much): "Really?"

The tee was worse than imagined. Smelly and dirty and wrinkly AND obscene.

"You're all right with this?" (Fine! She'd taken the damn bait. She hated herself. Satisfied?) (But here was the thing, and the important difference between herself and her husband: while she knew about the change of clothes [that she hoped was] in the backpack, she didn't believe *for one second* that Kwame knew, and so he *was*, in fact, perfectly all right with their son going out in the street looking—and SMELLING—*like that*.)

And as if to prove her point, Kwame said:

"If my man wants to wear a dirty-ass shirt, let him wear it. Long as I don't have to smell it."

"That 'dirty-ass shirt' has at least three words printed on it that will get him suspended. And you can be the one that answers when the principal calls."

"Turn around, son," his father ordered.

Jason threw his arms out and swanned around as if he were showing couture on the runway in Paris.

"Yeah, not happening." He waved his son in the direction of the stairs, and Jason flashed his "gotcha" grin. At *her*.

"Did you see that? Did you see that look he gave me? That's what I'm talking about, right there." (*As if she were the bad cop here!*)

"Don't feed in. Sometimes you got to ignore the fool."

"*You* were going to let him go out like that. If I hadn't said anything. You were going to let him go."

"He wasn't going anywhere."

"How do you know that?"

"Well, you see, I used to be a teenage boy."

You see.

As if she were some second-rate second-year in his torts seminar.

One in a whole catalog of Kwame Anderson phrases, each designed to make Amy homicidal:

Let me break that down for you.

Perhaps if I explained it to you this way.

A reasonable person would...

She loved *and* hated debating him. The enormous pleasure he derived from verbal sparring had attracted her to him in the first place. Still, Kwame simply could not resist the rhetorical low blow, innocent-seeming flourishes tagged onto the beginnings of sentences, designed to communicate his (perceived) intellectual superiority—(*to a women's studies scholar, no less!*).

She sighed (not an actual sigh but a performative one, that infuriated him as much as his dismissive sentence starters did her) and gathered up some paperwork to drop off at the office. To Kwame, sighing indicated there was a whole backlog of perfectly sound reasoning NOT being employed against him—therefore depriving him of the pleasure of crushing it with his own (dare he say) more dazzling rhetoric. To Kwame, sighing was... dirty pool.

And as close to a "win" as Amy got in these set-tos. As if there could be a win against his "I was a teenage boy" card.

Say nothing of the unspoken: I was a *black* teenage boy.

Meta message: You, dear wife, are a middle-aged white woman. You may have given birth to this person, but let's not kid ourselves; you're in over your head with the likes of "us."

What to do but sigh and walk away and leave them to their truth. Some things it was better not to know.

Parting shot on the way out the door: "You might want to fish your good cologne out of his backpack. Just saying."

She didn't stick around for the rebuttal.

*   *   *

At the restaurant, Amanda was already seated and waved Amy over to the table. They did something resembling a hug, and sensing Amanda's pique at the tardiness (five minutes, for Pete's sake!), Amy doubled down on her apology.

"One of these days you'll find out what it's like with teenagers. Most days I'm lucky if I don't come running into my classroom after the slackers."

(Amy had never in her life been late for a class. Never.)

"That Jason again, huh?" Amanda canted her head knowingly. It hadn't really been a question.

Amanda's tone rubbed Amy the wrong way—always—and in lieu of a response she asked if the waiter had announced any specials. Not that it mattered; she'd be ordering the crab cake appetizer and a fresh melon salad—her usual at Blondel's.

"I can't imagine what it'll be like when Deidre and Deanna get to that age."

"And girls, no less," Amy added, ominously, partially to get a dig in and partially because she genuinely believed that teenage girls were worse than teenage boys, personal hygiene notwithstanding. Like her husband, she'd had personal experience with the matter.

Amanda was the mother of first-grade twins. Her feigned fears about the upcoming teen years were nothing more than a feeble attempt at chitchat. Amy doubted this woman gave them one thought while she was at the university—while they were home being coddled by an au pair. She was sure the feeling was mutual. From what Amy had seen, the Detweiler twins were the sorts of

DAVID HAYNES

girls who in ten years would buy themselves sleeves of tattoos, move to LA, and start rock bands. After which, Amanda would find herself in the seminar room, cueing up their music on the phone—a pathetic attempt to earn street cred from her students. Occasionally she would feel compelled to stage family reunions that none of them really wanted to attend. On the twins' suggestion, they would hold them at the Hard Rock Casino in Las Vegas, which would provide useful distractions for the daughters' skeevy husbands.

"You all have plans for the summer?" Amy asked, less the "mentor" steering the discourse than the civil member of the party attempting small talk with a person raised by wolves.

"Ted and I were talking about a trip. Australia and the South Pacific. I've been in touch with a woman at a university in Brisbane doing fascinating work on aboriginal peoples and their access to health care."

Amanda specialized in cultural studies with a focus on critical race theory. She spent a lot of time looking for manifestations of racism in the pop culture of other nations—anti-Roma graffiti in Western Europe, skinhead metal bands from New Zealand. Her writing was solid and even engaging, but like a lot of people in her field, her scholarly pursuits tended to bleed into her daily existence: she couldn't watch an episode of a singing competition without posting to her blog (*Skinny White Bitch*) about "the appropriation and decimation of black culture." Amy always wanted to say: "Calm down, sister, it's a game show."

Amanda continued: "I'm not so much interested in the health-care part, but this Aussie has been analyzing poetry

HOW TO BE SEEN IN PUBLIC

and street lit. From the mental-health aspects. Not on its own terms, of course. Pathologizing both the artists *and* the creative product. You know how they do. And you know me: can't resist a good street fight. Thought I'd go over and see what I can get stirred up."

You could say this for Amanda Detweiler: she was nothing if not scrappy. Distressed with the burden of every -ism known to humankind, Amanda is on the case. She'd recently and notoriously spearheaded a grassroots campus campaign to expel the entire basketball team and immediately hire them as professionals—and should anyone accuse her of damaging their futures, she had ample data that proved her salary proposal—money funneled from "the proceeds of these workers' exploited labor"—would in every case outpace their future potential earnings as C-minus graduates with degrees in health club management. Amanda presented as an odd mix of strident and snide, pontificating and pounding the table with a sneer on her face that to Amy came off as simply phony. Amanda picked away at a Caesar and lectured on the evils of race relations down under. Amy tried to recall if she knew any Aussie academics whom she might give a heads up about the shitstorm scheduled to arrive on their shores.

Amy savored her crab cakes and Amanda switched the subject to her belief that the chair lacked enthusiasm for her style of research. Between outbursts, Amanda pecked at tidbits of lettuce. Amanda was one of those rail-thin academics: hipster glasses, unstructured pixie haircut (over highlighted, if you asked Amy). Amanda *never* inquired about Amy's work. Amy guessed that as far as Amanda was concerned, Amy's only role in the world was to shepherd her successfully to promotion. With that all but guaranteed, mentorship now focused on suggestions for close-in neighborhoods with "progressive" schools and where to find a decent bagel.

"Listen to me go on," Amanda apologized (half-heartedly). "You know how I am. Earlier you were saying something about your son, as I recall. Before we got off on *my* stuff." Amanda pointed to herself in a way both ironic and self-satisfied. (What else would they be talking about, after all?)

"Jason is... Jason," Amy replied. A busboy leaning in to clear the remains of their meals saved Amy from further elaboration; she had no intention of discussing her family with this woman. Amanda's promotion would be announced sometime next month. Today's "mentorship" lunch—another of many bad ideas from their dean—was also their swan song: these horribly uncomfortable soirees soon to be a thing of dark memory.

Amy asked the waiter for a cappuccino and said, "I'm feeling like a celebration is in order. Let's split dessert."

"Oh... sure," Amanda replied. "You pick."

Four years of forced communal dining had taught Amy that food was not one of Amanda Detweiler's pleasures, so Amy chose something she loved: a crème caramel.

Amy commented on the weather. She noted the capacity lunch crowd at Blondel's. She complimented Amanda on her lovely leather briefcase (or was it a messenger bag or perhaps just another of those enormous purses that women carried these days?).

Amy hated small talk. Here they were, two intelligent and well-published PhDs: couldn't they be—shouldn't they be—talking about... something? Well, perhaps if either of them actually gave a crap about anything the other one had to say.

Amanda clamped her hands on top of Amy's and said, "It's not an easy thing. We all know that. Everybody's pulling for you."

(What the hell?)

Amanda kept going. "It's hard when the odds are against you. With a kid such as Jason."

"A kid such as Jason such as what?"

Amanda lifted her hands in a fake-demure, "naughty me" way. She rolled her eyes the same way the sorority girls did when Amy attempted to have them consider that their choice to come to class with a bare midriff might not advance the cause of women in academia.

"Okay, then," Amanda said, echoing those girls.

"I prefer directness, please." Amy feared her voice had taken on an edge. The ventilation in the restaurant seemed to have failed.

Amanda moved through a series of expressions, from piety to pity to "What could I have done to deserve your wrath?" (a Jason favorite, that particular one), eventually landing on something akin to run-of-the-mill academic condescension.

"I know this is a touchy subject." She shook her head with ersatz compassion. "I didn't know *how* touchy." Another sigh.

An inhale. "You know the statistics for young black men..." she proffered a hand that was apparently to be seen as full of universal truth about young black men.

Amy went slack-jawed, her eyes shone with fury. She should have said something, but everything she thought to say seemed wrong or offensive.

A bit slipped free:

"But Jason's not..." She stopped the words—at that most unfortunate place, alas. Attempting a corrective, she added, "I don't mean to say he's not..." Again, she stopped: another unfortunate break.

So, she turned away, exasperated.

Why was this woman getting to her? She owed this person... nothing. Some damn scrubby millennial who had learned everything she knew about everything from Buzzfeed and from listening to bad papers at MLA. Amy forced a smile.

"I've given you the wrong impression. My Jason: he's a good guy. He's a good person."

"Well," Amanda scoffed smugly. "You know that, and I know that."

"Meaning?"

Amanda turned toward the wall of doors that were open to the sidewalk.

"Take a look," she suggested. "Out there." She pointed to the midday crowd bustling past the windows.

Amy shrugged.

"Over there," Amanda cajoled.

Amy saw Vintage Vinyl, where Kwame would buy his music when they had relocated to St. Louis so he could attend law school.

"In front. How can you not see them?"

Taking them in, Amy realized she had been hearing them for some time—had somehow been taking in the aggressive and melodic conversation that through the restaurant's accordion French doors had been underscoring the ambient noises of dining. Her son's age, these young men, their pants sagging; hulking, blocking the sidewalk: they were poster children for the kind of urban mass nightmare shared by almost everyone in Blondel's. She should have spoken in their defense, but she couldn't find the words. The part that could not speak was the same part that felt relieved that her son was not out there with them.

"Let's be honest," Amanda said. "It's human nature. I'll admit it myself: If I get on a plane and see a guy in a turban or someone sort of... swarthy-looking... I don't know. It makes me nervous. Sometimes. Despite my training—and you of all people know my training—and just imagine what it's like for most people. People who haven't examined these issues with anywhere near the depth that you or I have."

So typical of Amanda, this casual xenophobia, this lumping together of things: the two of them as "cultural allies," her son and whichever straw man was most conveniently at hand, including those boys across the street.

"So now my son's an international terrorist?" The custard embittered on her palate, and she dropped her spoon onto the china with a clatter. She was nauseated at the idea of her own utensil pushing through the same puddle of caramel as her "colleague." She wanted to slap Amanda Detweiler back to wherever the likes of her were hatched. And still, the bitch pressed on:

"You know that's not what I mean. Look, I'm just trying to offer my support. I know you've been having trouble with him and…"

"We are not having trouble with our son, and I resent your saying so."

"Apologies. I guess I got it wrong. It's just that, every time we talk, you've got some new horror story."

"That is not true."

(Was it?)

Clearly offended at being called a liar, Amanda struck back.

"The odds are not in your favor, Amy. Or, rather, not in his. We want you to know that we're on your side here. We want you to know that we *know,* and we *understand.*"

"We?"

"People talk." Amanda shrugged nonchalantly and shielded her eyes to signal her fake embarrassment. As if she'd taken a big naughty swipe with her finger through the dregs of the dessert and loudly slurped as she licked it clean.

And then Amy found herself star of the sort of scene she hated—where some out-of-control woman scrambles to find her bag and her papers and her wrap and whatever the hell else she needs in order to storm pointedly from the room. The twenty-dollar bills she wanted to fling onto the table snagged against something else in her wallet.

"You just wait, Amanda Detweiler. Give those damn daughters of yours five years, and you'll... Well, I don't know what a person like you would do. I can't even imagine."

"I meant no offense. And I don't think you're hearing me. I'm not talking about Jason at all, really."

Amy had already started toward the door, but she could not let this slight pass unremarked.

"Oh, the hell you aren't. This is why I should just stay out of that damn office. I make a few jokes now and then about my son. The same silly, stereotypical parental banter that everybody else over there engages in. But because it's *my* son, suddenly you've got him thugging around the streets with the likes of... that." She pointed to where the nightmare boys had been, but her finger found instead a security guard, the one who had no doubt moved the crew along to its next station.

"You're not hearing me." Amanda raised her voice, her own frustration brimming over. "It's not about those boys. It's about what people *think* about those boys."

"Shut up, Amanda. Just shut the hell up."

Telling a colleague to shut up: fairly much the end of the relationship. And so be it: good riddance.

Months later, remembering this scene filled Amy with a mixture of rage and embarrassment. The rage was mostly at herself—at her loss of control, at her inability to hear or understand what Amanda Detweiler had been trying to tell her.

Amanda had been right.

And it would occur to Amy that she should apologize to her coworker.

(The fact that she'd never cared for Amanda Detweiler in the first place made that a nonstarter.)

The shame had been caused, first, by having participated in the ridicule of a group of young black men outside a restaurant in University City. That those young men had no longer been present when Amy called them out—or, for that matter, the fact that, as was the case for many such scenes, few if any of the other diners paid one bit of attention to an approaching-middle-age academic type quietly bickering with another, if younger, academic type over overpriced custard—did little to assuage the guilt she felt over her own disgusting behavior.

The greater shame—the confusing, confounding part—had been precipitated by her exit from the restaurant. Without a doubt she had been out of control, blind with anger and frustration. She didn't even know where she was going—except the hell away from that vile woman and her evil ideas.

She vaguely remembered someone at the host station saying, "Thank you," and telling her to enjoy her afternoon, but she also wondered if she'd merely conflated this restaurant departure with the thousands of others she had exited in her life.

Out the door, she'd turned to the left, the direction for walking to the office, but—remembering she'd driven to

Blondel's—she'd done a hasty pivot on her heels. And that was when she walked right into them—the boys from the other side of the street. Now on her side—and she'd walked right into them. Into one of them.

Into the largest of the boys, she'd walked, or into the one she remembered as the largest of the boys, but they'd all blurred together, and they'd all seemed large in that moment. Huge.

She'd expelled a noise. (Had it been a gasp?) (No, not a gasp: she remembers an "umph" sound.) As if she'd been punched in the gut, although it had been she who had barreled into him—she was clear on that much—and she who'd startled, she who'd done a double-take and said, "Oh," as her papers floated to the ground.

"Whoa! Hey, now!" the young man had said. Something like that, he'd said, and she thought he'd gone to shove her back, but realized later—too late—that what he'd actually done was extend his arms to slow her, to keep her from pushing into *him*. After which he'd reached for her as she bounced away to keep her from falling.

She'd guessed he was the same age as her son, give or take a year. About the same height, but he was larger, muscled and solid in a way that Jason was not. His shirt had been open almost to the waist almost—it had been hot that afternoon—and he was sweaty—she could smell it on him. What she'd first read as chest hair she realized had been tattoos, barely visible and blue in rococo curlicues against his dark skin. (Well, not that dark, maybe. Darker than her son.) (Who was not dark.)

"Hey, now," he'd said again. More softly that time, and she realized he'd been calming her and that she had been waving her arms. Waving him away as if fending off an attack.

"Lemme get that for you," he'd said, reaching for her files, and she'd said, "No!" Had said it emphatically, had said that she could handle her own things, had continued to wave him away.

"All right then," he'd replied. "Eyes in front from now on, okay?" He'd pointed at her and winked. One of those others had laughed. Another one said something that sounded like "dumb white bitch."

She gathered the essays she'd graded the night before, and she thought she might have run to her car, but she had no recollection of that.

She'd been in one place and then she'd been in the other.

It would be a day or so before she understood her disrespect to the young man—the way that she had swatted at him as if he were pestilent, her failure to apologize for her own inattentiveness on the sidewalk. Her refusal of his help, her unwillingness to meet his eyes. It didn't take much to imagine what he must have thought of her: certainly, it wasn't the first time he'd caused someone to cower. Perhaps he even got some pleasure from it—all in a day's entertainment: cruising the Loop and making the white folks shiver in their boots. She'd certainly played her part well.

And so there it was, the rest of the shame—a quirky and gentle kind, as it happened. Like the nasty rush one got after executing the fine sharp retort during a childish email spat with a loathed coworker, one laced with the perfect literary allusion. Or the low-budget thrill of beating your husband and son to the kitchen in the morning and wolfing down the last slice of leftover pizza.

Sitting in her car after running into the boy, checking for her phone and her wallet and her purse and her files, she'd realized that what she'd expected to be relief was instead a kind of... exhilaration. In a way that continued to surprise her, she had been delighted to have gone head-to-head with America's worst nightmare and—save a bruised ego—to have come away from the encounter mostly unscathed. This was a trashy pleasure, to be sure, but in its own way a substantial and powerful one, strong enough to linger long after the moment; powerful enough in that moment to mask and to somewhat mitigate her mortification at how genuinely and specifically the young man had been repulsive to her.

THE WEIGHT OF THINGS

ONE YEAR EARLIER, ON a rainy morning in October, Lou Wilson emerged from a deep slumber and attempted to nudge awake the man to whom she had been married for over four decades. He did not respond. Later, after she'd called 911 and accepted comfort from a young paramedic, she brewed a pot of coffee and laid out some things for the undertaker to dress him in. After which she set to the difficult task of making the necessary calls to family and to his many, many friends. Wilson had lived a long and only occasionally troubled life, as full of sometimes backbreaking labor as it had been rich in acquaintances and admirers and clubs and parties and... And the list went on. Her husband's relentless need to be part of a constant social whirlwind for all those many years had exhausted her, and while she'd fed into the official story that his heart had given out, she continued to believe he had burned himself out, succumb to decades of relentless... fun. All those good times had simply driven him into the ground—as would their neighbors do the Chryslers he spent all those years building out at the auto plant in Fenton.

THE WEIGHT OF THINGS

The year passed, and tired of living inside of what often felt like nothing more than a memorial to Wilson's many pleasures—the souvenir shot glasses and cocktail shakers, the wardrobe of chef's aprons he'd worn when inviting "the gang" over for an impromptu barbecue, each bib emblazoned with a tastelessly smutty double-entendre—she had resolved to rid herself of the detritus that had accumulated on every shelf and inside every drawer. Taking a cue from former neighbor and garage sale queen Martha Garrison, she outlined the carport with a string of party lights (tagged, as were many of the odds and ends, with a red "make me an offer" sticker) and festooned the trellises that bordered the driveway with all manner of forlorn wardrobe from their closets and from their daughter's. (Carolyn had flown the nest years before but insisted on using Lou's house as an annex to accommodate her own overstuffed life.)

A festive bouquet of pink and gold Mylar balloons floated above the concrete cherub who guarded the intersection of her driveway and St. Benedict Court. Sometime in the late sixties, Wilson (never in her life had she heard him called by anything other than his last name) brought that angel home from an excursion to the Grandpa Pigeon's store out on the Rock Road. She remembered he'd seemed more than usually disappointed at her less than lively response to yet another spontaneous "gift"— "Don't you like it? I saw it and it reminded me of you"—but how much enthusiasm ought one muster over a hunk of concrete so poorly molded that a jagged spine of teeth protruded from its gray and bulbous ass? The years had not been kind to "Old

Bessie," as Wilson had taken to calling her. That oldest Johnson boy had bounced a stolen moped off her left side, clipping the tip off her wing and leaving the bike pretty much unusable. Thirty years of exposure to the constantly changing Missouri weather had left her looking these days like what might happen if a gargoyle mated with a fireplug.

On this, the final Saturday that her permit allowed her to set her wares in the yard, "Old Bessie's" balloons bounced listlessly on the asphalt. When she'd started this mess back in September, one might have imagined them lofting that monstrosity out of her life forever. Today they quite accurately reflected her waning enthusiasm for the whole fiasco. She hung the remaining clothes on the trellis and arrayed the assortment of basement junk on two folding tables. She sat in a lawn chair (five dollars or best offer), its itchy plastic webbing reminding her why she'd always hated the damn thing. She picked up one of those Oprah Book Club novels that Carolyn had foisted on her sometime back in the nineties and settled in for one last long dull day of waiting for someone—anyone—to take the rest of this mess off her hands.

What in God's name would have made her think it was a good idea to invite armies of strange and rude and trashy women to trample her lawn and snoop around her carport and pick with their grubby fingers through things that she—or more likely her husband or her daughter—had at some point cherished?

"Where are the baby clothes?" they would ask. All of them asked that. Just one of the many nuances of the garage sale industry she'd neglected to research before she'd started down this awful road. What little she knew of such affairs came entirely from observing (with annoyance) Martha regularly and seemingly spontaneously turning her lawn into a vulgar, open-air thrift market. An odd old bird, but the woman did seem to know how to throw a sale. Cars would vie for parking on the cul-de-sac, and everyone, it seemed, left with an armload of goods. Here Lou sits, her own operation looking less like a viable retail concern than someone with too much time on her hands airing out a few items before storing them for the winter.

It hadn't all been a bust: the first weekend a man in a raggedy, once-blue pickup and with what looked like a homemade camper on the back gave her fifty bucks and hauled away Wilson's tools and what she believed to be the second newest of the weedwhackers. Sloan, from up on the other court, took a molded plastic Santa that lit up from the inside. Its reds and whites had faded until it was almost transparent: she'd just given him the damn thing—after all, he helped her string the lights for the sale, and since Wilson's death, he would come by now and again to check on her and to see what might need doing.

A white woman with a brusque attitude took about half the things hanging on the trellis—and then had the nerve to scold Lou for leaning them against the wisteria, which Wilson had planted there "for privacy" (damned lot of good that did). "I doubt these will bloom for you this year," the woman had sniffed. Lou had given her the finger (to her back, of course).

By the time she opened the previous weekend, the "good" stuff was long gone, and the word was out that the sale on St.

Benedict was hardly worth one's time. Business trickled to nothing. An occasional car would circle the cul-de-sac, most not even stopping to browse. A Mexican woman with what felt like a half dozen toddlers in tow signaled to the side door, assuming the real deals must be elsewhere, but Lou had waved her toward the stacks of magazines and paperback books—and the damn woman seemed genuinely offended—but she had given Lou ten bucks for a perfectly good blender, an extra one that Wilson had on reserve "only for margaritas."

Today there was no one—not one damn browser, even—and around noon, Lou called it quits. Lifting the lid of the garbage, she chucked in a shoebox full of assorted cables and cords (to God knew what) and another, overflowing with ancient cassettes. A few of those had been store-bought, with luridly wrapped cases, and she had found them and swept them from a shelf in Carolyn's room—music of now obscure but once infamous soul crooners from the eighties—but the bulk were the mixed tapes that Wilson would play at his barbecues. The man would spend hours on the floor in front of his stereo components, coordinating the needle-drop with the record button, and she'd hesitated briefly before releasing the box from her grip.

(Maybe... she'd thought.)

(But, no.)

The plastic clattered to the bottom of the bin. On top of which she deposited the now-deflated balloons, without even bothering to release what little helium might remain.

THE WEIGHT OF THINGS

Folding across her arms the few remaining items from the wall of wisteria, it occurred to her that she had sold more than she had believed. Things seemed to have trickled away across the weekends, not at all like the Martha Garrison frenzy she had imagined, but more like the slow drip of a leaky faucet, which was fine. Remaining were a couple of boxes of knickknacks and kitchen gadgets; books, which she decided she would put in a bag for the Goodwill.

She placed on the bed in Carolyn's old room an opaque plastic bin containing several of the "kits" that Cousin Pearl liked to make as Christmas gifts: sewing kits, first-aid kits, travel kits, emergency kits. Each tucked into its own uniquely and hideously decorated pouch. She'd wrap the lot of them in festive paper and drop them off the next time her daughter got the urge to throw one of her way-too-frequently held "white elephant" parties. Her father's daughter, that one: Carolyn loved inventing reasons for people to hang out at her house out in Creve Coeur.

She picked up the stack of *Ebony* magazines she'd meant to add to the recycling last week. A dozen or so that she'd retrieved from a variety of closets and shelves and drawers on her search for things to sell.

"How much?" a woman asked. A woman in her living room. The pile of *Ebony*s tumbled from Lou's arms.

God in heaven: Martha Garrison.

Hadn't Cynthia Garrison placed her mother out in the Delmar Gardens "Home for Active Seniors" last year? That's what everyone said. (Those, that is, who hadn't said she'd run away to California or been abducted by aliens.) Here she was, NOT in a nursing home NOR on a spaceship, but in Lou's front room, bigger than life, picking things up, turning things over, and putting them back wherever the hell she felt like.

"You surprised me, Martha," Lou said, pushing the magazines into a messy pile with her foot. "Sale's over. Everything's sold. All gone." Lou yelled those phrases in the same tone she had to the Mexican woman with all the toddlers.

"How much is this?" Martha asked, holding up the silver-framed family portrait of Lou and Wilson and Carolyn, taken on a cruise organized by the UAW. It is the only decent photo of their family of three after Carolyn became an adult, and Lou started toward her, prepared to wrestle it from her fingers, but Martha set it down and moved over to the TV cabinet to inspect the items there.

"I meant to come by earlier, but, girl, you know how the time gets away from you. You sell all the baby clothes?"

"Why on earth would I have baby clothes, Martha? Where've you been keeping yourself? I haven't seen you in…"

How long? Six months? Closer to a year, surely: she had disappeared just after Wilson's funeral. She remembered Martha arriving at the visitation so elegantly dressed that Lou hadn't known who she was. (Which Carolyn exploited as another opportunity to chide Lou for being out of touch with "the community"—*Good God, Mother, you've only lived next door to the woman most of your life.* But the woman who had come to offer her respect to her husband resembled in no way this mess in her living room today.)

THE WEIGHT OF THINGS

"So many nice things you have," Martha sighed, browsing around the media cabinet as if she were in the housewares department at JCPenney. "You've always made such a lovely home. Just look!" She pets one of a pair of glossy black cougars who had been sentinel over this room since Carolyn was in grade school. Wilson had won them from the owner of some bar over in U City where he had been a regular back in the day. Martha's caress is practically obscene.

Everyone in Breckenridge Hill's worst nightmare: Martha Garrison. She'd as much as move into your damn house if you let her. Door-to-door, she'd go, every damn day, up and down Coles Avenue, around the first court and around St. Benedict. A relentless evangelist, housecoat over her nightgown, her hair wrapped in a do-rag. Before Cynthia Garrison put her away (or whatever the hell had happened to her) any given morning would find Martha looking for a newspaper not retrieved from the driveway or a screen door left slightly ajar; anything remotely resembling an opportunity to be thanked and invited to come in and sit for a spell. For a decade the neighbors had planned their days around this woman's obnoxiousness.

("Oh, the poor girl's just lonely," Wilson would say, but Wilson hadn't ever had to spend the morning trying to get "the poor girl" to move the hell on.)

Martha had segued into rifling through a collection of old compact discs that had not been played since God knows when. Lou had considered selling the damn things, but they had become part of the décor, and she'd been unable to imagine that cabinet without the shiny face of Luther Vandross smiling from his plastic case. Martha also discovered Wilson's cache of souvenir coasters, collected over decades; from bars and beer halls and corner taverns and nightclubs. Martha pressed her flat fat hands into her face in the expression of shocked delight that people give at their own surprise birthday parties.

Lou followed her from item to item the way the salespeople did the black customers in a lot of the stores in the area. "Nothing in here is for sale," she enunciated. She waved her hand toward the front door, lest the old fool had forgotten where it was. Time for you to GO!

By all evidence this had been interpreted as an invitation to make a run for the kitchen.

"Um, Martha, uh, no," Lou had tried, but before the words cleared her throat, Martha was rounding the corner and was elbow deep in a cupboard. Either everyone in Breckenridge Hills stored their coffee cups in exactly the same place, or the rumors were true: Martha actually did roam the streets after midnight, sliding herself in unlatched windows and pawing through people's things. After inspecting a half dozen, she selected a mug that met her standards and filled it with the cold dregs of the breakfast brew. She hauled back a chair from the dinette and stated:

"Just like I predicted, another one of them Holmes girls, in trouble again." Martha's own belly lent an ironic edge to her miming of the poor child's misfortune. Non sequiturs having been something of a specialty of her late husband, Lou rolled with the flow.

"You don't say?" had been her response.

"She's a fast little wench," Martha added, and closed her eyes solemnly, before launching into a story about how frustrating it was that the store with the best fresh greens didn't also carry Bon Ami scrubbing powder—among a dozen other individually named products, specific sizes and a range of costs appended to the itemization.

Wilson, rest his soul, also preferred the "starting mid-sentence" school of conversation, would walk in that carport door, perch his jacket on a peg and announce, "Because if you don't rough in the light assembly before you attach the hinge, the whole thing's coming off the line anyway."

"Good evening to you too," she would reply, to which he'd add: "Everybody knows this."

Lord, what she wouldn't give for even one more moronically meandering conversation with that man.

Martha, who was a substitute only in the same way a toothache might substitute for a headache, was now on the subject of out-of-control pets.

"And, I'll tell you what," she was saying. "Let Geraldine's mutt wake me up one more night and see if Fido doesn't get a taste of mama's special pork chops." She winked at Lou, who thought, Well, another rumor confirmed. At least the general topic of neighbors and the neighborhood had been broached; as useful an opening as any to ask how the hell she had escaped the nursing home. (Or wherever the hell else she might have been.)

"Martha, let me ask you something..."

DAVID HAYNES

Which for whatever reason prompted Martha to raise a "stop sign" hand, lean back slightly in her chair, and freeze in position with a big simper on her face.

God almighty, thought Lou. I guess I'll wait.

And she waited. And waited. And while she waited, she found herself thinking vile and uncharitable and even bigoted thoughts about the woman in front of her. Which got Lou to regretting the way in which every woman with a do-rag and lovely brown skin gets reduced to awful stereotypes. Which got her to thinking about racism, which got her to thinking about the NAACP, which needless to say, Wilson had been a member of. Which got her to thinking about what a joiner that Wilson had been! Urban League. The UAW. The PTA. The Washington-Reed Improvement Association. Last year, when his heart gave out, she'd fished a wad of memberships as thick as a deck of cards from his wallet. The man carried them everywhere. What was he expecting? That he might be stopped by the president of the Cheese-of-the-Month Club and ordered to show his papers?

Martha's face: still frozen in that Jemima simper. Which got Lou to thinking that she had just as well avert her eyes.

So she glanced down. Which would have been her next mistake of a day where mistakes seemed to be lining up like cars for a funeral.

Question: What is the proper etiquette for suggesting to a neighbor—a mere acquaintance, really—that she really might want to fasten her housecoat, thereby covering up the clearly-visible-through-her-nightgown floppy titties, right there in your face, like two juicy grapefruits crammed inside a pair of knee socks and about to make you spit up your breakfast?

Answer: She needed to get this bitch out of her house.

"Martha," she said, "I'm still clearing up from the sale, and the permit says I've got to..."

And suddenly Martha was up and off, kid-in-a-candy-shop mode, back to the front room: bargains waited for no woman!

"Ooh!" she said. "Ooh, ooh, ooh!"

An angel figurine. A (mostly unintentionally) ratty bird's-nest basket full of potpourri. A spindly rack packed tight with old *Jet* magazines. "Ooh!" she cooed, and she bobbled her head in the direction of each coveted treasure. She ran a finger lightly across the flank of a porcelain poodle, the same way Wilson would sometimes caress Lou's forearm. Some things she manhandled: that brass apple—the one Lou's daughter had gifted her decades ago on Mother's Day, a typically unsentimental (probably boosted) Carolyn gift. Martha hefted the thing, testing its weight. "Ooh!" she said. "Ooh!" The degree of head bobbling indicated the level of enchantment with any given item.

A tarnished replica of the Empire State Building with a stopped clock pressed into its base; the ceramic pair of Japanese ladies with their sad crumbling umbrellas. A brass lobster-shaped ashtray, a macramé doily. Why hadn't all of this crap been set out on sale with the rest of the unwanted garbage?

Martha Garrison's head bobbled obscenely, and Lou willed her to make her an offer and take every last bit of this junk off her hands. Every wretched scrap of it. That bookend, the chipped ceramic candy dish, that giant pinecone, that vase. This, that, this.

Not the snow globe. Not Wilson's snow globe.

Martha tested its weight. A dispiriting representation of a dreadfully dispiriting place: the city of Detroit in the 1980s, appearing quite as much as it had to Martha in real life, a colorless cramming of undistinguished buildings, harried by oversized flakes of snow, a souvenir of Wilson's big trip to the UAW convention. Don't you even dare, Lou thought, and just as she had that thought, up the paperweight went; up and over, up and out of Martha Garrison's right hand and over her head and down into her left. Martha Garrison's eyes widened with delight.

"Now just a damn minute," Lou stepped toward the neighbor woman.

And up and over it went again, this time left to right it flew.

Lou froze. She didn't dare alarm this creature; wouldn't risk the snow globe's demise.

Dear God, how Wilson had loved that paperweight. She couldn't even remember how long it had sat right there, on the end table next to his recliner. She'd find him sometimes shaking it and watching the snow fall. Sometimes he'd just place it on his thigh while he watched TV.

There it went: up and over. And up and over again.

Here was the thing: Martha Garrison wasn't even looking at it. Up and over it would go, and the crazy woman caught it in her palm, and grinned like a Las Vegas showgirl, and didn't take her eyes off Lou for one second. She'd toss her head as if to say, "Ta da!" and Lou could hear her dentures snapping into and out of position.

Up from the left it went, and up from the right. Left, right, left, until—for the finale—Martha Garrison popped open the pocket of her housecoat, leaned out slightly to the side, and Lou gasped as the snow globe, through some miracle or some modicum of insane illogical luck, dropped into place, resting its bulbous mass right where Martha intended it to, a third floppy titty, this one a few inches south and slightly to the right of the other two.

Martha gathered her fingers delicately to her chest, demurring the nonexistent ovation for her performance. "My daddy taught me that," she announced. "He was circus people, you know. For a while, back in the day, anyway, he was. You remember I told you all about that."

"What?" Lou said. It came out more harshly than she intended it to, a kind of astonished bark.

"That's how they got out of Mississippi, Daddy and them." Martha folded with grace down into Wilson's old leather recliner, her housecoat and nightgown billowing out and away, despite the snow globe still weighing down one side. She lounged back and opened her arms as if welcoming the sun on a hot day. In for the long haul, by all evidence, Lou settled herself on the couch opposite from her. She'd allow Martha the courtesy of an hour, perhaps, before calling Cynthia Garrison to come see about her mother.

"He was cropping with his family," Martha continued, "when they came through. What do you call it? The minstrel show. Daddy'd been tossing peaches and all manner of things since he was this big, and it just come natural to him. Showed them show folks what he could do, and they said, 'Come on then.' Got on that wagon and took my Aunt Sable with him and did not look back. Are you going to open a window in here or what?"

Lou stood and lifted the sash next to the TV stand and decided she didn't have an hour to waste on this wench—not for this, no way in hell—and she turned and asked, "Is your Cynthia still working at..." but Martha Garrison snored, with her open arms gone slack along the crackling worn rests of Wilson's chair.

Well, I'll be damned.

Lou became of two minds: part that wished to knock this bitch upside her head and tell her to wake the hell up and move the hell on. Another—a surprising part—wanted to lay a quilt across the poor thing, maybe tuck her in a bit.

It surprised her, too, that she mostly believed the story about Martha Garrison's father and his unlikely departure from the South—believed it despite contradictory versions of the family history from the woman's own mouth.

Years ago, back in the days of the annual community picnic, hadn't Martha Garrison planted herself in a lawn chair next to Lou and Wilson and told some long-ass story about how her father had been a merchant over on the East Side? (Owner of a men's clothing store, hadn't it been?) Hadn't there also been some story about the

South Side of Chicago, something about a bank? The many versions all shared the same feature: the young Martha (what might her maiden name even have been?) as some variety of privileged princess—a debutante, even, in some accountings—the finest of everything and, needless to say, her pick of eligible suitors.

And what might have happened to all those future captains of industry? Martha's husband spent forty-five years doing the regular mail run to Chicago, and any number of times hadn't Wilson driven this woman to retrieve Donald Garrison from Union Station at the end of an overnight shift?

Wilson had always insisted the woman was full of herself, "Just ordinary folks, like the rest of us, but that ain't good enough for her."

Lou couldn't be sure. Wilson, it embarrassed her to admit, did have his colorstruck side, and it just might have been the case he'd been unable to imagine brownskin people rising in the world. What a gorgeous woman she'd have been back in the day, and surely Wilson had seen this. And, yes, most certainly she'd carried herself well and with refinement, passed those elegant traits onto her daughter, Cynthia.

Likely all of the stories contained some element of truth. Measuring his life in the fields, a young man jumps at the main chance—juggling, prize fighting, whatever it might be, whenever it might happen into his path. He works over here, does a little something else over there. The goal: That his children not know one minute of the life he left behind, breaking his back and shredding his fingers to line someone else's pockets.

That she might have ended up here (blissed out, is it?) in Lou's dead husband's comfy recliner, in a pleasant little house in a quiet suburban enclave, a place where even on its worst day all would agree was far from the worst place on the planet: Could the juggling boy in the cotton fields have imagined this for his daughter?

Not knowing what to do with a plus-sized woman passed out in the front room, Lou headed to the kitchen, where she shifted to the recycling bin a few of the remaining photocopied garage sale notices she'd failed to find a place to tack up.

Yes, she probably should call Cynthia—Come see about your mother, please—but how to explain to Martha's daughter exactly what the problem was?

Oh, nothing, really. She's escaped from wherever you had her committed and is now asleep and drooling in my living room. I would like her gone.

Hardly neighborly, when you put it that way.

And hadn't that been her late husband's biggest knock against her?

Wilson's credo: "We got to do right by each other."

The part of him that was a joiner. The part that ran a Boy Scout troop (even though they had no son of their own in the crew), the part that worked the polls on election day, the part that ran the community picnic as if it were the Normandy Invasion.

That Damn Community Picnic: broke his heart when it petered out. Petered out because people got older and the kids grew up and moved away and folks just got tired of the same damn mosquitos and the same old gossip and the same old same old, year after year.

Wouldn't Wilson be proud of her now, grinning and bearing it with crazy old Martha? Among the myriad tensions that erode the edges of any marriage, for Wilson it had been Lou's "selfishness" that set the hardest. Selfishness: that's how he had construed it. He'd been fine, for the most part, with her not-infrequent mishaps with various autos, and only slightly miffed with her inability to stew up a proper pot of collards, but what he saw as her being... "inhospitable" would set him aquiver with rage.

"We could have some people in now and then, is all I'm saying." His standard phrase for punctuating the running argument about whether a home was a public or a private place, and beneath his always stoic surface as they debated, she could feel the anger roiling. She'd come back at him with a list of holiday parties and other special occasions she'd hosted every year.

Which had never been his point, she knew.

And, no, as far as that went, she did not ever understand why a person would want to have her doors wide open on a regular basis for whoever took a whim to come in and take a load off—because just look there, in her front room, what happened when you did. People took liberties. This was a known fact.

On a given weekend she'd come in from errands, and here Wilson would be, set up around this this very table, leaned up on his elbows, his buddies arrayed to the left and right of him, a second or a fifth round of beers on offer.

"I'll thank you to stop giving our guests the evil eye," he'd scold her with a laugh, and she'd roll her eyes at him. That four or five greasy fools in T-shirts and overalls didn't fit her description of "guests" was hardly worth arguing over.

His little impromptu six-pack circles, his lodge meetings, that damn community picnic: oh, how Wilson missed that picnic. On and on he would go about how they should bring it back, and nothing she could say would make him believe it had run its course.

Then came Carolyn's graduation from Ritenour, and along with it, the guest list that had no end—the man wanted everyone and his mama included (and that the girl had barely made it through—so busy chasing boys, she was—hardly seemed to matter to him).

"We'll do it here, out in the backyard," she'd conceded, and she prayed for a sunny evening, because there was no way all those folks would be up in her house. Hell, no.

For what it was worth, Lou had been an accommodating hostess, thank you very much. She'd loaded up tables with every manner of nibbles, from chips to chicken wings (and hadn't it been just like that Carolyn to lament the lack of "taquitos," whatever the hell they were, and hadn't she told that little heifer that she best count her blessings and also to start looking for work, because her lazy behind wouldn't be sitting up in *here* all day with nothing to do, and she could take that to the bank!). She'd stationed Wilson at the grill—at a whole series of grills, lined up side by side—where the man was in his element—in absolute heaven: flipping ribs and burgers and spearing up hot dogs by the dozen for the little ones.

From out of this window, she had watched them for a while: Carolyn—in the new floral sundress she'd insisted be bought for the ceremony—swanning around the yard, plucking gift cards from the guests—and Wilson there at the grills, his cronies gathered around, beers in hand and voices raised in laughter. Lou's sisters had volunteered to keep the food and drinks moving, and after a while all the merriment just became tiresome. She retreated to their bedroom, where Wilson discovered her later in the evening.

"What you doing, sleeping in here?" he'd asked, and if there'd been any pique in that question it had been buried beneath his euphoria at having pulled off his dream of the perfect neighborhood festival.

"Was I sleep?" The question had been genuine. She'd been in some kind of other state, that's for sure; something like a dream, but somehow more visceral.

She'd been back in that four-family flat on Page, remembering all the people who had lived there—her mother and several of the mother's sisters, assorted husbands of those aunts, various cousins. People came and went constantly from that apartment; came and went from jobs, from errands, from failed marriages, from stints in Korea. It had been the same with every other flat in that building, as well. When Wilson had interrupted, she had been sitting on a piano bench (could there actually have been a piano in there with all those people?) and some drama

DAVID HAYNES

involving a borrowed sweater was in the process of boiling into a full-fledged argument. Who were all those women?

"Come on," Wilson had encouraged her. "Come on and sit with us. We're all just sitting. Just enjoying the evening."

"All right," she'd responded, and she smiled for him, and he told her to take her time and he'd see her out there. "Ain't nobody in a hurry tonight. Take your time."

If he had seen her tears, he had not mentioned them.

They hadn't really spoken of that evening, nothing more than a quiet series of "thanks" he'd offered her late that same night, along with a kiss on the cheek as she helped him pack away the trash and the few odd scraps of food that had not been eaten or carried away in go-bags.

That kiss! Nothing more, really, than a chaste peck on the cheek: the memory of its sweetness undid her every time, fires an acid surge of pain to her chest; enough every time to make her reach to her sternum as is if to smother the flame.

Behind her something metallic slapped into a palm, and Lou turned just as Martha reached to add a real apple to the flying metal one and its snow-globe companion.

"It's the different weight of things, that's the tricky part, Daddy always said."

On her face was the unconditional pleasure of a person doing something she loved and doing it well and with ease. It was the pleasure she would see on Wilson's face at his conventions and at his picnics and around this table with his buddies.

"Do you remember the picnic, Martha?"

THE WEIGHT OF THINGS

Martha set her face in puzzlement and—one, two, three—she snagged her implements from the air and planted them gently on the counter, searching around with her eyes as if "picnic" were the name of a long-lost friend. Placing the referent, her eyes bugged open and her face filled with a grin.

"I remember chopping all night on six giant heads of cabbage from the farm stand for the best damn coleslaw anyone around here ever ate."

"You always made a nice slaw, Martha. That you did." The dressing would bite your tongue in an almost tingly way, some secret ingredient that Lou could never quite decipher.

And suddenly Martha was patting her pockets and turning up her wrists to check the time on a watch that wasn't there. "I just remembered," she said, and she headed to the carport door.

"Before you go," Lou said, not quite believing that she was delaying the woman's departure. Martha, too, seemed shocked—else her expression was her version of annoyance at the nerve of someone keeping her from her appointed rounds.

"Martha, I was thinking, what if I had a little backyard barbecue? Like we used to do. Like Wilson used to do, back in the old days."

"Like the picnic?" Martha snatched up the Granny Smith apple into her palm.

"Something like that," Lou said. She would call a caterer, of course (and wouldn't Wilson die, everything not being homemade).

"That's an idea." Martha responded in a way that indicated she most definitely approved. She stroked the brass apple obscenely. "While we're all still here. All us from the old times."

"Maybe I'll do that," Lou whispered. "Maybe I will."

Martha patted Lou's arm. There was something condescending about it, but it comforted her all the same. Martha's eyes returned to her new favorite toys, arrayed on the counter, tempting her toss.

"One man's trash…" she opined, again picking up the brass apple again and examining it for a price tag. Lou's hopes that she would somehow forget about the snow globe were quickly extinguished.

"Some things are just the right heft," Martha said with almost a reverent whisper, raising and lowering Detroit and making the snowflakes swirl around the skyscrapers. Martha parked the globe next to the brass apple and tested the heft of a different Granny Smith.

Lou remembered the icy streets of the city and a seemingly endless walking tour of the old River Rouge plant; the way Wilson just couldn't seem to shake enough of the hands of his union "brothers."

"It's just a big happy family, darling," he'd said. "Just a big happy family everywhere." He'd been practically weepy.

She and Martha reached for Detroit at the same time, but where Lou balked, Martha seized the city and grasped it tight and said, "You want me to teach you? I can do that."

"You can?"

"Like Daddy says, it's all right here, in the wrist." Detroit popped up and down as easily and as smoothly as a boat bobbing on a gentle wave.

"And you always catch it like you mean it, like the ball has no place else to go but right here." The snow globe snapped down securely into her palm. "Just like Daddy says."

"I'm a terrible catch," Lou confessed, but Martha just shrugged and grinned. She scooped the brass apple into the left pocket of her housecoat, a Granny Smith into the right, all the while popping the snow globe up and down in an easy and constant rhythm.

"Mama's got places to be," she said. She flourished Detroit and twisted it with a dramatic shimmy.

"Martha..." Lou reached for the globe, but Martha bustled away, toward the front door this time, sharply pointing as she passed at this coveted thing and at that coveted thing. At another still and then another.

"Before I forget I'm gonna dig out that coleslaw recipe." She waddled down the front walk, bowing in admiration at the beat-up old cherub.

She turned and gave Lou a perch-mouthed look that simply dripped with judgment and then winked at her and ordered her to "chill out," saying that everything would work out for the best, saying that you just have to focus down and put your hands up and be ready for anything.

Lou was not really listening to what was now nothing more than a wavering watery blob.

"Hear me, now!" Martha barked.

"What I said. Now!" Martha ordered. "Hands up, now! Make them like a bowl."

Four or five Marthas at the end of Lou's fingers were giving Lou orders, each one of them bouncing her arms up and down mechanically and with a wide grin on her face.

"It's all in the wrist," the Marthas said, and just like that, a snowy spinning world arced up and over and headed impossibly towards Lou's outstretched fingers.

ON THE AMERICAN
HERITAGE TRAIL

ANOTHER DAY AT THE Mount Vernon Economy House Motel, and a season of optimism has of recent taken root. Carlos and his crew of sheetrockers have more work than they can handle. At six they return to the motel flush with cash, white dust powdering brown faces and wiry black hair. Several of the boys gather at the desk, miming for Humphrey their desire to purchase the international calling cards Patel keeps on a console next to the lottery ticket display. Most of that cash they'll wire home, those boys—wherever the hell home is—the rest they'll spend on bootleg CDs and cheap wine from the shop up the way with the Spanish signs in the window. Or on the working girls, whose own response to the good times is a noticeable extra wiggle in the walk and, on more than a few girls, a new pair of fishnets to replace ones ratty from wear.

Humphrey works the evening shift at the motel's desk, officially four to midnight, but on most nights he's here until at least two. Patel works the balance of the hours, though his mother, who owns the dump, would just as soon her son live behind the desk. The old woman, a shrill, hawk-nosed harpy, storms into the motel office now and again, as she makes the rounds of her sundry properties up and down Route One, from here down to well past Quantico. She'll breeze in, shrouded in layers of shiny loud fabrics and start into her son about one thing or another, finger in his face, rapid-fire delivery. Now and again, she'll swat him upside the head. Humphrey doesn't know a word of their language, but he knows that this is one unpleasant old broad, and he also knows that all the son ever says in reply to her is Yes, ma'am, whatever you want, ma'am, right away, ma'am. After she leaves, the poor guy will sit at his desk, head in his hands, mumbling.

Somehow, two years back, Patel had convinced the mother to allow him to bring on someone to take a shift behind the desk— on the guise, Humphrey imagined, that doing so would free up Patel to supervise the endless and badly needed renovations that are also his responsibility. Occasionally, while Humphrey oversees the comings and goings in the lobby, Patel will rip the carpeting from one of the "casual" rooms, toss a threadbare bedspread into the skip out back. Most of the time he sleeps.

Humphrey isn't entirely sure why he'd been offered the job or, for that matter, why he'd accepted. A couple of hours out of DC lockup on a bum shoplifting rap, and he'd found himself wandering Route One, looking for a cheap bed. He'd heard about this place, although the nightly rate Patel had quoted hadn't been exactly cheap. He'd inquired about the small "help wanted" sign, figuring it was worth a shot. If he'd learned anything in the workhouse, it was as a so-called ex-con, you took every shot that came your way and more or less expected to come up short in the game.

"You seem presentable enough," Patel had said, and had added, "I believe you to be someone I might trust." No questions, no history, no references. The Economy House is that kind of place. At the time and to this day it seems to Humphrey some kind of miracle he'd chosen to walk in here that afternoon. Minimum wage, barely, but the room is included, as it is also included for the housekeepers, of which they are down one as of late—that Josepha girl having slunk off into the night sometime in the past week (to who knows where). Generally speaking, they don't come back, those girls. Humphrey has picked up some of the slack himself, running the industrial washers and the vacuum. He draws the line at changing beds. He knows what goes on back there.

Misti stops by the desk on the way back from the nail salon in the ratty little strip mall across the highway. Misti is freelance these days, on the run and hiding here from her latest pimp.

"Yo, Hump, what you think?" she asks, waving her ten new tips in his face. Misti's maybe twenty, looks thirty. Each tip is a different psychedelic design.

"Looking good," he tells her. He's pleased for the distraction. It's the last night of the month, and Patel's left Humphrey the job of preparing the long-term manifest: who's paid in full for July and whose locks would be changed in the morning.

Misti snaps her gum, snaps it again. She beckons Humphrey to lean closer.

"Between you and me, some of them Mexican boys like it a little rough." She makes one hand into a claw, flutters an eyelid and waggles her tongue limply from the corner of her mouth.

"I'm not sure those boys are from Mexico," he tells her, recalling Carlos's litany of other places Humphrey remembers vaguely from middle school geometry: El Salvador, Guatemala, Honduras.

"Whatever," Misti replies. (*Snap. Snap.*) She taps a paisley nail into a DayGlo-striped one. Misti is vaguely ethnic herself, in that pop-star kind of way: tan, petite, and with a bundle of platinum-frosted brown hair clipped Kewpie-doll style atop her head.

A three-toned whistle trills around the corner—human-lipped riff on whippoorwill—and Misti rubs her fingers together to indicate a pending transaction.

As per instructions, Humphrey sees nothing, hears nothing. He returns to his manifest, scans down the list to room 317. M. Jackson. July paid in full. Good girl, he thinks. Safe bet her name is neither Misti nor Jackson, though chances are good her initials are M. J. Your AKAs tend to keep things simple that way.

Across the lobby Mrs. Ralph Wallingford riffles through a rack of brochures hyping dinner cruises on the Potomac and tours of obscure plantations. The sound of any car engine causes her to bolt to the window and brush open the vertical blinds.

The vertical blinds are ancient and turned a yellow tone from neglect and from decades of cigarette smoke. Each of Mrs. Ralph Wallingford's forays to the plate glass sends a cloud of dust Humphrey's way. Mrs. Ralph Wallingford is not paid in full. Has not been so for more than a few weeks.

"Oh, dear," she sighs, when the ride is once again not for her. She drops herself to a love seat and resumes paging through the June issue of *Hospitality Today*. Too cheap for real magazines, Patel's mother stocks the lobby with industry rags only. Mrs. Ralph Wallingford has surely read this one cover to cover by now, could recite from memory, surely, recent trends in occupancy rates and suggestions for turning your property's pool into a tropical oasis.

"I was sure that would be my son-in-law," she says. Humphrey is the only one in the lobby just now, so he imagines this is directed at him. And although he knows better than to respond to her, he turns his hands up in a way that he hopes indicates that he's sorry, that it isn't his fault, that it's beyond his control, and that, no, there have been no messages left at the front desk for her today just as there also have been none for the past ten weeks since she was dropped off here by cab.

Humphrey had been on duty the night she'd checked in. Drop-ins are rare in the spring. Now and again a road warrior would pull in, recognizing the corporate logo, but those old boys are no fools. They take one look at that courtyard, get an earful of the pumping rap music, take a gander at who lingers inside the open doorways, and know immediately they've made a mistake. Unless there is an ice storm, or they're up for extra-curricular fun, they'll head on down Route One looking for something more appropriate. Patel's policy: a cheerful refund. The mother makes enough on the monthlies she couldn't care less about the dozen rooms the franchise requires be open for "casual" traffic. Rent em by the hour to the whores, she'd said. (Well, since Humphrey doesn't speak their language, he can't prove she'd said exactly that, but it's another one of those things he'd take book on.)

She'd printed "Mrs. Ralph Wallingford" on her guest card, the woman had, her handwriting of the cheerful and confident variety. Well-formed and well-spaced, the sort of signature he imagined graced million-dollar contracts or presidential pardons.

"I'll be needing three nights, if that's okay," she'd informed him and she'd placed on the counter the first of what would soon become a whole series of maxed-out credit cards.

Humphrey remembers at the time having the same inclination he always has when someone such as her happened in off the road: he had wanted to beckon her closer so he could whisper to her that she might want to think again about her choice of accommodations. A fine lady such as yourself, he had wanted to tell her. Her hair, a one-tone brownish red, had been recently coiffed into one of those middle-aged-white-lady styles that is all layers of fat curls, and she'd been wearing one of those nice pantsuits women her age wore to the doctor's office or to PTA meetings.

It mostly happens during the summer tourist season that these straight types wander in here, often a young family on a budget, come east to show the kiddies their nation's heritage, including the first president's home, conveniently located a few short miles away. Hell, you could walk there from here. Often enough, around midnight, the weary father, frustrated at the ongoing boogedy beat in the courtyard, storms down to the lobby to ask Humphrey what kind of joint he thought they were running around here. Humphrey would throw up his hands and invite him to speak with the management in the morning. In the morning Patel would pass along his mother's business card. Case closed.

"Some of these people..." Humphrey had suggested at the time. "We should warn them maybe."

Patel's reply: "That would imply that you were aware that there were activities going on here that might cause concern to our guests. We are not aware of anything of the sort, are we?" As is always the case he had not looked up from the task of the moment. He had addressed Humphrey in a voice that a British professor would employ on some PBS show about ancient Rome. Humphrey had assured Patel that he was as unaware as the next person. A job was a job after all. And ignorance was a relative quality—and a highly prized commodity in some markets.

The courtyard smells of ganja and curry. When flush, the sheetrock boys now and again enjoy something stronger than wine, and as for the curry, cousins of Patel's hold down the two rooms nearest the laundry. Hot, noisy, and hard to rent, those two rooms house maybe a dozen folks, always cooking something on their electric burners, and always with the door open. Just across the way the working girls cluster on the patio tables by the pool, where they trash talk each other's costumes while awaiting their whistles. Another ordinary day in the cradle of democracy.

Upon check in, Mrs. Ralph Wallingford already had that deer-in-the-headlights look in her eyes, so there was no telling if the Economy House scene caused further distress. Two months in the motel have taken their toll on the poor creature; the neatly arranged hair gone matted for lack of styling tools, blouses now a dingy off-white from too many washings in the sink with the brick-hard wax that the Economy House passes off as soap.

Another car engine revs in the parking lot. Mrs. Ralph Wallingford, Humphrey notes, takes a moment longer than usual to hop up, then does so sluggishly, just as Carlos comes in the courtyard door. Carlos stands at the desk, fingering through the bills in his wallet in that way he has, mumbling to himself some song in Spanish. Humphrey goes and stands at the counter on the off chance Carlos wants something other than what he usually wants—which is simply someone to shoot the breeze with. ("Humid tonight." "Slow this evening." "You catch those Wizards?")

Mrs. Ralph Wallingford comes and stands behind Carlos. She does this whenever there is another guest at the counter. Large purse over one elbow, she stands, patient—the way she has been taught—working to catch Humphrey's eye. This was her technique for asking to use the phone. She seems to figure that when the clerk is busy with another guest, he'll be too preoccupied to give her request a second thought. She persists, despite the fact that Patel cut her house phone privileges a week ago.

To avoid making eye contact, Humphrey finds and then slides a *USA Today* article Carlos's way—one about amnesty for aliens.

"Every one of my boys is legal." Carlos laughs. Now and again, for spite or for sport, someone would call the INS to the construction site and Carlos would return that evening with an empty van. He and Humphrey would load the boys' rag-tag possessions into a few boxes and set them in storage. None had ever found his way back here for anything. The next evening Carlos would return with a brand-new set of boys.

Mrs. Ralph Wallingford clears her throat, demurely.

"Excuse me, señora," Carlos says, stepping away with a bow. She gives him the false and cautious smile that here lately has become her trademarked reply to his Latin charms. Even after two months she's unsure what to make of what she'd no doubt refer to as one of "those people."

"I was wondering if I might..." Mrs. Ralph Wallingford stage-whispered, and she made the universal sign for phone call—thumb at the ear, pinky at the lips.

The words "You know what Mr. Patel says" start from Humphrey's mouth; instead, he sighs, places the machine on the counter, pushes the outgoing button for her. "Local only, remember."

Mrs. Ralph Wallingford smiles, bats her eyes in a way that suggests he's being foolish to think a quality person such as herself would even consider mounting unauthorized long-distance charges. She begins dialing from the numbers on her list.

Here lately, this past week or so, no one answers whatever phones those numbers correspond to and apparently everyone has also disconnected his or her voicemail.

"Oh, dear," Mrs. Ralph Wallingford says. She sighs. She dials the next number on the list.

Carlos gives Humphrey one of those "the mystery of women" looks, a combination of raised shoulders and rolled eyes. Just then Patel shuffles in, his house slippers rasping on the floor, rumpled blue-striped pajamas open to the naval. He scratches at his hairy stomach, nods and grunts at the men. Seeing Mrs. Ralph Wallingford on the phone, he grunts again at Humphrey, proceeds to look on the desk for whatever he'd risen from the middle of his own personal night to find. He signals Humphrey to follow him out the courtyard door.

"That woman..." Patel seethes. No need to say much more, really, at least not as far as Humphrey is concerned. Something about her really sets the man off, certainly not the least being the fact Mrs. Ralph Wallingford hadn't paid a cent in rent for the past three weeks.

"A phone call," Humphrey pleads. "I figure what could it hurt."

Patel harrumphs. "People like her..." he mumbles. He ruffles his own hair some more. "I tell you what, Humphrey," Patel always pronounces Humphrey's name as if it contained no *F* sound—Humpree, he calls him. "You tell that woman she must go. Tonight. No more extensions. No nothing."

Humphrey is not surprised, had hoped that however it happened with the poor woman it would happen while he was across the courtyard sound asleep. For whatever reason he finds himself pleading her case.

"Give her another couple of days," he suggests.

"Couple of days for what? I'll tell you for what. I've seen her kind. She goes. I'm ordering you. You tell her."

"Me tell her?" Humphrey complains. "You're ordering me?"

Patel paces over to the back courtyard entrance and glances in. Mrs. Ralph Wallingford, Humphrey is sure, is still in there dialing her little heart out. Humphrey meets Patel's eye with a wry smile. They have the kind of communication developed only between people who have been together up to their elbows in other people's human waste.

"Okay, okay," Patel says, raising his hands to indicate he's backing down. "I don't say order. I say implore. I implore you. Please. Show this woman the door. Otherwise, what choice?" Patel rubs his hands together, washing them of the whole matter.

"Or until we need the room," Humphrey proffers.

Patel scoffs. "Or until my mother." He barks the word *mother* in Humphrey's face as if it were a swear word. "Mother comes tomorrow at two." Patel places a hand on the ledger for emphasis. Once a month the crone spends the afternoon teasing through the books, quibbling over every dime. Humphrey knows what will happen. She'll find 207, note the arrears, swat Patel upside the head, and then personally dump Mrs. Ralph Wallingford right in the middle of Route One. He'd bet on that—and there, finally, would be one bet that he could win.

"I implore you," Patel repeats. He shuffles back toward his apartment. He nods at another half-asleep man, scuffling toward the candy machine wearing only his BVDs. It's that kind of place.

Between dials, the desk phone rings. Mrs. Ralph Wallingford says, "Oh, my," and hands the phone to Humphrey. As good an excuse as any to relieve her from her pointless routine. Trooper that she is, Mrs. Ralph Wallingford raises her eyebrows with hope. The voice on the line jabbers something rapidly. Humphrey shakes his head, causing Mrs. Ralph Wallingford to step away from the desk.

"Don't understand!" he yells into the phone.

"One thirty-one," comes the crisply enunciated reply, and Humphrey connects them to that room. He'd been surprised his first days in this place how few calls came on the house phone. He'd figured he'd spend his days like a receptionist on a bad TV show, parroting the name of the motel over and over again, but in fact the ancient black console almost never rings. When it does, it's either Patel's mother shouting her son's name or a wrong number.

Many years ago, in a biology course at UDC, back during Humphrey's short-lived college career, he learned about ecological bioregions, self-contained worlds within worlds. The Mount

Vernon Economy House could be such a place. Busses to the city stop out front, delivering and returning those who have jobs—else people head off with Carlos or someone just like Carlos. Folks like himself and Misti and Lisette, the Haitian maid, work right here. All of them eat fast food from the convenience store. There are no calls because everyone they know is already here—else far enough away to be as theoretical as dreams.

The kid named Kyle comes into the lobby. He and Carlos exchange nods. They are professional rivals: Kyle is hooked up with a crew doing an interior build-out over in Springfield.

"Settle up," Kyle says, not a threat, rather an offer to get it over with. He splays on the counter the pages of invoices accounting for his last month's keep. The manifest indicates he has nothing down on the month ahead, but Kyle insists he's good through the tenth.

"See, here," the kid says. He points to a place on one of the pages where the printer seemed to have stuttered, then to another where Patel's initialed a credit of what looks like two hundred bucks. Kyle's right arm is all tattoos, from his wrist up to his shoulder blade. Both ears contain a lot of metal. He's a "local" Humphrey knows, has people over in Dumfries. They threw him out or he threw himself out—same difference. He lives here now.

"They keeping you busy?" Carlos asks the kid, who blows air through his lips, nods. He's not much on words, ever, this Kyle.

"You let me know, okay? I always got room for a good worker."

ON THE AMERICAN HERITAGE TRAIL

Humphrey doubts Kyle will work for whatever crumbs Carlos metes to his boys, but it's not his concern. Humphrey skims down the manifest and clears Kyle through the tenth.

Just then Misti comes limping around the corner. She's lost the heel from one of her platform shoes and is whimpering. Blood leaks from a swelling lip.

"Damn animal," she hisses. The kid Kyle steadies her against the counter.

Carlos purses his lips and raises his eyebrows, more bemused than concerned it seems.

"Are you okay?" Humphrey asks her. Officially he's to ignore this sort of thing. Officially there's no such thing as "this sort of thing."

"One of those Mexican boys. I gave him a half and half, and he started yelling about *más* and about his *dinero*. Then he went psycho."

She tells Carlos the room number. It's one of his boys so Carlos heads back there to check it out. That's how this world works: you see to your own mess.

Misti's really working hard to be tough—spews an accomplished string of vulgarity and choice threats about what she'll do to "Juan" when she gets her hands on him again—but Humphrey sees that she is trembling hard and that her eyes have gone wide like a little girl's might at a horror movie. That is what she is, in fact: a little girl.

Just then, Mrs. Ralph Wallingford comes with a towel and some ice from the machine. She gathers Misti into her arms.

"Come over here, sweetheart," Mrs. Ralph Wallingford says. Misti collapses sobbing into her arms and Mrs. Ralph Wallingford leads her to a couch.

Later, after Carlos reports that the boy—whoever he had been— is long gone, after Misti decides to take the rest of the night off, Mrs. Ralph Wallingford sits on her regular couch, leafing through her regular magazine.

Humphrey turns the dead bolt on the door to the street. After ten, it's transactions through the night window only. He sits down next to Mrs. Ralph Wallingford. Flipping the lock is his signal for her to leave the lobby, but tonight she doesn't budge. She peruses the magazine solemnly, the bloodied damp towel on the end table beside her.

"A little excitement there, huh?" he says to her.

"That poor young woman," Mrs. Ralph Wallingford responds, and she clicks her tongue. Some of Misti's makeup has adhered to the front of her blazer, sparkly flecks here and there among the herringbone.

Humphrey should be asking her for rent money, should be finishing up that manifest, should be clearing today's receipts, should be over behind the desk just chilling. But it's okay to sit here a minute. It feels just fine for some reason.

Mrs. Ralph Wallingford speaks.

"Can I ask you a question, Mr.... Why I've seen you all these many days and I realize I don't know your name."

"People call me Humphrey."

"That girl, that young woman. She's a prostitute, am I correct, Mr. Humphrey?"

"I believe that she is."

"Yes." Mrs. Ralph Wallingford says, quietly, sadly, nodding her head. Her hands are folded in her lap like an honor student waiting her turn outside the principal's office. Her nails, Humphrey notices, had at some point been manicured. Several are now tattered, edged and rimmed an angry-looking red.

The traffic on Route One slows this time of night. Humphrey can hear an engine now and again roar through the valley. There's almost no chance one of those cars will pull in. He could sit here all night with no reason to move.

"Mr. Humphrey, did you ever in your life think you'd end up in a place like this?"

Her question roils him slightly, visibly.

"Did I startle you? Forgive me."

"Oh, ma'am… you didn't… it's just that…"

"Myself: I did not. I doubt that surprises you."

Humphrey shakes his head. He wants to tell this woman that there are many worse places in the world than this one. Much worse. He understands that such an observation would be beyond the point, really.

Over the past two months he has often imagined the people at the other end of the calls she makes, the ones where she wonders if she might trouble this one for a bed for a few nights or whether that one might have a spare room. There is a son, evidently, but he's proved difficult to locate. Works itinerant, probably overseas. There is bad blood with the daughter that the mother now wants—needs—to heal. These one-sided conversations are hard to read; even so, any fool could see that Mrs. Ralph Wallingford has left in her wake a broad legacy of hurt feelings and broken connections. This is a woman who wears her difficultness on her sleeve and with a great deal of pride. She might be impossible to love.

"Bridges get burnt, the world turns. And here we are," she proclaims this matter-of-factly and without the slightest bit of bitterness. If anything, she sounds philosophical.

As a boy, Humphrey had dreamed of doing medical research—of being one of those people who discovered the secret mechanism inside the cancer cells that had taken his mother when he was sixteen. Schools—the schools little black boys attended—did not prepare you for careers in oncology. Instead, he has removed dead tree limbs; changed tires and oil; flipped burgers and drained hot fish fillets; stocked shelves at CVS; detailed cars at the Mazda dealer in Charles County, Maryland; delivered pizzas and summonses and legal briefs; unloaded exotic produce from the bellies of 747s at Dulles Airport. Twice in his life he's worked as a bouncer at a club. For a week-and-a-half he'd been an "exotic dancer." The pay had been good, but he'd broken out from the oils he'd been required to slather on to make himself glisten under the spotlights. He's made cold calls selling newspaper subscriptions and long-distance service and aluminum siding; ran the machine in the Walgreen's for the old people who still believed in old-school cameras; washed dishes, chopped vegetables, driven third-world ambassadors between appointments, and most recently, after having the misfortune of being in the wrong place at the wrong time, made license plates for the citizens of the District of Columbia.

And now he was here. And so was Mrs. Ralph Wallingford. Who says:

"I despise this place. When I step out of bed in the morning, I have the feeling that I am up to my ankles in insect life. And the less said about the shampoo and the raspy towels the better." She says this with an off-kilter smile, Mrs. Ralph Wallingford does, whispering it to him almost from the corner of her mouth as if they were sharing secrets.

She rises, presses at the wrinkles in her suit. The irons here have all been stolen—sold at the flea market in Woodbridge no doubt.

"Another day passes," she says. She lifts her key from her purse.

"Wait," he says to her back. There's something he needs to say to her that needs to be said right away.

The next day Humphrey finds himself head-to-toe covered in stinking crumbles of foam padding; Patel has offered him a few extra hours' work to strip the rooms on two east of their moldering carpet. He takes his time dragging the foul-smelling carpeting to the skip—there's only this one room on the to-do list today. He'll sweep out the filthy fragments, slather the floor with disinfectant and bug juice, then lock it up. It will sit empty like the other ten he's done; apparently Patel's mother spends half her time ragging him to get the rooms updated, the other half refusing to sign off on costs to update them.

By the laundry room Patel's female cousins are gathered around a patio table, prepping some strange pod-like vegetable that Humphrey doesn't recognize.

"Good day, Mr. Humpree," they nod shyly, the same *F*-less version of his name Patel employs.

Humphrey organizes the chairs and tables in the area where Misti and the girls gather for their morning cigarettes and Cokes. It's well past two, but it's only the start of their workday.

"Hey, Hump," Misti calls to him. He steps over. Her bruised lip she's shrouded in pink gloss with a pearly finish. If anything, their bee-stung quality has been enhanced.

"Mai and I was just discussing among ourselves here whether or not a person could get a driver's license in Virginia without a birth certificate. What you think?"

Humphrey shrugged. "I wouldn't know about anything like that," he told them. Mai is an Asian girl—Vietnamese he thinks, or that might be the other one there—Kim, he believes she goes by. There's a Russian or Polish girl who comes and goes and sometimes shares a room with Misti. "One of you girls thinking about driving?" he asks.

The girls all laugh like that's some big joke. The cost of even the cheapest vehicle, he guesses that's the funny part.

"Up over there that convenience store, the one with the cheaper beer, gots a new guy running it, some Arab dude. He won't sell without a state ID. Ain't that a blip?"

Humphrey's pretty sure the guy's Pakistani, not that it matters. "There's always the Spanish store," he suggests, teasing some of the yellow foam from his hair.

The girls scoff. "We're boycotting them," Mai announces. They look at each other with resolve and take drags off their cigarettes.

Kyle struts by, giving the ladies the eye. He nods at Humphrey. The contractor he works for lives out past Manassas and is always on the job well before dawn. Kyle's already put in his full day. The girls smile their cheap smiles at him. He gets a freebie now and again, according to Misti, because, in her words, "Every now and then you get a taste for white meat."

"Just another day at the ranch," Misti announces. There's no trace of irony in her voice. The girls tilt their heads back and soak up the scorching summer sun.

"Check out the new maid," Misti suggests.

Across the way Lisette the Haitian maid removes the padlocks from the supply closet and angles the two carts close to the door. She mimes for the woman where she should place the soaps on the cart and how to stand the matchbooks in the ashtray.

Mrs. Ralph Wallingford nods, watches, inventories the items on her own cart while Lisette does the same.

At first Patel had balked at the arrangement—the woman truly sets him off—but Humphrey had prevailed.

DAVID HAYNES

It is a trial run only. Patel had been fussing with the ledgers for his mother's review. He'd been nervous, sweaty, irritable, saving his energy for the bigger fight on the horizon. "One problem, she goes," he warned.

There'll be none, Humphrey knows. Like everyone here, Mrs. Ralph Wallingford has her resources. She can make a bed, scrub a toilet, run a wet cloth across a pasteboard TV stand. Is it glamorous? No. But like everyone here, she'd weighed the alternatives and cut the best deal she could—here on Route One, where the first world on its way down meets the third world, holding on by the fingernails to wherever they gain purchase.

"But it's just so degrading," Mrs. Ralph Wallingford had said to him last night when he'd told her the plan. A weaker woman would have wept, but while she might have issues, this one had an iron will. She'd lamented her fate with the hard-edged bitterness of a washed-up gambler who'd lost his last hundred on the over under.

Humphrey's response to her judgment had initially been to go ahead and show her the door, but he understood she had only been speaking the truth. Here *is* a long way from wherever she'd come from. Now and again, he would think of that pleasant little house in Petworth where he'd lived as a boy, the one that the medical bills ate. Yes: it takes some getting used to, this life. But that's what one did. Get used to it.

Across the way, Mrs. Ralph Wallingford and Lisette the Haitian maid fold dryer-hot towels into efficient bricks. The ones that don't fit on the cart they stow away in the supply room.

Mrs. Ralph Wallingford fumbles with a face cloth. She can't make the neat shape Lisette does and she tosses the thing away with frustration.

Humphrey watches Lisette come over behind her and lift the next one from the bin into which they unload the dryer. She moves her hands slowly, demonstrating for the older woman the elegance of the fold. Like this, Humphrey imagines Lisette saying, even as he is also fairly sure that those are not the words she uses.

This way. Like this. One side meets the other, then turn it again. Then again. Then another. This is how we do it here. This is the way it's done.

ABOUT THE AUTHOR

DAVID HAYNES is the author of eight books for adult readers and five books for younger readers. He is an emeritus professor of English at Southern Methodist University, where he directed the creative writing program for ten years. From 1996 through 2024 he taught regularly in MFA Program for Writers at Warren Wilson College. His most recent new novel is *A Star in the Face of the Sky*, and in 2023 he published a thirtieth-anniversary edition of *Right by My Side* as part of the Penguin Classics series. David serves as board chair for Kimbilio, a community of writers and scholars committed to developing, empowering, and sustaining fiction writers from the African diaspora and their stories.

OF THE DIASPORA

A BOOK SERIES FROM McSWEENEY'S

OF THE DIASPORA is a series of works in Black literature whose themes, settings, characterizations, and conflicts evoke an experience, language, imagery, and power born of the Middle Passage and the particular aesthetic which connects African-derived peoples to a shared artistic and ancestral past. The first novel in the series is *Tragic Magic* by Wesley Brown, originally published in 1978 and championed by Toni Morrison during her tenure as an editor at Random House. It's followed by *Praisesong for the Widow*, a novel by Paule Marshall originally published in 1983 and a recipient of the Before Columbus Foundation American Book Award. The third book is a collection of editorial photography by Lester Sloan framed within a conversation with his daughter, Aisha Sabatini Sloan.

The series is edited by Erica Vital-Lazare, a professor of creative writing and marginalized voices in literature at the College of Southern Nevada. Published in collectible hardcover editions with original cover art by Sunra Thompson, the first three works hail from Black American voices defined by what Amiri Baraka described as a strong feeling "getting into new blues, from the old ones." OF THE DIASPORA–North America will be followed by series from the diasporic communities of Europe, the Caribbean, and Brazil.

Other books in the OF THE DIASPORA *series:*

PRAISESONG FOR THE WIDOW
by Paule Marshall

Avey Johnson—a Black, middle-aged, middle-class widow—has long since put behind her the Harlem of her childhood. Suddenly, on a cruise to the Caribbean, she packs her bag in the middle of the night and abandons her friends at the next port of call. The unexpected and beautiful adventure that follows provides Avey with the links to the culture and history she has so long disavowed. Originally published in 1983, and a recipient of the Before Columbus Foundation American Book Award.

CAPTIONING THE ARCHIVES: A CONVERSATION IN PHOTOGRAPHS AND TEXT
Photos by Lester Sloan; text by Aisha Sabatini Sloan

In this father-daughter collaboration, photographer Lester Sloan opened his archive of street photography, portraits, and news photos, and noted essayist Aisha Sabatini Sloan interviewed him, creating rich, probing, dialogue-based captions for more than one hundred photographs.

Available at bookstores, and at store.mcsweeneys.net